THE

DREAMER

ALSO BY SHELDON SIEGEL

Mike Daley/Rosie Fernandez Novels

Special Circumstances
Incriminating Evidence
Criminal Intent
Final Verdict
The Confession
Judgment Day
Perfect Alibi
Felony Murder Rule
Serve and Protect
Hot Shot
The Dreamer

David Gold/A.C. Battle Novels

The Terrorist Next Door

THE DREAMER

A Mike Daley/Rosie Fernandez Thriller

SHELDON SIEGEL

Sheldon M. Siegel, Inc.

Cover Photo by Lala Gavgavian

ISBN: 978-0-9996747-6-5 E-Book
ISBN: 978-0-9996747-7-2 Paperback
ISBN: 978-0-9996747-8-9 Hardcover

In loving memory of my grandmothers:
Elkie Bloom Garber (1893-1969),
Sylvia Isaacson Siegel (1905-1933),
and Mollie Cooper Siegel (1910-1992),
— all of whom were Dreamers.

In loving memory of Cheryl Holmes (1943-2019),
my longtime secretary, colleague, mentor, and friend.

1
"HERE WE ARE AGAIN"

The Honorable Elizabeth McDaniel glanced at her watch, rested her chin in her palm, and spoke to me in a world-weary tone still bearing a trace of her native Alabama. "Always nice to have you back in my courtroom, Mr. Daley. I didn't expect to see the head of the Felony Division of the San Francisco Public Defender's Office at a pretrial motion."

"Co-head," I reminded her. "The Deputy P.D. handling this case is dealing with a medical situation for her mother."

"Nothing serious, I hope."

"Everybody is fine."

"Glad to hear it. Are you here to request a continuance?"

"No, thank you. I'm up to speed."

Betsy McDaniel was a thoughtful jurist who ran a tight courtroom and expected the attorneys appearing before her to be prepared and concise. Now approaching seventy, the former Assistant D.A. had gone on senior status to spend more time with her grandchildren, take pre-dawn Pilates classes, teach criminal procedure at Hastings Law School, and travel the world. From time to time, she pinch-hit for her colleagues when they went on vacation.

She added, "Please give my best to our distinguished Public Defender."

"I will." My boss, Rosita Carmela Fernandez, was San Francisco's first Latina P.D. She was also my ex-wife and former law partner. We had met during our first tour of duty at the Public Defender's Office almost a quarter of a century earlier. "Rosie asked me to tell you that she'll see you at the gym tomorrow morning."

"Excellent."

At eleven-thirty a.m. on Thursday, October third, the gallery was empty in Judge McDaniel's stuffy courtroom on the second floor of the Hall of Justice. We were the last case on her docket, and the usual ragtag assortment of retirees, courtroom junkies, homeless people, and other hangers-on who passed the time in court had already left for lunch, which required a little more planning than it used to since the cafeteria in the basement and the McDonald's down the street had closed.

The Hall was no longer as busy as it was when I was a baby P.D. The drab fifties-era edifice at Seventh and Bryant next to the I-80 Freeway had been declared unsafe from earthquakes, and it was being vacated at a leisurely pace. The P.D.'s Office had moved down the street in the nineties. The D.A.'s Office was located in a remodeled building about a mile south of the Hall, near the foot of Potrero Hill. The Southern Police Station was now housed in the sparkling new headquarters near the ballpark. The Medical Examiner had relocated to a state-of-the-art facility in India Basin. For now, the Homicide Unit remained in its longtime home on the third floor, but it was only a matter of time before the inspectors moved to updated quarters. They were prepared to sacrifice the convenience of working in the same building as the courtrooms in exchange for reliable plumbing. There was ongoing chatter among the politicians about tearing down the old warhorse and replacing it. The chances of it happening in my lifetime were remote.

The veteran judge addressed the Assistant D.A. standing at the prosecution table. "Why are we here, Mr. Erickson?"

"Reggie Bush, Your Honor."

"Again?"

"Afraid so."

Now pushing forty, Andy Erickson was a lanky lad who had taken the traditional path of many San Francisco attorneys: high school at St. Ignatius (also my alma mater), followed by college and law school at USF. His dad worked at the City Attorney's Office. His mom taught second grade at Dianne Feinstein Elementary School near Stonestown Mall. Smart, well-connected, and, most important, politically savvy, Erickson was a conscientious career prosecutor who had a shot at heading the Homicide Unit someday if he continued to play his cards carefully. I gave him a little more deference than many of the hardworking public servants at the D.A.'s Office because he was a reasonably straight shooter and a fundamentally decent guy. He also let me use his father's seats behind the Giants' dugout a couple of times a year.

The judge's tone revealed its first hint of impatience. "I take it this means you haven't been able to resolve this matter?"

Erickson feigned disappointment. "I'm afraid not, Your Honor. Mr. Daley insisted on a hearing to discuss his motion to dismiss the charges."

"Lack of evidence," I said.

Judge McDaniel tugged at her shoulder-length hair, which was a distinguished shade of silver. "Is your client here, Mr. Daley?"

"Yes, Your Honor."

And here we go. I nodded at the bailiff, who escorted Reggie Bush from the holding tank to the defense table. Reggie was no relation to the star running back and Heisman Trophy winner at USC with the same name. My Reggie was a star shoplifter who lived in a tent encampment beneath the I-80 Freeway across the street from the Hall. If we had a frequent flyer program at the P.D.'s Office, Reggie would have been a member of the platinum club.

I leaned over and spoke into his left ear, which worked better than the right one. "You ready to roll, Reg?"

"Yeah, Mike."

A native of the hard streets of Hunters Point and a one-time all-Bay Area power forward, Reggie's dreams of playing big-time college basketball ended when he blew out his knee in the City title game against Mission. He bounced between junior colleges for a couple of years before he began drinking and doing crystal meth. At forty-nine, he had ballooned to almost three hundred pounds, and his leathery face bore the scars of two decades living on the street.

"Follow my lead," I reminded him.

"I always do."

Judge McDaniel glanced at the clock. "It's almost noon, Mr. Daley. Do we have time to deal with this before lunch?"

"This will take just a few minutes."

"Fine." She spoke to my client in a maternal tone. "Haven't seen you in a while, Reggie."

"Been trying to stay out of trouble, Your Honor."

"Yet here we are again." Her voice turned pointed. "Last time I saw you I let you out on your own recognizance on a shoplifting charge, didn't I?"

"Yes, Your Honor."

"You went downstairs and broke into my car, didn't you?"

His eyes turned down. "Yes, Your Honor."

Reggie's ill-timed break-in to Judge McDaniel's Lexus in full view of two cops demonstrated his less-than-stellar judgment and profoundly poor timing. The incident made the front page of the *Chronicle* and earned him a week in the lockup. To his credit, he apologized to the judge. To hers, she accepted.

She pointed her reading glasses at Reggie. "We aren't going to have a repeat of that unfortunate episode, are we?"

"No, Your Honor."

"Good." She turned back to Erickson. "Charges?"

"Indecent exposure and committing a lewd act in public."

She looked over at Reggie again. "Seriously?"

"It was a misunderstanding."

"Seems you've had more than your share over the years."

He had. On the other hand, Reggie had never been convicted of anything more serious than stealing food or breaking into cars, and he had never hurt anyone.

"Your Honor," I said, "Mr. Erickson has blown this matter out of proportion. As we noted in our motion, while it is true that Reggie took a bag of Skittles without paying for it, there is no evidence that he exposed himself."

"Care to enlighten us about the details, Mr. Erickson?"

"Yes, Your Honor." He cleared his throat. "On Monday, September twenty-third, at two-forty in the afternoon, the defendant entered a convenience store in the Chevron station at Sixth and Harrison, where he stole a bag of candy. This act of blatant shoplifting was captured on a surveillance camera. He walked over to the bus stop in front of Bessie Carmichael Elementary School on Seventh Street, where he sat down. As a Number 19 Muni bus arrived, he exposed himself. The fact that he was within a hundred feet of a grammar school makes this a felony."

"Did any of the children see him?"

"Not as far as we know."

"Witnesses?"

"The bus driver."

I interjected. "Her statement was inconclusive."

Erickson fired back. "We also have surveillance video from the bus."

"Also inconclusive," I said. "Reggie acknowledges that he

stole a bag of Skittles. He is very sorry, and he is prepared to make full restitution of three dollars and ninety-nine cents, plus tax."

Judge McDaniel nodded. "That should resolve any potential shoplifting charges. What about the more serious issue of indecent exposure?"

"Mr. Erickson left out some important facts. As Reggie was leaving the convenience store, he hid the Skittles in his pants in the area below his navel."

The judge rubbed her eyes. "I get the picture, Mr. Daley."

"As the bus approached, Reggie removed the Skittles and ate them."

The judge shifted her gaze to Reggie. "True?"

"I was hungry."

"And how do we get from Skittles to indecent exposure, Mr. Daley?"

"We don't, Your Honor." *How do I say this delicately?* "The surveillance video shows Reggie removing the bag of Skittles, but it doesn't show any of his, uh, anatomical features. As a result, as a matter of law, he cannot be guilty of indecent exposure."

"Perhaps we should look at the video."

"Fine with me."

Erickson shook his head vigorously. "I think it would be better if Your Honor reviewed this evidence in chambers."

I shot a melodramatic glance at the empty gallery, then I turned back to the judge. "There's nothing to see, Your Honor. Besides, nobody else is here."

"Counsel will approach."

Erickson and I came forward and stopped in front of the bench.

Judge McDaniel turned off her microphone and spoke to us

in a whisper. "Let's see it."

Erickson's eyes grew wide. "I still think it would be better to view it in chambers."

"I want to see it now, Mr. Erickson." She pointed her finger at me. "Just so we're clear, Mr. Daley, if I see even the tiniest part of your client's, uh, junk, I'm going to deny your motion and hold him over for trial. Understood?"

"Yes, Your Honor." In my long and occasionally illustrious career as a defense attorney, I had never heard a judge use the term "junk" in court. For that matter, in my short and frequently unsatisfying prior career as a priest, I had never heard it there, either.

I put my laptop on the bench and ran the grainy footage in slow motion for the judge, who studied it intently. It was less than five seconds long.

Judge McDaniel shooed us back to our respective places. She turned on her microphone and addressed Erickson in her prosecutor's voice. "You believe this video provides corroborating evidence that Reggie exposed himself?"

"Yes, Your Honor."

"What did you see, Mr. Daley?"

"Nothing. Reggie unzipped his pants, removed the bag of Skittles, and re-zipped his pants. It was undignified and inappropriate, but it wasn't lewd. And it certainly wasn't illegal."

Erickson tried again. "Mr. Bush exposed himself in broad daylight in front of a grammar school."

"No, he didn't," I said. "You get a glimpse of his underwear, but you can't see his, uh, stuff. This is serious. If Reggie is convicted, he will have to register as a sex offender for at least ten years. It will be impossible for him to find employment or a place to live. In effect, it would be a life sentence for stealing a bag of Skittles."

"We can't just let this go, Your Honor."

"Sure you can," I said. "And you should."

Betsy McDaniel took a deep breath and spoke to Erickson. "I find Mr. Daley's take on the video substantially more persuasive than yours. Are you getting my drift?"

"Yes, Your Honor."

"Mr. Daley, do you have a suggestion as to how we might resolve this matter?"

"I do. In exchange for Mr. Erickson's agreement to drop the indecent exposure charge, Reggie will plead guilty to misdemeanor shoplifting, replace the bag of Skittles, and apologize to the shopkeeper at the convenience store and the bus driver. His sentence would be limited to time served."

Erickson held up a hand. "He's been here for only ten days."

"He stole a bag of Skittles, Andy."

"Thirty days, Mike."

"Three additional days.

"A week."

I leaned over and whispered into Reggie's ear. "You okay with a week?"

"I'm going to need at least two weeks, Mike."

"You want to do *more* time than he's asking for?"

"I need to get a couple of fillings replaced. The regular dentist is on vacation."

It wasn't the first time that one of my clients had agreed to a longer sentence to finish some dental work. I looked over at the judge. "Two weeks works for us, Your Honor."

"Mr. Erickson?"

"Fine."

"I think we have a resolution."

The criminal justice system tends to work most expediently

right before lunchtime.

Judge McDaniel smiled triumphantly. "Nice to see you, Mr. Daley. You always manage to find a way to bring a certain amount of practicality to our proceedings."

"Thank you, Your Honor."

"We're adjourned."

* * *

"Any word on when they'll send somebody over to fix the air conditioner?" I asked.

My secretary, process server, paralegal, and occasional bodyguard, Terrence "The Terminator" Love, was sitting at his desk outside my office at one-thirty on Thursday afternoon. "Hopefully by Monday."

It was almost a hundred degrees inside the P.D.'s Office, which was housed in a remodeled auto repair shop on Seventh Street, a block south of the Hall of Justice. When we moved over here, our new space had been a substantial upgrade from our drafty old digs on the second floor of the Hall. After two decades of deferred maintenance, our windows leaked, the plumbing was temperamental, and the air conditioner had more bad days than good. This was especially unfortunate in October, when summer weather finally arrived in San Francisco.

Beads of perspiration covered The Terminator's shaved head. At six-six and three-hundred and thirty pounds, the former smalltime heavyweight prizefighter and recovering alcoholic had been a steady customer during my first stint at the P.D.'s Office. Ten years earlier, I hired Terrence as the receptionist at the law firm that my ex-wife and I were running at the time. It was part of a plea bargain deal that I had negotiated with Judge McDaniel in settlement of an assault charge after Terrence got into a shoving match with another man in a dispute over a roast chicken. To our unending delight, the gentle giant became one of our most valuable employees, and we insisted on bringing him with us when we returned to the P.D.'s Office three years ago. To his unending credit, he hadn't touched a drop of malt liquor in almost a decade.

"How did Reggie's hearing go?" he asked.

"I got the indecent exposure charge dropped. He agreed to do two weeks for shoplifting."

"Seems a bit steep for stealing a bag of Skittles."

"It would have been shorter, but he wanted to finish some dental work."

"Been there." He adjusted the collar of his navy polo shirt, which was drenched in sweat. His expression turned serious as he pointed at the office next to mine. "Rosie wants to see you right away. New client. I overheard something about a murder trial. That's all I know."

It was unusual for her door to be closed. "How long has she been inside?"

"Five minutes."

"By herself?"

"With her mother and another woman."

"Sylvia's here?"

"As far as I know, she's Rosie's only mother."

My ex-mother-in-law, Sylvia Fernandez, was an eighty-five-year-old force of nature who was still as sharp and opinionated as she was when I met her more than two decades earlier. With two new hips and two new knees, she had also regained most of her mobility. While she was always delighted to give Rosie advice about her job and her personal life—especially her relationship with yours truly—Sylvia rarely came down to the P.D.'s Office.

"What's going on, T?" I asked.

"It's probably better if you go inside and ask Rosie yourself."

2
"SHE'S A DREAMER"

The Public Defender of the City and County of San Francisco was sitting in her leather chair behind a government-grade metal desk in her workmanlike office with a view of the paint store across Seventh Street. Unlike many of her contemporaries in the political world, there were more photos of our children than politicians on her walls.

My ex-wife, Rosie Fernandez, flashed the smile that I still found irresistible a quarter of a century after we'd met in the file room at the old P.D.'s Office. "Come in, Mike. We need to talk."

I closed the door behind me. *First things first.* "Kids okay?"

"Yes."

Our twenty-one-year-old daughter, Grace, had recently graduated with a film degree from USC and was working as a production assistant at Pixar in Emeryville. Our fifteen-year-old son, Tommy, was a sophomore at Redwood High School in Larkspur.

"Your brother?" I asked.

She touched the sleeve of a cream-colored Michael Kors blouse that was an upgrade from the days when she wore jeans and denim shirts to the office. When she ran for P.D., she'd bought fancier clothes and had her hair shortened into a stylish shoulder-length bob. "Fine."

So far, so good.

Rosie's mother, Sylvia, stood up to greet me. "Good to see you, Michael."

I hugged her. "Are you okay?"

"Fine."

Although she was stockier and grayer than Rosie, they were mirror images of each other. Sylvia was born in Monterrey, Mexico and came to the U.S. shortly after she got married. Her husband, Eduardo, a carpenter, had died a few years after I met Rosie.

I kept my tone even. "I didn't know that you were coming in today."

"Something came up."

It was out of character for my ex-mother-in-law to be so coy.

She pointed at the petite woman standing next to her. "This is my neighbor, Perlita Tejada."

I extended a hand. "Mike Daley."

"Pleased to meet you, sir." With her straight black hair and soft features, I guessed that she was somewhere in her mid-thirties, but the crow's feet at the corners of her eyes suggested that she was older. She was wearing a gray hoodie, faded Levi's, and worn Converse All-Stars. The grip from her calloused right hand was firm. She spoke deliberately in lightly accented English. "Thank you for seeing me. Sylvia thinks very highly of you as a lawyer."

"Thank you." *From time to time, she thinks a little less of me as a person.*

We took our seats. The room fell into an uneasy silence as an overworked fan pushed around the humid air. I glanced at Rosie, who nodded.

I spoke to Perlita. "How can we help you?"

Sylvia answered for her. "Her daughter needs a new lawyer."

I kept my eyes on Perlita. "What's her name?"

"Mercy."

Sylvia interjected again. "Mercedes."

I recognized the name. Mercedes "Mercy" Tejada had been a student at City College who worked at El Conquistador, a trendy restaurant on Valencia Street in the gentrified part of the Mission. Mercy had been charged with first-degree murder after her boss, an up-and-coming chef named Carlos Cruz, was found stabbed to death in the alley behind the restaurant. The case had received a lot of attention because Cruz was about to receive a James Beard Award and was going to star in a show on the Food Channel. There were rumors that Mercy was a jilted lover. After Cruz's death, El Conquistador had closed.

I spoke to Perlita again. "I thought Luisa Cervantes was representing your daughter."

"She was. Luisa was diagnosed with breast cancer. She needs to start treatments right away."

"Sorry to hear that."

I darted another glance at Rosie, who had fought her own battle with breast cancer a decade earlier. Luisa was a respected attorney who had grown up a few blocks from Rosie in the Mission. She had graduated near the top of her class at my alma mater, the law school at UC-Berkeley. Instead of opting for a six-figure salary at one of the big firms downtown, she set up a solo practice in the Mission where she handled criminal cases, eviction issues, and immigration matters.

Sylvia spoke up again. "Luisa isn't going to be able to handle Mercy's trial. That's why we came to see you and Rosita."

"Happy to help," I said, "but you know that we are only allowed to represent clients who have financial need."

"We took up a collection to pay for Mercy's defense, but we ran out of funds. Luisa generously continued working *pro bono*. Perlita doesn't have the money to hire another private lawyer, and we don't have time to do another fundraiser."

I shifted my gaze to Perlita. "Do you or your daughter have any savings or other sources of financial support?"

"No. Mercy has been in jail for almost a year. I clean houses, but I live day to day. My husband was killed in a construction accident three years ago."

"I'm sorry. Any other children?"

"A four-year-old daughter named Isabel."

Being a single mother of a four-year-old was stressful. Dealing with an older daughter facing trial for murder was unimaginable. "Other relatives?"

"No. My parents are gone. My brother and sister live in Mexico, but they can barely support themselves. I have cousins here in the City, but they have trouble making ends meet."

"Where do you live?"

"In a basement apartment across the street from St. Peter's. When I'm short, Father Lopez helps me with the rent."

St. Peter's Catholic Church had served the Mission for over a hundred years. My parents were married there. Rosie and I were, too. The parish was now predominantly Latino.

Sylvia reached over and squeezed Perlita's hand. Then she turned to her daughter. "You'll take care of this, Rosita?"

"Of course, Mama."

"Then it's settled."

Perlita's eyes filled with appreciation. "Thank you, Ms. Fernandez."

"Rosie. Anything else we should know?"

Perlita cleared her throat. "Is this conversation covered by the attorney-client privilege?"

"Yes."

Technically, this wasn't true. Perlita was not our client. Nevertheless, Rosie wanted to hear her out, and so did I.

"What did you want to tell us?" Rosie asked.

Perlita's eyes filled with tears, and she couldn't answer.

Sylvia spoke up for her. "Perlita is undocumented."

Rosie addressed Perlita in a maternal tone. "Obviously, that presents a potential complication. Have you ever been contacted by ICE?"

"No."

"Do they know you're here?"

"Probably. I've tried to keep a low profile—especially since Mercy was arrested."

"It's better that way. We'll try to avoid doing anything that would give them a reason to talk to you. On the other hand, your daughter's case has already generated media attention, which is likely to become more intense as we get closer to trial. Ideally, it would be better for you to remain out of the public eye."

"Can I visit her?"

"I can't order you *not* to visit your daughter, but it could make things complicated for you and Isabel."

"Can I go to Mercy's trial?"

"Yes, but it will also increase your chances of being detained."

"I'm prepared to take the risk."

I would have answered the same way. "Perlita," I said, "was Mercy born here?"

"No. We brought her here when she was a baby."

"Is she a U.S. citizen?"

"No, she's a Dreamer."

Deferred Action for Childhood Arrivals (DACA) was a controversial immigration policy adopted by the Obama administration in 2012. It permitted certain young people to apply for a renewable two-year period of deferred action from deportation and obtain a U.S. work permit. To be eligible, participants could not have felonies or serious misdemeanors on their records.

"When does her 'Dreamer' status expire?" I asked.

"December thirty-first."

It meant that even if we got an acquittal, Mercy could still be deported a few months later if her Dreamer status was not renewed. "Has she ever been convicted of a crime?"

"Not even a parking ticket."

"Good. What about your younger daughter?"

"Isabel was born here, so she's a U.S. citizen."

Whose life will become very complicated if Perlita is detained or deported.

Perlita took a deep breath. "Are you allowed to represent Dreamers?"

"Yes." *Well, maybe.* The law wasn't settled. It was the policy of the Public Defender's Office, as handed down by the Public Defender (Rosie), and as implemented by the co-head of the Felony Division (me), that we would represent Dreamers who otherwise qualified for our services. Rosie and I had agreed that we would continue to do so until a court ordered us to stop. The risk of that happening in San Francisco was relatively slim.

A flash of hope appeared in Perlita's eyes. "What happens next?"

"We'll want to meet Mercy. She'll have to complete some paperwork to appoint us as counsel and fill out some financial disclosures, but that won't prevent us from moving forward. We'll also want to talk to Luisa."

"She assured me that she would help with a smooth transition."

"Great. Does Mercy have a trial date?"

"October twenty-eighth."

It was only three and a half weeks away. "That's a tight timeframe for us to get up to speed. We may want to ask for a continuance."

Sylvia interjected again. "Perlita and I would be very grateful if you would move forward as soon as possible, Michael."

It was "Sylvia-speak" for "Perlita and I expect you to go to trial in three and a half weeks." "We'll do everything in our power to move forward on schedule."

"Thank you."

We spoke for a few more minutes before Rosie and I escorted Sylvia and Perlita to the reception area. Rosie and I returned to her office, where we took seats on opposite sides of her desk.

"We need to get on this right away," I said. "We should also talk about staffing."

Rosie's eyes narrowed. "I'm going to try this case myself."

3
"THIS ISN'T A POPULARITY CONTEST"

"Excuse me?" I said.

Rosie's cobalt eyes had turned to hard steel. "I'm going to handle it myself."

"You don't try cases anymore."

"I'm going to try this one."

She was one of the best trial attorneys I'd ever known, but the P.D. is primarily a politician and administrator who sets policy and supervises other lawyers—including the co-head of the Felony Division. She was already working eighty-hour weeks running the office, preparing budgets, and raising money for her re-election campaign. The demands would become even more acute as we got closer to the election, which was only six weeks away.

"It wouldn't be an optimal use of your valuable time," I said.

"The Public Defender needs to multi-task."

"You know how it goes. There aren't enough hours in the day to do a murder trial and everything else."

"I'll find a way. I always do."

"Let me do it."

"You don't try cases anymore, either."

My role was also primarily administrative, but Rosie and I had agreed that I could do trial work on occasion as long as I stayed out of her hair and didn't screw up. "We decided that I could do one or two a year."

"Not this one."

"Why are you doing this?"

"Mama asked me."

More accurately, Sylvia told her. "Why is she so interested in this case?"

"It's personal. Mama has looked after Perlita since her husband died. Perlita cleans Mama's house. She's found a way to put food on the table for Mercy and Isabel."

"How well do you know Perlita?"

"I met her once before today."

"You just said that she's close to your mother."

"Undocumented people keep a low profile. Friends of undocumented people need to be careful about introducing them to others."

"Including their daughter?"

"Mama was probably trying to protect me. It wouldn't enhance my standing among certain voters if word got out that the mother of the Public Defender was helping an undocumented person."

"It's going to get out now."

"We'll deal with it."

"Who takes care of Isabel when Perlita is working?"

"She goes to pre-school at St. Peter's. Father Lopez waived tuition. In the Mission, people still look out for each other."

The same was true when my parents were growing up there in the thirties and forties when the neighborhood was still home to working-class Irish and Italian families. When many of the Irish and Italians fled to the suburbs in the fifties and the sixties, the Latino families moved in. The Mission started gentrifying in the nineties during the dot-com bubble.

"This case would be perfect for Rolanda," I said.

"No."

Rosie's niece, Rolanda Fernandez, was the co-head of the Felony Division. The talented young woman whom Rosie and I had once babysat was one of our best trial attorneys. Her father,

Tony, was Rosie's older brother. He ran a produce market on Twenty-fourth Street around the corner from St. Peter's.

"It would be a good experience for her," I said.

"She's in trial. And I'm not going to jeopardize her career by putting her on the front line of a case that could become a political fireball."

"It could ruin yours."

"I can take care of myself."

Although the early polling indicated that Rosie had a substantial lead over her opponent, there were no sure bets in San Francisco politics. "The election is next month. The only way you can lose is if you make a serious unforced error."

"Doing our job isn't an error."

"You don't have to take the lead."

"This isn't a popularity contest."

"The trial isn't, but the election is."

"We don't make staffing decisions based on political calculations. Besides, this is San Francisco. I'll get more grief if we *don't* take this case."

Probably true. "You don't have to do it yourself."

"I *want* to."

"Is there any way that I can persuade you to change your mind?"

"No."

Didn't think so. "Anything I can do to help?"

"I want you to sit second chair."

Just like old times. "Why me?"

"Because you're good. And experienced. And you can get up to speed in a hurry."

Good to hear.

She smiled. "And I don't want to ask anybody else in the office to potentially sacrifice their career."

"You're willing to sacrifice mine?"

"We'll manage."

"I'm a year and a half away from being eligible for my pension."

"You'd be bored out of your mind if you retired."

True. "If you lose the election, I'm going to get fired by your successor."

"Then we'll stand in line together at the unemployment office."

It was my turn to smile. "Sounds like a fine back-up plan."

"We can always re-open our law firm in a converted martial arts studio above a second-rate Chinese restaurant."

My mind flashed back to the original office of Fernandez and Daley in a crumbling walk-up above the Lucky Corner #2 Chinese Restaurant around the corner from the old Transbay bus terminal. After Rosie and I got divorced, we left the P.D.'s Office. She started a solo practice, and I spent five miserable years working for a mega-firm at the top of the Bank of America Building. She took me in after I was fired because I failed to develop a sufficiently lucrative book of business, and we'd been working together ever since. Over the years, we had settled into a permanent "ex-spouses-with-benefits" relationship, which had lasted longer than our marriage.

"It had its charms and a working air conditioner," I said. The Lucky Corner was a distant memory, and the walk-up had long since been torn down to make way for a high-rise.

"Are you in?" she asked.

"Of course."

"Then it's settled."

"We'll need an investigator."

"I don't want to use any of our in-house people. They have families to feed."

So do we. "Did you have somebody in mind?"

"Pete."

My younger brother was a former cop who became a P.I. after he was fired for using too much force breaking up a gang fight in the Mission. "You sure?"

"Yes. For one, he's very good. For two, he's family. For three, he used to work at Mission Police Station, so he knows everybody in the neighborhood."

"Standard or family rates?"

"Standard."

"Does the P.D.'s Office have the budget to pay him, or is this going to be on our own dime?"

"I'll find the money," she said.

"I'll talk to him. It would also make sense to have one of our younger attorneys help us with research, motions, and trial prep."

"Did you have somebody in mind?"

"Nady."

Nadezhda "Nady" Nikonova was a whip-smart and tenacious graduate of the law school at Berkeley who had joined the P.D.'s Office two years earlier.

Rosie nodded. "Fine with me if she has time."

"I'll talk to her, too. Where do you want to start?"

"We should go introduce ourselves to our new client."

.

4

"I DIDN'T KILL CARLOS"

The young woman's wide face had a yellow cast from the fluorescent light dangling from the ceiling. "Are you my new lawyers?"

Rosie answered her. "Yes. I'm Rosie Fernandez."

"Sylvia's daughter?"

"Yes."

Mercy Tejada looked like a younger version of her mother. Her features had a youthful softness, but her brown eyes had a hardened edge reflecting the stresses of a year in jail.

Rosie pointed at me. "This is Mike Daley. He's the co-head of our Felony Division. We met with your mother earlier today. We're going to be handling your case."

"I didn't expect the Public Defender."

"You qualify for our services. And you and your mother are special to my mother."

At four-thirty p.m., we were meeting in an airless consultation room on the ground floor of County Jail #2, the Costco-like structure that was jammed between the Hall of Justice and the I-80 Freeway in the nineties. The cops nicknamed it "the Glamour Slammer." It was the only facility in the County Jail system where women were housed. The utilitarian building was an upgrade from the dingy cells on the top floors of the old Hall next door, and it had a functioning air conditioner. Then again, a newer jail is still a jail.

Mercy's eyes narrowed. "How's Mama?"

Rosie answered her. "Holding up okay under the circumstances. How often does she come to see you?"

"Once or twice a month. We talk by phone more often."

"She doesn't visit more frequently?"

"She can't. She's afraid that somebody will report her to ICE. That would create a big problem for her and an even bigger problem for my baby sister." Mercy swallowed. "How is Isabel? I haven't seen her in over a year."

"Your mother assured us that she's doing okay." Rosie gave Mercy a moment to regain her bearings. "How are you getting along?"

"Not so well." She played with the sleeve of her orange sweatshirt. She said that her health was generally good, she was getting enough to eat, and the other inmates left her alone most of the time. "I'm taking my insulin to keep my diabetes under control."

"Are you getting any sleep?"

"Not much." Mercy's lips turned down. "Can you get me out of here?"

That's always the first question.

Rosie's voice remained even. "We understand that your bail was set at a quarter of a million dollars. We'll ask the judge to reduce it, but the odds aren't great."

Rosie understood the importance of managing a new client's expectations. As a practical matter, even if we persuaded a judge to lower bail substantially, Mercy wouldn't be able to afford it unless a sugar daddy intervened. It was also unlikely that she could raise ten percent of the bail to buy a non-refundable bail bond from one of the entrepreneurs across the street.

Rosie moved on to setting ground rules—an exercise I had seen dozens of times. "Rule number one: you need to be absolutely truthful with us. We can't represent you effectively if you don't tell us the full and unvarnished truth. You can't leave anything out, either. Understood?"

Mercy nodded.

"Second, I don't want you to talk to anybody about your case other than Mike and me. Not the guards. Not the cops. Not the other inmates. And don't talk to anybody about your case on the phone. The calls are recorded and may be reviewed."

This warning was coming late. We couldn't undo anything that Mercy had already said.

"What about Mama?" she asked.

"I don't want you to tell her anything about your case. I don't think the prosecution will call her as a witness, but I don't want to put her in a position where she might consider lying under oath."

"Okay."

Rosie glanced my way. Time for a fresh voice.

I started slowly. "Why don't you tell us a little bit about yourself?"

"I didn't kill Carlos."

"Good to know."

Actually, it was a mixed bag. If we discovered otherwise, it could limit our ability to maneuver. In the unlikely event that we decided to have Mercy testify at trial, Rosie and I couldn't let her lie. While defense attorneys contort themselves to bend this rule, it was better to avoid the issue altogether.

I kept my voice measured. "We'll get into the details of what happened that night in a minute. For now, why don't you tell us a little more about yourself?"

"I went to elementary school at St. Peter's and graduated from Mission High. I was in my second year at City College when Carlos died. I was planning to transfer to State to study nursing."

"You lived with your mother and younger sister?"

"Yes." She confirmed that they shared a basement apartment in the ungentrified corner of the Mission. "I started working at restaurants when I was fourteen to help Mama pay the bills."

I admired her sense of responsibility. It was also illegal to hire a fourteen-year-old, but her employers needed cheap help, and Mercy and her family needed the money. "How long did you work at Cruz's restaurant?"

"About a year."

"What did you do?"

"Whatever Carlos wanted. I bussed tables, helped with the dishes, took out the trash, and ran errands."

"Did you like your job?"

"No."

"Did you spend a lot of time with Cruz?"

"Everybody did. El Conquistador had only forty seats. We had a small staff. Carlos micromanaged everything."

"Was he married?"

"To the restaurant."

"In a relationship?"

"With the restaurant." She read my expression. "The restaurant business is insanely competitive—especially in a foodie town like San Francisco. One week, El Conquistador is the hottest place in town. A month later, everybody has moved on."

It reminded me of the high-end restaurant that a couple of my former law partners had opened near the ballpark to great fanfare and closed six months later. They always said that the way to make a small fortune in the restaurant business is to start with a big fortune and bleed money until you're left with a small fortune.

"How was the food?"

"Very good. Mexican-Asian fusion with French nuances. Organic and locally sourced."

"Pricey?"

"Two hundred and fifty dollars for the prix-fixe dinner."

Yikes. "Was it worth it?"

"I didn't think so, but the tech bros in the Mission will pay for trendy." Her expression turned somber. "Some people thought it embodied everything that's going wrong in the Mission. Landlords are jacking up rents. High-end places like El Conquistador are taking over spaces from neighborhood businesses. The mom-and-pop shops can't afford to stay open."

"Did Cruz have any formal training?" I asked.

"No. He worked at his parents' taqueria on South Van Ness for a few years. Then he bought a second-hand food truck that he parked near the Salesforce Tower. He developed a reputation among the tech crowd. He ran a pop-up restaurant in an empty storefront on Twenty-fourth for a year. It got good reviews and word-of-mouth, so he was approached by an investor to open El Conquistador."

"How much did the investor put in?"

"Millions. He designed and built out the space on Valencia."

"Seems like a big investment in a young chef. What's the name of the investor?"

"Jed Sanders. He used to run a couple of high-end restaurants in L.A."

"Did you ever meet him?"

"A few times. He was at the restaurant the night that Carlos died."

"Working?"

"Eating. And checking on his investment."

We would track him down. "What was Cruz like as a boss?"

"He was a dictator. You did it his way or you were fired."

"Abusive?"

"At times."

"Did he ever cross the line?"

"Many times." Her eyes turned down. "He called me fat. And stupid. And ugly. He threatened to fire me. He said that he would report my mother to ICE."

"Did you ever complain?"

"I needed to keep my job."

"Did anybody else complain?"

"A couple of people who were then fired. There was nobody else to complain to other than Carlos. His brother was supposed to be the business manager, but he was afraid of Carlos."

Rosie interjected in a maternal tone. "I admire you for sticking it out."

This was Rosie-speak for "Your boss was a pig."

Mercy shrugged. "I needed the money."

Rosie leaned forward. "Did he ever touch you inappropriately?"

"Yes." A pause. "He liked to pat me on the ass. He tried to kiss me."

"How many times?"

"Dozens. It started on my first night at work. I told him that I wasn't interested. He stopped for a few days, then he started again."

"There were rumors that you and Cruz were involved in a relationship."

"When your boss tries to kiss you against your will, it isn't a relationship."

"Did he try to kiss you on the night that he died?"

Mercy nodded.

"Did anybody see it?"

"I don't know. I told him to keep his hands off me."

"That's it?"

"I didn't kill him."

"Mercy," I said, "why don't you tell us what happened that night."

5
"I TRIED TO HELP HIM"

Mercy squeezed the armrests of her chair. "It was like every other night at El Conquistador."

Except the star chef was dead. Rosie and I remained silent, hoping that Mercy would keep talking.

She did. "The restaurant was packed. Carlos was in a good mood—for him. He had just gotten word that he was going to receive a James Beard Award. The *Chronicle* had included us in its list of Top 100 Restaurants in the Bay Area."

"What time did you get to work?" I asked.

"Two o'clock. I unloaded the produce that Carlos always picked out himself. I helped prep the salads and the appetizers. I folded napkins and laid out the silver. The first seating was at six. The second was at eight-thirty. The hardest part was getting the people at the early seating to leave so we could turn the tables."

"How many employees were working that night?"

"About a dozen." In addition to Cruz, she noted that there was a sous chef, a pastry chef, two waitresses (one of whom left early), a maître d' (who also served as the sommelier and managed the front of the house), a dishwasher, and Mercy. I jotted down their names.

"Anybody else?"

"Carlos's brother, Alejandro, the business manager. And Jed Sanders, the investor." Mercy explained that the last customers left around eleven p.m. The staff stuck around to eat leftovers and clean up. "It took us about an hour and a half to do the dishes, put away the food, and get ready for the next day. We had a good team. Everybody helped."

"Even Cruz?"

"He was always the first to arrive and among the last to go home."

"What time did he leave?"

"Twelve-thirty a.m."

"Was anybody else still there?"

"Just me. I locked up and went out the back door to the alley where I left my bike. I found Carlos on the ground next to his car. Someone had stabbed him. The knife was sticking out of his stomach. There was a lot of blood."

I had little to offer except the obvious. "That must have been horrible."

"It was. Carlos was still breathing. I screamed for help. I pulled out the knife and covered the wound with my sweatshirt."

Which means they found your fingerprints on the knife and his blood on your sweatshirt. "Did you call the police?"

"A woman who lived across the alley heard me and came outside. Her name is Juanita Morales. I told her to call nine-one-one. Mission Station was a block away. The police came right over. An ambulance arrived a few minutes later. Carlos died at the hospital."

I asked if she saw anybody else in the alley.

"No."

"How soon did you leave after Cruz?"

"Five minutes. Maybe less."

"Did you hear anything outside? Arguing? Fighting?"

"Nothing."

"Do you recall when the other employees left the restaurant?"

She took us through the timeline. The first waitress left

around ten-forty-five. The pastry chef left a few minutes later. The sous chef departed at eleven-fifteen. Then the investor. Then the maître d', followed by the second waitress. The dishwasher left at twelve-fifteen. Then Cruz's brother. Then Cruz. Then Mercy.

"Is it possible that one of them was waiting outside for Cruz?"

"Sure."

I eyed her. "Was anybody angry at him?"

"Everybody."

"Enough to kill him?"

"I don't know."

"Did anybody argue with him that night?"

"*Everybody* argued with him *every* night. Carlos was insanely demanding. He was physically and verbally abusive."

"You said that he tried to kiss you."

"He did. I pushed him away and swore at him."

"Did anybody hear you?"

"Probably. There were other people in the kitchen when it happened."

I looked over at Rosie, who picked up the cue.

"I presume that you talked to the police that morning?"

"Yes. They took me to Mission Station. I gave my statement to Inspector Ken Lee."

Rosie and I knew him. Lee was a veteran homicide inspector. We had been on opposite sides of several high-profile cases. We didn't always enjoy each other's company, but I respected him. The former undercover cop was smart, tenacious, and scrupulously honest.

"What did you tell him?" Rosie asked.

"The same thing that I just told you. I found Carlos in the alley. I tried to help him."

"You didn't confess to anything, did you?"

"No."

"Good. How long were you at Mission Station?"

"A couple of hours. Then Inspector Lee took me down to the Hall of Justice and we went over everything again."

"For some reason, he concluded that you killed Cruz."

"I didn't."

"They must have found your fingerprints on the knife."

"I just told you that I pulled it out of Carlos's stomach. I was trying to stop the bleeding."

"There must have been blood on your hands and clothing."

"There was." Her eyes narrowed. "But I didn't kill him."

"They arrested you that morning?"

"Yes. First-degree murder. Mama asked Luisa to handle my case. I couldn't make bail, so I've been here ever since."

"Did Luisa discuss a plea bargain with the D.A's Office?"

"The Assistant D.A. said that they might be willing to go down to second-degree murder. I told Luisa that I wasn't going to plead guilty to killing somebody when I didn't."

"Would you like us to raise the possibility of a deal?"

"You think I'm guilty?"

"No, but we should consider all of our options."

"I am not going to be plead guilty to a crime that I didn't commit."

Rosie reached over and touched Mercy's hand. "What aren't you telling us?"

"Nothing." There were tears in her eyes. "You know what else really bothers me? I did everything right. I worked hard. I stayed in school. I got good grades. I was finishing my second year at City College. Mama and I never took a penny of government money—not one cent. I got Dreamer status. I helped take care of Mama and Isabel. I found a job and put up with endless crap from Carlos. And then somebody stabbed Carlos, and they blamed me. It isn't fair."

"No, it isn't." Rosie frowned. "Inspector Lee must know something that we don't."

"You'll need to ask him."

* * *

"What did you think?" Rosie asked.

"Mercy is smart," I said. "And she's scared."

We were sitting in Rosie's office at six-thirty on Thursday night. The air was heavy, but slightly cooler than earlier in the day.

She took a sip of Diet Coke. Fine wine, fancy chocolate, and Diet Coke were her only vices—all of which she consumed in moderation. "Do you think she was telling the truth?"

"For now. Guilty people shade their stories. Innocent people get mad. Mercy didn't hedge. Either she didn't do it, or she's convinced herself that she didn't."

"Or she's a convincing liar."

True. "Not the way I saw it."

"For what it's worth, I'm inclined to agree with you—for now."

"You really think we have an innocent client?"

"I'll give her the benefit of the doubt until I have reason to believe otherwise."

Rosie always said that it was scarier to represent somebody who you believed was innocent than somebody you thought was guilty because there was a chance that a jury would convict them anyway—which was even worse than letting a guilty person go free.

Terrence appeared in the doorway. "We just got the files on Mercy's case. I set them up in the conference room."

"We'll be right there."

6
"THERE'S ALWAYS SOMETHING"

At seven-thirty on Thursday night, the conference room in the P.D.'s Office smelled of leftover pizza and fresh coffee. I turned to the intense young woman sitting across the table who was absentmindedly tugging at her shoulder-length blonde hair. "Is this all of the case files?"

"Yes." Nadezhda "Nady" Nikonova confirmed that we had received the police reports, autopsy report, forensics, blood spatter analysis, and witness statements.

"Looks a little thin. Which A.D.A. is handling the case?"

"DeSean Harper."

The Chief Assistant District Attorney was second-in-command to our D.A. He was smart, meticulous, and honest.

"We'll talk to him," I said. "Anything useful in the police reports?"

She responded with a confident smile. "There's always something, Mike."

Nady and her mother had liberated themselves from Uzbekistan when Nady was seven. They found their way to relatives in L.A., where Nady picked up English quickly and graduated at the top of her class at UCLA and law school at Cal. She paid off her student loans by slaving away at a big law firm downtown for a few years, whereupon Rosie and I persuaded her to help us slay dragons at the P.D.'s Office, a job she found more to her liking.

"Surveillance video?" I asked.

"A camera by the front door of the restaurant provided nothing useful. A camera in the rear was broken. Unfortunately, the action took place in the back. There were no cameras in adjacent businesses or in the alley."

I looked at the unshaven and pockmarked face of my brother, Pete. "Have you talked to anybody down at Mission Station?"

"Working on it, Mick."

He was the youngest and stockiest of the three Daley brothers. Our older brother, Tommy, had been a star quarterback at St. Ignatius and Cal before he died in Vietnam. Pete was two years younger than I was, but the wear and tear of a decade as a cop and twenty years as a P.I. made him look older. A scar ran from his droopy mustache to his full head of gray hair, and he walked with a slight limp.

"Anything you'd care to share at this point?"

"No." He took off his ever-present bomber jacket and draped it over an empty chair. Even though it was ninety degrees outside, Pete never left home without it. "I'll let you know when I have something useful."

Rosie took command of the room without raising her voice. "We have only three and a half weeks until trial, Pete."

"I'll get you everything you need."

She turned to Nady. "Let's start with the decedent."

"Carlos Cruz. Thirty-two. Born in the Mission. Parents ran a restaurant on Twenty-fourth. Graduated from Mission High. No college. Never married. Bisexual. No long-term relationships."

"Short-term?"

"Several. Men and women—sometimes at the same time. As far as I can tell, he wasn't seeing anybody at the time of his death."

"Did any of the old relationships end badly?"

"Several."

"Any of his former boyfriends or girlfriends angry at him on the night he died?"

"Nothing mentioned in the file."

Pete nodded to indicate that he would look into it.

Nady confirmed that Cruz had worked at his parents' restaurant before he bought a second-hand food truck and later opened a pop-up restaurant. Good buzz among the tech crowd elicited interest from Jed Sanders, an L.A. restaurateur of some note. Sanders agreed to bankroll El Conquistador, which opened to stellar reviews and sold-out crowds.

"Profitable?" I asked.

"You would think so, but impossible to know. If you believe the *Chronicle's* food critic, there were some preliminary discussions about opening a second location in L.A. The plan ended when Cruz died."

"Any mention of any friction between Cruz and Sanders?"

"No."

"Mercy said that Cruz wasn't an easy guy to deal with."

"The *Chronicle* called him a 'volatile creative genius.'" Nady's mouth turned up. "That's usually the euphemism for 'asshole.'"

"If I had a dollar for every chef accused of being an egomaniac, I would be rich. Any claims of sexual harassment?"

"Nothing on the record."

"What about off the record?"

"Nothing in the police reports."

Not surprising. "Any undocumented employees?"

"Can't tell."

"If anybody is here illegally, they'll be reluctant to talk to us."

Pete made his presence felt again. "I'll find them."

I turned to Nady. "Do the police reports say that Mercy got into it with Cruz that night?"

"A couple of witnesses said that she and Cruz had been going at it for weeks."

"Any mention of Cruz hitting on Mercy?"

"No."

"Other than Cruz and Mercy and the customers, who else was at the restaurant?"

Nady studied her list, which matched up with the information that Mercy had provided. Two waitresses, one of whom left early. Jed Sanders, the investor. Christine Fong, who ran the front of the house. A sous chef named Olmedo Rivera. A pastry chef named Maria Garcia. A second waitress named Carmen Dominguez. A dishwasher named Junio Costa. And Cruz's older brother, Alejandro. The information about their respective departure times matched up with the timeline provided by Mercy.

"Why did Mercy stay after Cruz left?" I asked.

"She said that she used the bathroom."

"I count eight people who left shortly before Cruz. All of them had issues with him. Any one of them could have stabbed him."

Rosie looked up. "You're thinking of a 'SODDI' defense?"

"SODDI" was lawyer-speak for "Some other dude did it."

"Until we come up with something better," I said.

"Always good to give the jury options. Any evidence that somebody else stabbed Cruz?"

"At the moment, no." I pointed at my brother. "That's why we have Pete."

He looked up without saying a word.

Rosie turned back to Nady. "Where was Cruz's wallet?"

"Next to his body. According to the police report, there was no money inside."

"The suggestion of a robbery could get us a long way toward

reasonable doubt."

"It may be difficult to prove. Millennials don't carry cash."

"We don't need to prove it; we just need to suggest it. Murder weapon?"

"A knife from a matching set of six, one of which was missing from the drawer when the police did their inventory."

"Is it a common type of knife?"

"No. It's a high-end model used primarily in restaurants. A Messermeister Meridian Elite Stealth chef's knife. They cost about two hundred and fifty dollars each."

"Not a likely weapon of a neighborhood punk."

"Correct. On the other hand, anybody who was inside the restaurant could have taken the knife and stabbed Cruz."

"Including our client," Rosie said. She looked at Pete. "We need you to go down to the Mission and work your magic finding these people." She then turned to me. "We need to talk to Mercy's former lawyer."

7

"HE WAS AN EQUAL OPPORTUNITY SEXUAL PREDATOR"

Luisa Cervantes extended a hand to me. "Thanks for coming over."

"Thanks for seeing us."

Wearing faded jeans and a Warriors T-shirt, Mercy's former lawyer wasn't imposing physically, but her eyes had an intensity similar to Rosie's. At forty-four, her short black hair was flecked with gray, and the worry lines on her forehead reflected two decades of trench warfare in the rougher corners of the legal world. She was married for a short time when she was in her twenties, but it hadn't worked out. A more recent long-term relationship ended when her boyfriend moved in with another man. She always reminded us that life was complicated.

"How's your mother?" she asked Rosie.

"Getting around better since she had her second knee replacement. Except for the usual aches and pains associated with being eighty-five, fine. Yours?"

"Except for the usual aches and pains associated with being eighty-one, fine."

At nine-thirty the following Sunday morning, Rosie and I were sitting on the sofa in Luisa's cluttered office, which doubled as the living room of her ground-floor flat down the block from the house where Rosie had grown up. The built-in bookcases, working fireplace, and plaster walls embodied the craftsmanship of the nineteen-twenties. The century-old plumbing and kitchen cabinets were overdue for an upgrade.

Rosie's voice was soft. "How are you feeling, Luisa?"

"Not great, but you do what you need to do." She explained that her breast cancer was similar in type and degree to the cancer that Rosie had fought off a decade earlier. "They found it early and it's treatable. There are no guarantees, and the treatments are, uh, difficult."

"When do you start?"

"Tomorrow."

"Do you need a ride?"

"My sister has it covered."

"You'll let us know if you need anything?"

"Of course."

We sat in silence for a moment. Luisa sipped her herbal tea. Rosie held a glass of water. I looked out the window at the kids playing soccer in Garfield Square Park across the street.

Luisa cleared her throat. "Thanks for helping Mercy. Have you gotten any blowback for representing a Dreamer?"

"Not yet," Rosie said.

"You will. People forget that Mercy is a human being with a mother and a baby sister."

"We got your files. The police reports are pretty thin."

"DeSean Harper sent over what he was legally obligated to give us—nothing more."

The D.A. was only required to provide evidence that would tend to exonerate our client.

"Any chance DeSean might be willing to go down to manslaughter?" Rosie asked.

"Absolutely not. We talked briefly about a deal for second-degree murder, but that's as far as he would go."

"He's usually more reasonable."

"His boss is running for mayor. Nicole is taking a hard line on everything—especially cases involving undocumented people and Dreamers."

"The mayor's race shouldn't impact strategic decisions at the D.A.'s Office."

Luisa shrugged. "Politics. You know how it goes."

"Unfortunately, I do."

Our long-time District Attorney, Nicole Ward, had branded herself as a law-and-order zealot and the last line of defense between the people of San Francisco and anarchy. Smart, photogenic, and media-savvy, the political opportunist had set her sights on the mayor's office by staking out hardline anti-crime and anti-immigrant positions that initially seemed contrary to the prevailing vibe in San Francisco. On the other hand, she had astutely calculated that in a primary field of a dozen candidates, the eleven liberals would divide the vote among themselves, leaving her an easier lane to a runoff. With her substantial name recognition from years of TV appearances, she came in first in the primary with a less-than-whopping eighteen percent of the vote, while her closest competitors were in single digits. She was running neck and neck against her more progressive opponent in what was lining up as a hotly contested race.

Rosie scowled. "Nicole is using Mercy's case to score political points?"

"Nicole would lock up her twin daughters to score political points. You might be better off asking for a continuance until after the election. If Nicole wins, DeSean will probably become acting D.A. He might be willing to consider a more reasonable deal."

"Mercy's Dreamer status expires on December thirty-first. If we delay, she could be deported before we ever get to trial."

"Then you'd better be ready to go to trial on a first-degree murder charge."

Rosie exhaled. "Where was the premeditation?"

"There wasn't any."

"What did DeSean *say* constituted pre-meditation?"

"Mercy thought about killing Cruz all evening. At the end of the night, she grabbed a knife, followed him outside, and stabbed him to death."

"She told us that she didn't."

"She told me the same thing."

"Do you believe her?"

A hesitation. "Yes, but it's complicated. She didn't like him."

"She told us that nobody liked him. How much did *she* not like him?"

"A lot."

"Enough to stab him?"

"I don't think so, but there are other employees who are prepared to testify that Mercy and Cruz were arguing that night."

"Did she threaten him?"

"She swore at him. The jury will decide whether it was a threat."

"It still doesn't prove that she stabbed him."

"There's motive, means, and opportunity."

"True," Rosie said. "Let's take a step back. Tell us a little more about Mercy."

"She's like her mother: smart, ambitious, direct, fearless. Nobody has given her anything, and she doesn't take crap from anyone."

"Criminal record?"

"None. No arrests, either."

"Substance issues?"

"Not as far as I know."

"Temper?"

"She was suspended from high school for punching a boy who tried to kiss her."

"I might have done the same thing. Did she hurt him?"

"Bloody nose."

"Any other similar behavior?"

"Not as far as I know. Then again, according to several of her co-workers, if you crossed her, she wasn't afraid to let you know how she felt."

"We understand that Cruz wasn't easy to deal with."

"He was an equal opportunity sexual predator."

"He hit on her?"

"Yes. And she wasn't the only one."

"More than comments?"

"A lot of uninvited touching. El Conquistador was Cruz's show. Unlimited power and unchecked ego often make for a hostile work environment."

"She could have quit."

"I know that you grew up around the corner, but it's been a long time since you've lived here day to day. Mercy is a Dreamer. Her mother is an undocumented single mother of a four-year-old. You put up with a lot of crap when you need money to eat."

"Did any of the other employees mention sexual harassment?"

"Not on the record."

"Off the record?"

"Yes."

"Are they willing to testify?"

"No."

"Why not?"

"It might suggest that they had motive to kill Cruz. A couple are undocumented. If they show up in court, they risk being detained."

"Names?" Rosie said.

"A waitress named Carmen Dominguez and a dishwasher named Junio Costa. Their last contact information is in the file. As far as I know, they're still in the area."

We would ask Pete to find them.

Rosie moved in another direction. "Was the restaurant making money?"

"I think so, but Cruz was late with payroll a couple of times."

"We understand that there was an investor named Jed Sanders."

"He put up a hundred percent of the money and owned a ninety percent interest in El Conquistador. Cruz owned the rest."

"Cruz couldn't get a loan?"

"It's difficult to obtain financing for a restaurant—especially when it's run by someone of color. In some cases, in order to obtain a bank loan, a new restaurant is required to bring in what is colloquially known as a 'White Savior.'"

"A white guy with money?"

"Exactly."

"That's wrong."

"Welcome to the real world."

"Was Sanders happy with his investment?"

"According to an interview with the *Chronicle*, he was thrilled with the critical response, but concerned about cost overruns. Evidently, his suggestions to Cruz about cost control were not well-received, so he brought in his girlfriend, Christine Fong, to run the front of the house. She had previously managed one of Sanders's restaurants in L.A."

"I presume that she was also there to spy on Cruz?"

"Precisely. It made for a toxic environment. Cruz and Fong

barely spoke to each other."

"Did Cruz hit on her, too?"

"She didn't mention it to me. Then again, she probably wouldn't have said anything because it would have suggested motive for her, too."

"And Cruz's older brother?"

"He's pleasant enough. Alejandro graduated from Mission High and San Francisco State. He got an MBA from USF. He was nominally the business manager at El Conquistador. In reality, he took orders from his brother and Sanders."

"Married?"

"Divorced."

"Criminal record?"

"None."

"Bad behavior?"

"Not as far as I could tell. Alejandro was the good son."

"How did he get along with his little brother?"

"He did whatever Carlos said."

Rosie pushed out a sigh. "What happened that night?"

"Cruz and Mercy were at each other's throats. Cruz could be vicious. Mercy gave it right back. Cruz was the second-to-last person to leave. Mercy was the last person out the door. She found Cruz in the alley with a knife in his stomach. The knife matched a set from the restaurant. They found Mercy's prints on the knife and Cruz's blood on her clothes."

"She told us that she removed the knife from Cruz's stomach and tried to help him. That would explain how her prints got onto the knife and how his blood got onto her clothes."

"True. You'll need to sell it to the jury."

I finally spoke up. "Did anybody see Mercy walk out the door with a knife?"

"It wasn't mentioned in the police reports. Then again,

they're only required to provide potentially exculpatory evidence. If they have a witness who saw her pick up a knife, that wouldn't be exculpatory. You'll need to talk to Ken Lee. And DeSean. And everybody who was working that night."

"We're thinking of a SODDI defense."

"So was I. The problem is that other witnesses are going to point the finger at Mercy."

"They have incentive to lie."

"If Harper puts up a half dozen people who implicate Mercy, it's going to be hard to rebut their testimony. You can try to point out inconsistencies in their stories, but the only person who can refute them is Mercy."

True. "Putting Mercy on the stand would be a less-than-ideal scenario."

She smiled. "I learned it from you at a seminar that you taught when I was a law student at Berkeley. You said that you should never put a defendant on the stand unless you're desperate."

"It's still the right advice."

"I agree. On the other hand, if the prosecution has a couple of witnesses who are prepared to testify that they saw Mercy grab a knife, you *may* be desperate."

8
"SEEMS YOUR CLIENT LEFT OUT
SOME RELEVANT FACTS"

The veteran homicide inspector adjusted the lapel of his charcoal Men's Wearhouse suit jacket. "Rosie okay?"

"Fine," I said.

"Looks like she's going to win re-election."

"That's the plan."

"Kids?"

"All good. Tommy is a sophomore in high school. Grace is working at Pixar."

"Must be nice to have one out of college."

"It is." When you're trolling for information from a homicide cop, you need to go through the motions of exchanging banal pleasantries for a few minutes. "Yours?"

"Both girls are still in high school and generally okay. Life is complicated when you share custody. They're starting to show interest in boys."

"Nobody gets through the teen years unscathed."

At nine-thirty the following Tuesday morning, Inspector Ken Lee was sitting behind his desk in the sweltering bullpen housing the Homicide Unit on the third floor of the Hall. An overworked fan next to the open window pushed the scalding air smelling of stale coffee and mildew from one side of the room to the other. Most of San Francisco's two dozen homicide inspectors sat facing each other at cluttered desks that were pushed together. Twenty years ago, the homicide cops were all white and male. Nowadays, almost half were female and/or people of color. Despite the heat, the men were wearing suits and ties, and the women were dressed in conservative pantsuits. They always dress respectfully in case they're called to a crime scene.

"What brings you here on such a lovely morning?" Lee asked.

Rosie and I decided that I should make the first contact and play nice. If Lee stonewalled, she would try again another time. "Mercedes Tejada," I said.

"Mercy."

"Uh, yes."

At forty-five, the native of Chinatown had been a homicide inspector for a decade. In an earlier life, he had worked undercover in the crowded neighborhood where his parents had run a spice shop. His cover was blown when he brought down one of Chinatown's most notorious gangs. He was rewarded with a promotion to homicide, where he was trained by my father's first partner, the legendary Roosevelt Johnson. Since Roosevelt retired, Lee had worked alone.

He stroked the scar that ran along his chin line—a souvenir from his undercover days. "I thought Luisa Cervantes was representing Ms. Tejada."

"Luisa was diagnosed with breast cancer, so she won't be handling the trial."

"That's terrible. She going to be okay?"

"I hope so. She started treatments yesterday."

"Give her my best." He meant it.

Notwithstanding our inevitable differences when we had faced off in court, I respected his honesty. The system works better when everybody plays by the same rules.

He cleared his throat. "I gave Luisa everything that she's entitled to from me."

I didn't expect him to be wildly forthcoming. "Anything else you'd like to hand over?"

"Not at this time. You'll need to check with the D.A. about a witness list. You going to ask for a continuance?"

"Haven't decided."

"Trial starts in three weeks."

"We'll be ready."

"So will we. Anything else?"

Here goes. "Mind telling me why you arrested Mercy for first-degree murder?"

"I'm under no obligation to talk to you."

"Please?"

"No comment."

"Professional courtesy?"

"No comment."

"Just a few highlights?"

"This is where I'm supposed to tell you to read my report."

"I'll buy you a cup of coffee."

"I'm not allowed to accept gratuities from defense attorneys."

"Then we'll skip the coffee. Give me five minutes and I'll leave you alone."

His sat in silence for a moment while he tried to decide how much, if anything, he wanted to reveal. "What did Mercy tell you?"

"She didn't stab Cruz."

"She told me the same thing. Seems your client left out some relevant facts."

They always do. "Such as?"

"Did she mention that a neighbor found her kneeling over Cruz's body with a bloody knife sitting on the ground next to her?"

"Somebody else stabbed Cruz. Mercy was trying to help him."

"Did she mention that she and Cruz had been fighting all night and they had a huge shouting match right before he left?"

"What were they supposedly fighting about?"

"Money. Hours. Real and imagined slights. She thought he was a jerk. He thought she was lazy. Maybe they were both right. Either way, it had been going on for months."

"Why didn't he fire her?"

"It's hard to find people for minimum-wage jobs. Nobody can afford to live here. Besides, he was doing his part for the community by hiring her in the first place."

"He thought that being abusive was magnanimous?"

"Everybody who worked there—including your client—knew that he had a big ego."

"It doesn't make it right."

"It didn't give her an excuse to kill him."

"She didn't."

"Says your client."

"Do you have any eyewitnesses who saw what happened outside?"

"No comment."

"What about surveillance video?"

"I sent everything over to Luisa. Nothing relevant."

"A first-degree murder charge requires premeditation."

"You'll need to take it up with DeSean."

"I will." I invoked my best "Can we please cut through the crap" tone. "What do you have, Ken?"

"We found a bloody knife with her fingerprints next to the body. We didn't find anybody else's prints on the knife."

"She removed it from Cruz's stomach and tried to help him."

"Sure."

"Smudges or unidentifiable prints?"

"None. Her clothes were covered in blood. Our spatter expert will testify that the pattern indicated that she stabbed him."

"Ours will come to a different conclusion."

"A witness saw your client pick up a knife shortly before she left."

"El Conquistador was a restaurant. Everybody used knives. It doesn't mean she took it outside and stabbed her boss."

"She took it into the break room. She didn't bring it back into the kitchen."

Uh-oh. "Who is the witness?"

"No comment."

"Come on, Ken. There's no reason to play games."

"I am only required to provide information that would tend to exonerate your client."

I eyed him for a moment. Either he was bluffing, which would have been out of character, he had a less-than-convincing witness, which seemed more likely, or his witness had disappeared, which meant that this evidence—such as it was— might never see the light of day. Either way, he wasn't going to give me a name.

"You can't prove that it was the same knife used to stab Cruz," I said.

"It was part of a matching set of six, one of which was missing from the knife drawer. We found the missing knife next to your client."

"It doesn't prove that Mercy stabbed Cruz."

"The jury will put the pieces together." He stood up and buttoned his jacket, signaling that our conversation was coming to an end. "You might want to ask your client about it."

9
"HE WAS BAD NEWS"

Mercy's eyes were red as she stared at me through the Plexiglas in the visitor area of the Glamour Slammer. "You're back."

"I am." Ordinarily, we would have met in a semi-private consultation area, but the pods were occupied, and I wanted to talk to her right away. The air smelled of disinfectant as I pressed the phone to my ear. "I talked to Ken Lee. He has a witness who saw you take a knife from the kitchen to the break room shortly before you left the restaurant."

"That's a lie."

"It was one of a matching set of six. One was used to stab Cruz. The other five were still in the drawer."

"I didn't stab Carlos."

"Did you take a knife out of a drawer?"

"I used knives every night. So did everybody else who worked there."

"Did you take a knife into the break room?"

"No."

"Is it possible that you took something into the break room that looked like a knife?"

"I don't remember."

"Any idea who the witness might be?"

"Anybody working at the restaurant that night."

"You're the only person who can rebut their testimony."

"I'm prepared to testify if you need me."

"It's generally a bad idea for the defendant to take the stand."

* * *

The cheerful bartender pushed the few remaining strands of his silver hair across the top of his pasty dome and spoke to me in a practiced—and phony—brogue. "Last call, lad."

"Guinness, please, Big John."

"Coming up, Mikey."

My uncle, Big John Dunleavy, used his massive right hand to pull the tap behind the pine bar that he and my father had built more than sixty years earlier. The longtime proprietor of Dunleavy's Bar and Grill on Irving Street and one-time All-City tight end at St. Ignatius had recently celebrated his eighty-sixth birthday, but he refused to slow down. He had turned over the day-to-day operations of his neighborhood watering hole to his grandson, Joey, but he still showed up every morning to make coffee and prepare the batter for his fish and chips.

"Joey told me that you're going to start taking Mondays off," I said.

"The kid's been working here for fifteen years. I figure that he can handle it."

The "kid" was thirty-eight years old. "You should take a vacation." Big John hadn't left town since my Aunt Lil had died almost twenty years earlier. "You could go to Ireland and check out our family's history in County Galway. Maybe I'll come with you."

"There was a reason that my granddaddy—your great-granddaddy—moved over here a hundred and twenty years ago. There wasn't much to see over there other than sheep."

"We can bring your grandkids and great-grandkids. It will help them appreciate how good we have it nowadays."

"Maybe I'll take you up on it—someday."

The wood-paneled saloon was almost empty at ten-thirty on Tuesday night. It was unseasonably warm outside, which meant that it was unbearably hot inside. Dunleavy's was located a block south of Golden Gate Park and about a mile from the ocean in the fog belt. As a result, it didn't have an air conditioner. A couple of off-duty cops were throwing darts next to the booth where my father and his partner, Roosevelt Johnson, used to wind down after their shifts. My mom, who was Big John's sister, wasn't crazy about their after-work ritual, but she knew that my uncle would make sure that my dad made it to our house around the corner safe and sound.

"You talk to Roosevelt?" I asked.

Big John nodded. "He came in last week. He's doing okay. So is Janet."

"Heard from my brother?"

"Petey is on his way. He said that he's going to help you with a new case. I was surprised that you weren't using an investigator from the P.D.'s Office."

"Pete is good."

"That he is. Rosie's okay with it?"

"It was her idea. We need somebody who knows the Mission." I took a draw of my Guinness. "We're representing Mercy Tejada. Luisa Cervantes was handling her case, but she had to drop out. She's starting treatments for breast cancer."

"Sorry to hear it." The phony brogue disappeared. "She going to be okay?"

"I hope so."

"You going to do the trial yourself?"

"Second chair. Rosie is going to take the lead."

"Seriously?"

"Yes."

"This case is going to be a heater, Mikey. Given the current political environment, representing a Dreamer is going to make some people unhappy."

"We'll deal with it."

His expression turned thoughtful. "Are you okay representing a Dreamer?"

"Sure."

"A lot of people don't like the fact that so many undocumenteds are living here."

"I'm just her lawyer, Big John. I leave the politics to Rosie."

"A little of the anger may spill over to you, Mikey."

"We'll deal with that, too." I took a sip of beer. "You okay with us representing a Dreamer?"

"Sure."

"What if she didn't have papers?"

"I'm just a humble barkeep, Mikey."

He was also a very successful one. Dunleavy's had put his four kids and ten grandkids through college.

"Besides," he continued, "I don't like all of the nastiness being directed at immigrants, legal or otherwise. It's mean-spirited. Most of them come here because they're desperate to find work and feed their kids—just like our ancestors."

"True enough, although it's better if they have papers."

"That it is. On the other hand, do you think all of our ancestors had papers?"

"I never asked."

"Neither did I, lad." He gave me a conspiratorial wink. "That didn't stop some of our relatives from sharing a little information with me. For example, I have it on good authority that a few of our forebears came here as a result of arranged marriages."

"Care to mention any names?"

"You know that a bartender would never engage in gossip—especially about family."

"For the next five minutes, let's pretend that you've hired me as your lawyer. Everything you tell me is confidential under the attorney-client privilege."

His round face transformed into a broad grin. "Let's just say that if your great-grandma hadn't agreed to an arranged marriage to your great-grandpa, they wouldn't have let her into the country, and neither of us would be drinking Guinness at this fine establishment today."

"You're saying the only reason they let Great-grandma Margaret come over here was because she had agreed to marry Great-grandpa Tom?"

"So I was told."

"By whom?"

"Great-grandpa Tom."

"Did he come here legally?"

"As far as I know."

"Had they ever met before they got married?"

"Absolutely."

"How long had they known each other?"

"Depending on who was telling the story, somewhere between fifteen and twenty minutes. They tied the knot at St. Peter's. Father Yorke performed the ceremony himself."

Father Peter Yorke was a native of County Galway who found his way to San Francisco and became the longtime priest at St. Peter's in the early twentieth century. In addition to his priestly duties, he was a labor organizer, newspaper editor, and rabble rouser. The street in front of the headquarters of the San Francisco Archdiocese is named after him. He was buried near my parents at Holy Cross Cemetery in Colma.

I was now intrigued. "Did money change hands when this marriage was arranged?"

"I wouldn't be surprised. Either way, it worked out pretty well. They were married for fifty-seven years. I was also told that a few of our 'cousins' who came over here under the sponsorship of my grandpa were rather, uh, distant cousins."

"How distant?"

"They weren't related to us. When the potatoes stopped growing, they did what they had to do. Things were looser in those days, and the Irish Catholics looked out for each other."

"We still do. Did they all get papers?"

"Eventually."

"Legally?"

"Beats me, lad." His eyes danced. "For all I know, Father Yorke knew somebody who provided immigration papers." He refilled my pint. "Look on the bright side, Mikey. You aren't running for re-election. Rosie will take most of the heat."

"If she loses, I'll be out of a job, too."

"My sources assure me that she's going to win."

His sources were very reliable. "There are no guarantees, Big John."

"Even if she loses, you won't be out of work for long."

"There isn't a huge market for a fifty-eight-year-old defense attorney and former priest."

"You can always tend bar for me."

I had worked part-time for Big John from the time I was seventeen until I finished law school. It wasn't legal until I turned twenty-one, but nobody complained. "Best job I ever had."

"You were the best barkeep I ever had. My regulars always liked you, Mikey. They were disappointed when you became a priest. They were devastated when you became a lawyer." He winked. "For Mercy's sake, I hope the jurors like you as much as my customers did."

A few minutes later, we were watching the highlights of the Warriors game on the big-screen TV when the back door swung open and Pete ambled inside, head down, eyes on his phone. He took a seat on the stool next to mine and spoke to our uncle. "You good, Big John?"

"Fine, Petey." My uncle poured him a cup of coffee. "Donna and Margaret okay?"

"All good."

Pete's wife, Donna, was a patient soul who was the chief financial officer of one of the big law firms downtown. Margaret—named after our mother and great-grandmother—was Pete's thirteen-year-old daughter. She was lightning smart and as tenacious as her father.

Pete took a sip of scalding Folgers and turned to me. "Rosie and the kids good?"

"Fine." We were now of an age where every conversation began with an inquiry into the health of our respective family members.

"You wanted to see me?"

"Yes." I filled him in on my conversation with Lee. "He claims that they have a witness who saw Mercy take a knife from the kitchen into the break room before she left the restaurant. He thinks she used the knife to stab Cruz."

"Got a name?"

"Not yet."

"Male or female?"

"Don't know."

"I'll see what I can find. Anything else?"

"I was wondering what you found out about Carlos Cruz."

"He was a dick." Pete played with his mug. "You remember how you used to tell me that the lawyers at that big firm where you worked were the biggest jerks on Planet Earth?"

"Uh, yes."

"And you recall all the lying sexist egomaniacs that you dealt with when you represented the woman accused of giving a hot shot of heroin to that Silicon Valley billionaire last year?"

"I do."

"Cruz was even worse." His tone was deadly serious. "He was bad news, Mick. He treated everybody like crap. He hit on anyone with a pulse: male, female, straight, gay, bi, trans. If they turned him down, he threatened to fire them. If they were undocumented, he threatened to report them to ICE."

"Have you talked to anybody who worked at the restaurant?"

"Working on it. The investor, Jed Sanders, is in Fiji with his girlfriend, Christine Fong, who was the maître d'. They're supposed to be back next week. Cruz's brother, the business guy, is working for a real estate agent. He must have known that his brother was a prick."

"What about the employees?"

"Working on that, too. Some of them have left town."

"Are you pretty sure that some of them were victims of sexual harassment?"

"No, I'm *absolutely* sure that *many* of them were victims of sexual harassment."

"Sanders didn't do anything about it?"

"It would have been bad for his investment if word got out that his star chef was a serial sexual harasser."

"How was the restaurant doing financially?" I asked.

"If you believe the press, it was printing money. If you believe my sources in the Mission, it was hemorrhaging cash." He arched an eyebrow. "My sources tend to be more reliable than the mainstream media."

True enough. "I need you to find everybody who was working at El Conquistador."

"Working on it." He finished his coffee and got up. "I'll be in touch, Mick."

10

"IT GAVE HER MOTIVE"

"You're up late," I said.

Our fifteen-year-old son, Tommy, was standing in Rosie's living room at twelve-thirty the following morning. He had been an unplanned but welcome surprise after Rosie and I had gotten divorced.

"Homework," he said.

Right.

I gave him a hug and took a seat on the sofa next to Rosie. We had rented the post-earthquake bungalow across the street from the Little League field in Larkspur after Grace was born. While we would have preferred to stay in the City, the leafy suburb ten miles north of the Golden Gate Bridge had excellent public schools. After we got divorced, Rosie kept the house, and I moved into a one-bedroom apartment a few blocks away behind the Silver Peso, one of the last dive bars in Marin County. After we got a death penalty conviction overturned for a one-time mob lawyer, our client expressed his gratitude by buying us the house. While Rosie and I were a permanent couple, I still spent a couple of nights a week at the apartment when we needed a little space. The arrangement had worked pretty well for us for almost two decades. In order to meet the legal requirement that the Public Defender live in San Francisco, Rosie's "official residence" was a rented studio apartment across the street from her mother's house.

"Homework finished?" I asked.

Tommy nodded.

He was more interested in football and video games than

schoolwork. I didn't expect him to obsess about his studies as much as I had, but I was concerned that his lack of focus would last into his forties.

After a recent growth spurt, he was now a lanky six-two, and he carried a hundred and seventy pounds on his wiry frame. His fair skin, blue eyes, and light brown hair suggested more Daley than Fernandez genes. He had inherited a powerful throwing arm from his namesake uncle, my older brother. Young Tommy was the starting quarterback at Redwood High and was leading the not-terribly-athletic Marin County Athletic League in passing. If he continued to develop and filled out a bit, he had a shot at walking on at a Division One college.

Rosie pointed at her watch. "Time to call it a night, Tom. Early practice tomorrow."

"I know, Mom."

She had always been the disciplinarian.

He started to head down the hall toward the room that he used to share with his older sister. He stopped abruptly, turned around, and pulled at the drawstrings of his faded UC-Berkeley sweatshirt which used to be mine. "You really going to handle Mercy Tejada's trial?"

"Yes." I exchanged a glance with Rosie. "You okay with that?"

"Uh, yeah."

"Something bothering you, Tom?"

"Somebody at school said that the City shouldn't pay for a lawyer for an illegal alien."

"She's here legally."

"Oh."

"It's our job to represent her. You okay with us handling her case?"

"Yeah."

"Good. If anybody else gives you any trouble, let us know."

"You coming to my game on Saturday?"

"Definitely."

His perpetual teenage scowl finally broke. "Good."

"You're starting, right?" I already knew the answer.

"Right."

"Excellent." I was silently hoping that he would decide to focus on baseball to avoid concussions and other injuries. Then again, since I had been a backup running back at S.I., I didn't think I could tell him that he couldn't play football.

"Uh, Dad?"

"Yes?"

"Do you think we can practice driving this weekend?"

"Sure. How about Sunday afternoon after church?"

His stoic façade finally cracked into the familiar smile. "Sounds good."

He walked the short distance to his room and shut the door behind him.

Rosie looked at me. "I'm a little surprised that the kids at school knew about Mercy."

"It's all over the media. It'll get even more attention as we get closer to trial—especially if our D.A. and soon-to-be mayor starts talking about it on TV."

"That's inevitable."

"Is Tommy doing okay?"

"As far as I can tell. He doesn't say much. I wish he would spend more time with his books and less with his phone, but there's only so much that we can do at this age."

"We'll get through it. Tommy is easier than Grace was at fifteen. She was already into boys. Wait until he discovers girls."

"He already has." Her eyes gleamed. "He just hasn't figured out how to ask them out."

"He will. Anybody in particular?"

"I think so."

"He'll muster the courage sooner or later."

Rosie's grin broadened. "Hopefully, it's later."

"It took me a couple of months before I asked you out."

"I asked you."

"No, you didn't."

"Yes, I did."

It was another argument that I was happy to lose. "Maybe you're right."

"I know that I'm right." She reached over and touched my cheek. "You're a good sport to take him driving."

"He needs practice. And he's more cautious than Grace. My hair turned half-gray when I taught her how to drive. By the time Tommy gets his license, it's going to be snow white."

"It makes you look distinguished."

"It makes me look old."

"You could color it."

"Then I'll look like a fifty-eight-year-old guy who dyes his hair."

She kissed me. "I like you just the way you are, Mike. And I think we've aged pretty well."

"I'd like to think so, too. How did it go tonight?"

"Better than expected. We raised about fifteen thousand."

"Not a bad haul." Between now and the election, Rosie would be spending most of her free time—such as it was—attending rubber chicken dinners. "How was the food?"

"Heavy hors d'oeuvres with some mid-priced wine."

"Could have been worse." I looked her in the eye. "Last campaign, right?"

"Right." She went into the kitchen and returned with a half-empty bottle of Pride Mountain Cab Franc and two glasses.

"You interested?"

"Not on a school night."

"You'll sleep better." She filled my glass and turned to business. "Did you learn anything useful from Ken Lee?"

"Not much." It was almost one a.m., but it was never too late (or too early) for Rosie to talk shop. "He has witnesses who will say that Mercy and Cruz were arguing. It gave her motive. There was a bloody knife on the ground next to her when the police arrived. Her prints were on the knife. She was wearing bloody clothes. It wasn't a stretch to suggest that she stabbed Cruz."

"She tried to help him."

"Says Mercy. Lee also purports to have a witness who saw Mercy take a knife from the kitchen into the break room shortly before she left the restaurant."

"Got a name?"

"Not yet."

"Let me guess: it's the same type of knife that was used to stab Cruz."

"Correct. It was one of a matching set."

"Let me guess again: Mercy denied it."

"Also correct. In addition, Pete says that Cruz treated everybody else at the restaurant like crap. It gave them motive, too."

"Only Mercy is charged with murder."

"Then we'll need to change the narrative. We should start with the District Attorney. DeSean Harper agreed to see us later this morning."

"Good." She finished her wine. "Are you going over to your apartment tonight?"

I reached over and squeezed her hand. "No, I'd like to stay."

11
"IT'S AN ELECTION YEAR"

The Chief Assistant District Attorney leaned back in his swivel chair. "Good to see you, Rosie."

"Good to see you, DeSean."

DeSean Harper glanced my way. "Mike."

"DeSean."

So much for the pleasantries.

At ten o'clock the same morning, Rosie and I were meeting with Harper in his spacious office in the D.A.'s new digs in a refurbished building at the foot of Potrero Hill that formerly housed a commercial catering operation. Since legal briefs aren't baked in ovens, the high-end commercial kitchen was removed at substantial cost. As a result, before a single lawyer moved in, the City had forked out over twelve million dollars, which was well over budget. Harper's mile-long commute to the Hall and less-than-stellar view of a welding shop across the street were a small price to pay for new bathrooms.

The alum of Cal and Harvard Law School had grown up in the Bayview near Candlestick Park. Harper was about my age, but three decades of prosecuting high-stress cases had taken a toll. He weighed more than two hundred and fifty pounds, and his closely cropped hair was now completely gray. His ex-wife was a federal judge. Their older daughter was a second-year law student at Stanford. Her sister was an engineer at Oracle. Their framed graduation photos were the only personal items in his office. His navy suit was complemented by a starched white shirt and a polka-dot necktie with a crisp Windsor knot.

Rosie looked at the bookcases filled with case reporters,

which were strictly for show. If Harper needed a citation, he would find it on his laptop. "Thanks for seeing us, DeSean."

"You're welcome. How is Luisa?"

"She completed her first chemo session. So far, the side effects have been minimal."

"Good to hear. I sent her a card."

"I'm sure she appreciated it." Rosie glanced at a poster-sized photo leaning against the wall. The stern image of Harper's boss, Nicole Ward, stared at us beneath a caption reading, "Tough on Crime." Rosie flashed a wry grin. "Seen much of Nicole lately?"

"She's busy running for mayor. I see her on TV more than in the office."

"She's ahead in the polls," Rosie observed.

"So are you."

"I take it that means that you're running things here?"

"For the most part."

Harper had been running the day-to-day operation of the D.A.'s Office for years.

"For what it's worth," Rosie said, "if Nicole wins, I would be pleased if you became our next D.A. It's always better to have somebody competent heading the office."

"Thank you." Harper glanced at his watch. "You wanted to talk about Mercy Tejada?"

"Yes."

"Trial starts October twenty-eighth before Judge Vanden Heuvel."

It wasn't a great draw for us. Judge Kathleen Vanden Heuvel was a former Alameda County prosecutor and one-time law professor at Berkeley. She was smart, prepared, and a stickler for rules. She was generally even-handed, but her views tended to tilt in favor of the prosecution.

"She's an excellent judge," I said.

"I've always gotten a fair shake. Pre-trial motions are due a week from Monday. Are you planning to ask for anything special?"

"Probably just the usual. You?"

"Same here. No TV cameras. No talking to the press."

Good. "What about a manslaughter instruction?"

"Haven't decided."

In a first-degree murder trial, the judge is required to instruct the jury that it may convict the defendant of second-degree. The judge also has the option to give a manslaughter instruction (voluntary, involuntary, or both). While the judge makes the final call, he or she usually gives some weight to the wishes of the lawyers. These decisions often have significant ramifications because it's generally easier for jurors to vote for a "compromise" verdict of manslaughter than to convict for first-degree murder. The judge wouldn't decide until after the evidence is presented.

"This isn't a first-degree case," I said.

"Yes, it is."

"There's no premeditation."

"Yes, there is."

"Mercy didn't stab Cruz."

"Yes, she did."

"You won't be able to prove it beyond a reasonable doubt."

"Yes, we will." He'd heard enough. "Are you going to ask for a continuance?"

"No."

"Change of venue?"

"Probably not."

"You going to try it yourself?"

Rosie spoke up. "I'm going to take the lead. Mike will sit

second chair."

"Really?"

"Really."

"May I ask why?"

"We think it would be in our client's best interests."

Good answer. Says nothing.

Harper arched an eyebrow. "You think that's wise in the middle of an election campaign?"

"We don't make staffing decisions based on political considerations."

Unlike Harper's boss.

"Are you going to try the case yourself?" Rosie asked.

"We think it would be in the People's best interests."

Touché.

Harper held up a hand. "I guess we'll see you in court."

"We'll need your witness list right away," I said.

"I'll send it over by the end of next week."

"Anybody other than the employees of the restaurant and Ken Lee?"

"Definitely the Chief Medical Examiner. Probably the first officer at the scene. Likely the neighbor who called nine-one-one."

"We're going to talk to everybody who was working at El Conquistador that night."

"I can't stop you, but they're under no obligation to talk to you."

"Are all of the employees still in the area?"

"As far as I know."

"Are any of them undocumented?"

"No comment."

"Anybody been picked up by ICE?"

"Not as far as I know."

"Are you planning to send over any other evidence?"

"Not at this time."

Thanks. "We'd like to take a look at El Conquistador."

"Be my guest. You can go over there and knock on the door. The space is still empty. Except for the fact that they've removed the kitchen equipment, it looks the same as it did on the night that your client murdered Cruz."

"Allegedly," I answered reflexively.

"Allegedly," he repeated, sarcastic. "Innocent until proven guilty, right?"

"Right. Are you planning to call the investor, Jed Sanders?"

"Possibly."

"Christine Fong?"

"Maybe."

"And Cruz's brother?"

"Haven't decided."

"We talked to Ken Lee. He said you have a witness who claims to have seen our client take a knife from the kitchen into the break room."

"We do."

"Mind giving us a name?"

"In due course."

Rosie cleared her throat. "Any chance you might be willing to discuss something a little more reasonable than first-degree murder?"

"What did you have in mind?"

"Voluntary manslaughter. Better yet, involuntary."

"No."

"This isn't a murder case, DeSean. Mercy didn't stab Cruz. And even if she did, there's no premeditation."

"Then it's second-degree."

"It's at most vol man—heat of passion."

"I can't do it."

"Says who?"

"Nicole."

"Why not?"

He glanced at the photo of his boss. "It's an election year."

12

"STAB WOUND"

The Chief Medical Examiner of the City and County of San Francisco pretended to remove an imaginary piece of lint from her white lab coat, tilted her head slightly, and spoke with her customary precision. "Good afternoon, Mr. Daley."

"Good afternoon, Dr. Siu."

I had met Dr. Joy Siu at least a dozen times in her office and a few times in court. At first, I always asked her to call me Mike, but informality wasn't her style. Nowadays, I didn't try.

The sunlight was shining through the picture window in her office on the second floor of the new Medical Examiner's facility in a warehouse-like building in the grimy India Basin neighborhood, about halfway between downtown and Candlestick Point. It wasn't as conveniently located as her old office in the basement of the Hall of Justice, but the state-of-the-art examination rooms and expanded morgue compensated for the less-than-ideal location and the less-than-stellar view of the recycling facility across the street on Pier 96.

"How can I help you?" she asked.

"I understand that you performed the autopsy on Carlos Cruz."

"I did."

She was sitting behind a glass-topped desk covered with folders in orderly piles. From her pressed lab coat to her meticulously applied makeup to her precisely cut black hair, she exuded exactness. Now in her mid-forties, the Princeton and Johns Hopkins Medical School alum and former research scientist at UCSF was a world-class academic and an internationally recognized expert in anatomic pathology. The one-time Olympic figure skating hopeful spent a quarter of her time travelling the world to consult on complex autopsy cases.

"I'm surprised that you didn't hand it off to one of your colleagues," I said.

"Mr. Cruz died when several of our people were on vacation or maternity leave. I happened to be in the office at the time."

She was one of San Francisco's hardest working public servants. "Cause of death?"

"Stab wound. I presume the D.A.'s Office provided you with a copy of my report?"

"They did."

"Then you know everything that I do."

Not quite.

"Anything else?" she asked.

"Just one stab wound?"

"Yes."

"Where?"

"It's in my report."

I looked at her hopefully.

She pointed at her midsection. "Abdomen. The knife pierced the stomach, colon, and gall bladder, resulting in substantial blood loss. The decedent had almost certainly lost consciousness by the time the EMTs arrived. He had a pulse for a short time. Then he bled out in the ambulance. He was pronounced at San Francisco General."

"Official time of death?"

'One-twenty-four a.m."

"Any chance he might have survived if they had gotten him to the hospital sooner?"

"Only if he had been stabbed at the hospital and they could have given him a transfusion and gotten him into emergency surgery immediately. There was extensive hemorrhaging and massive internal bleeding."

"You're sure the wound was caused by the Messermeister knife?"

She measured her words. "The wound was consistent in size and shape with one that could have been administered by the Messermeister."

"But you can't match up the knife precisely with the wound the way you can match expended bullet shells to a particular firearm, right?"

She responded with a grudging, "Right. The first officer at the scene found a bloody knife on the ground next to your client. I am not an experienced lawyer like you are, but I suspect that it will be a heavy lift to persuade a jury that another knife was used to stab Mr. Cruz."

We don't need to prove it. We just need to muddy the waters enough to give them another building block toward reasonable doubt. "Toxicology?"

"Traces of alcohol."

"How much?"

"Below the legal limit."

"Anything else?"

"Traces of cocaine."

"Enough that he would have been impaired?"

"Enough that he would have been mildly stimulated."

"Any evidence that he was a regular user?"

"Yes."

It was juicy information that may have explained some of Cruz's erratic behavior. On the other hand, we were not going to convince a jury that he died of an overdose.

"Were you able to identify any physical characteristics of the killer based upon your examination of the body?" I asked.

"The wound was made at a slight angle going from right to left. This suggests that the killer may have been right-handed." She quickly added, "The prints on the knife were from your client's right hand."

Mercy was left-handed. "Was he stabbed from in front or from behind?"

"In front. Based on the location of the body, it is almost certain that he was standing in front of his car when he was stabbed. There was no way that your client could have gotten behind him and reached around and stabbed him from the rear."

"Defensive wounds?"

"None. This suggests that he knew the killer."

"Maybe he was surprised and didn't have time to react. Or maybe he was distracted."

"Both are theoretically possible."

"Did you find any prints on the knife other than my client's?"

"That's a question for the evidence tech."

I studied the report. "The blood on my client's sweatshirt matched the decedent's?"

"Correct."

"A blood spatter analysis was completed?"

"Yes."

"And it's your view that the spatter on my client's clothing was consistent with your theory that my client stabbed Cruz?"

"That's another question for the evidence tech."

13
"YOUR CLIENT'S PRINTS WERE ON THE KNIFE"

The metal bookcases were crammed with three-ring binders with hand-written labels in the windowless office between the file room and the restrooms on the second floor of the Hall of Justice. The gray walls were covered by yellowed anatomy posters. In what passed for whimsy in this otherwise depressing area, a smiling plastic skeleton was sporting a Warriors jersey.

"I like your new office," I said.

"Thank you." The dignified woman in her mid-sixties stood up, extended a hand, and spoke with understated authority. "After sharing space for thirty-four years, this represents an upgrade. A private office without a window is better than a shared one with a view."

"Agreed."

The corner of her mouth turned up into a half smile. "Good to see you again, Mr. Daley."

"Good to see you, too, Lieutenant Jacobsen."

Lieutenant Katherine Jacobsen's badge was displayed in the breast pocket of the jacket of her gray pantsuit. Her makeup was subtle, her salt-and-pepper hair styled in a low-maintenance layered cut. The daughter of an IBM engineer had grown up in Atherton and spent her summers at the pool at the Burlingame Country Club. She turned down a tennis scholarship from Stanford to play water polo and to study criminal justice at USC, where she graduated *summa cum laude*. She earned a master's from Cal in forensic science and joined SFPD as an evidence technician. One of the first lesbians to work her way up the ranks, she had a national reputation on forensic evidentiary matters, with a specialty in blood spatter. A framed photo of her wife, Jill, a San Francisco firefighter, was on the corner of her desk next to her laptop.

She folded her hands. "I understand from DeSean Harper that you have some questions about the evidence relating to the death of Carlos Cruz."

"Yes." At least she didn't use the word "murder."

"This is where I'm supposed to refer you to my report."

"I know."

"You appreciate the fact that I'm under no obligation to talk to you."

"I do." The best defense attorneys are often accomplished grovelers. I was also certain that she wouldn't have been talking to me if she hadn't cleared it with Harper. "I am very grateful for your time."

"And I would be very grateful if you would keep this brief. I have another meeting."

"I understand that you processed the scene and collected the physical evidence."

"I did. You aren't going to be successful with a chain-of-custody argument, Mr. Daley."

I know. "We have no evidence of any such issues, Lieutenant."

"Good."

Then again, if we find any potential irregularities, we won't hesitate to ask you about them at trial. "You believe that Mr. Cruz was stabbed by a Messermeister Meridian Elite Stealth chef's knife?"

"Correct. That was the murder weapon."

It wasn't an ideal time to reminder her that there is no "murder" until the jury says so. "How many stab wounds?"

"Just one."

"You found the decedent's blood on the knife?"

"Yes."

"Anybody else's?"

"No. We did a DNA test."

"Where was the knife when the first officer arrived?"

"On the ground next to the body. Your client's prints were on the knife."

"Right or left hand?"

"Right."

"Anybody else's prints?"

"No." She confirmed that she found no unidentified or smudged prints.

"I understand that you also did a blood spatter analysis."

"I did. There was a heavy and contiguous bloodstain centered between the stomach and chest on your client's sweatshirt. It was consistent with an attempt to put pressure on an open wound to try to stop the bleeding."

"If she had just stabbed him, why would she have tried to stop the bleeding?"

"You'll need to ask your client."

"Why didn't she run?"

"You'll need to ask your client."

"Why did she call for help?"

She pushed out a melodramatic sigh. "I can provide information and answer questions about forensic evidence, Mr. Daley. I can't tell you what was going on inside your client's head."

Fair enough. I opened my laptop and showed her an image of Mercy's blood-stained sweatshirt displayed on a stainless-steel table. "You took this photo?"

"I did."

I pointed at a stain running from the stomach up to the

breast line. "That's the stain that you believe was created when Mercy attempted to stop the bleeding?"

"Correct. In addition, if you look closely, you'll see smaller droplets." She picked up a pencil and pointed at about a dozen droplets above the larger stain. "These are between one and four millimeters in diameter. It's a so-called 'projected pattern,' which is generally caused when there is arterial damage during a beating or stabbing and results in blood spraying toward the attacker."

"You're saying that my client stabbed Cruz in such a manner that it caused the smaller droplets to spurt out of his body and land above the larger stain?"

"Correct."

"Isn't it possible that those droplets were projected onto my client's sweatshirt when she removed the knife?"

"No, Mr. Daley."

"Why not?"

"If your client was telling the truth, the decedent was lying on the ground when she found him. If she removed the knife, she would have pulled it upward out of his stomach and toward herself."

"So?"

"Blood doesn't fly up in such circumstances, Mr. Daley. It would have defied the law of gravity."

We'll need to find an expert who would argue that the law of gravity doesn't apply. "Thank you for your time, Lieutenant Jacobsen."

"You're very welcome, Mr. Daley."

14
"IT'S NEWS"

Rosie looked at me over the top of the wire-framed glasses that replaced her contacts when she got tired. "Anything useful from Dr. Siu?"

"About what I expected. Cruz died of a stab wound." I filled her in on the details.

"And Lieutenant Jacobsen?"

"She'll testify that there is blood spatter evidence that Mercy stabbed Cruz. I'll find an expert who will come to the opposite conclusion. He'll have to say that the law of gravity doesn't apply in this case."

She smiled. "Wouldn't be the first time."

I looked over at Nady, who was kneeling in the corner of our conference room and rubbing the belly of her impeccably behaved Keeshond dog, Luna. With her plush, two-layer gray/black coat, pointed ears, and tightly curled tail, the thirteen-year-old canine had been a welcome addition to the only pet-friendly P.D.'s Office in California. Our unofficial mascot spent most of the day sleeping under Nady's desk.

"How's my friend?" I asked.

"Hungry."

"She's always hungry."

"That's her job. And she's an optimist. Every human is a potential bearer of food."

"She has good instincts." I reached into my pocket, pulled out a treat, and handed it to Luna, who devoured it enthusiastically, wagged her tail profusely, and looked up hopefully. "Sorry, pal. That's the last one."

The overgrown puppy's huge brown eyes filled with disappointment.

Our conference room smelled of coffee and dog food at nine-thirty on Wednesday night. We were two and a half weeks from trial, and we still had to cover a lot of territory.

I took a seat and spoke to Nady, who was now hunched over her laptop. "Did the judge respond to our request to reduce bail?"

"Yes. The answer is no."

I wasn't surprised. "Where do we stand on pre-trial motions?"

"We'll ask the judge to order Harper to provide additional evidence on an expedited basis. We'll want a gag order and no TV cameras. I don't think the judge will object."

"Neither do I."

"Have you given any more thought to requesting a manslaughter instruction?"

"At the moment, I'm inclined to do so."

"It may make it easier for the jury to find a path to a conviction."

"It's better than a murder conviction." I looked over at Rosie. "What do you think?"

"I'm inclined to agree with you—for now. Any word from Pete?"

"I'll let you know as soon as I hear from him. Did you go over and see Mercy?"

"Briefly. She's putting up a brave front, but she's getting nervous."

"Is she eating?"

"Not much. She's taking her insulin."

"Good. Have you heard from Perlita?"

"Mama talked to her briefly. She's also getting nervous. And she thinks somebody may be following her."

Uh-oh. "ICE?"

"I don't know. I told Mama to tell her to stay home unless she absolutely has to go out. Have you given any thought to our narrative?"

I knew this was coming. When I was a rookie P.D., Rosie emphasized that trial work is theater. You need to tell the jury a compelling story with a beginning, a middle, and an ending. It isn't always necessary to entertain them, but it helps. It's more important to play to their emotions. Jurors are more conscientious in real life than on TV. It was our job to convince them that they were doing the right thing by voting for an acquittal.

"It's simple," I said. "Mercy didn't stab Cruz."

"Bloody knife?"

"She found him lying on the ground and removed it."

"Her fingerprints?"

"She got them on the knife when she removed it. And the prints were from her right hand. Mercy is left-handed."

"What about the witness who said that Mercy took a knife into the break room?"

"They were mistaken or lying. Or she could have put it back. Or they were trying to set her up."

"And the witnesses who are going to testify that Mercy and Cruz were arguing shortly before she left the restaurant?"

"Cruz fought with everybody."

"And the claims that he sexually and verbally harassed Mercy?"

"It doesn't prove that she killed him."

Rosie frowned. "It would help if somebody can corroborate our version of the story."

"Pete's working on it. If he can't find anybody, we'll put

Mercy on the stand."

"That would be less than ideal."

"We'll make that decision later. We'll also argue that Mercy didn't behave like a killer. She tried to help Cruz. She didn't run. She called out for help. She cooperated with the police."

Rosie templed her fingers in front of her face. "This is going to be a tough slog unless we can find some hard evidence pointing at somebody else."

"We just need to blow enough smoke to get one juror to reasonable doubt."

Rosie's phone rang. She looked down at the display and her lips turned down. "My day is now complete."

"Who?" I asked.

"Jerry Edwards."

Edwards was the *Chronicle*'s longtime political columnist and investigative reporter. The award-winning journalist remained pugnacious after three acrimonious divorces and periodic trips to rehab for a long-running battle with alcoholism. Rosie and I had been on the receiving end of his barbs several times, and it was always painful. Nevertheless, I respected him for standing up for truth—most of the time.

"You going to talk to him?" I asked.

"It's better to get ahead of him and try to control the narrative. Who knows? Maybe he has something we can use."

She put her phone on the table, activated the speaker, and pressed the green button. "Hello, Jerry."

Edwards responded with a smoker's cough. "Ms. Fernandez."

"Rosie."

"Rosie."

"My colleagues, Mike Daley and Nady Nikonova, are here. How can we help you?"

"I understand that you're handling Mercy Tejada's trial."

"I am."

"And your ex-husband is going to sit second chair?"

"Correct."

"Do you think it's a wise use of taxpayer dollars to provide free representation to an undocumented person?"

"She's a Dreamer, Jerry. She's here legally."

"She isn't a U.S. citizen."

"She's entitled to representation from our office."

"You think that's right?"

"Yes. Anything else?"

He let out a violent cough. "We have information from a reliable source that Mercy Tejada's mother is undocumented. Could you please confirm that information for me?"

"No comment."

"We plan to publish this information in tomorrow morning's paper."

"That would serve no useful purpose."

"It's news."

Rosie made an obscene gesture at her phone. "I have no comment on the substance of this information, Jerry. However, I would note that our client's mother is also the sole source of support of a four-year-old daughter who is a U.S. citizen."

Edwards didn't respond.

Rosie lowered her voice. "If you report this information, Jerry, you're going to be responsible for ruining the life of an innocent little girl. Is that what you really want?"

"I'm just doing my job."

"This isn't a legal issue, Jerry. It's a moral one. You have kids. You understand what I'm talking about. I'm asking you to use your discretion."

"Let me think about it."

"I hope you decide to do the right thing." Rosie ended the call and spoke to me. "I'm going to call Mama. We need to talk to Perlita right away."

15
"WE HAVE A COMPLICATION"

Perlita took a sip of tea from a white mug. "Did you see Mercy this afternoon?"

Rosie's voice was gentle. "Yes. Given the circumstances, she's holding up okay."

"Is she taking her insulin?"

"Yes."

"Good." Perlita explained that she also dealt with diabetes and pointed out that it was complicated for an undocumented person to obtain insulin. "I was planning to go over and see her tomorrow."

"That isn't a good idea." Rosie reached across her mother's dining room table and touched Perlita's hand. "We have a complication."

Perlita waited.

"We got a call from Jerry Edwards at the *Chronicle*. He received a tip that you're undocumented. He's planning to publish the information tomorrow."

Perlita's voice filled with resignation. "I suppose it was inevitable."

The windows were open in Sylvia's house at ten-forty-five the same evening, a Wednesday. The fog had finally rolled in and provided a welcome respite from the heat. The aroma of Sylvia's chicken enchiladas wafted in from the kitchen. Perlita's younger daughter, Isabel, was in the living room watching a video of *Frozen*.

Perlita exhaled. "How did he find out?"

"I don't know. You had mentioned to Mama that you

thought that somebody was following you."

"I think so." Perlita described him as a young man of medium build with a mustache. "I noticed him on Twenty-fourth. He was wearing a Giants cap and a denim jacket."

"ICE?"

"I don't know. Is there any way that you can stop Edwards?"

"No." Rosie shot a glance at Isabel, then she turned back to Perlita. "I told him that if he reveals this information, it would make your life and Isabel's more difficult. In the meantime, we need you to be very careful and keep a low profile."

"Isabel and I will stay home for a few days."

"It may not be safe for you to go home."

"San Francisco is a Sanctuary City."

"It doesn't matter."

"Doesn't that prevent ICE from picking up people like me?"

"No. The Sanctuary City ordinance is more limited than people think. It prohibits city employees from using city funds to assist ICE. It also limits San Francisco police from giving ICE advance notice of when an undocumented person is going to be released from jail. And it prohibits SFPD from cooperating ICE with investigations and detainer requests."

"That's it?"

"That's it."

"The cops can't report me to ICE if I visit Mercy."

"True, but there is nothing to prevent ICE from waiting for you outside and detaining you."

"They don't know who I am."

"They do now."

Perlita darted a glance at Isabel. "We can't live on the street."

"Every time you go out, you risk being picked up by ICE."

"We have no place else to stay."

Sylvia spoke up. "You can stay here."

"No, Sylvia. I can't ask you to do that."

"I *want* to do it."

"You could get into serious trouble."

"I'm prepared to accept the consequences."

Rosie spoke up again. "Perlita is right, Mama. It's a bad idea."

"Doing the right thing is always correct, and I have an excellent defense attorney."

"It's too risky."

"You really think they'd lock up an old woman?"

"We live in challenging times, Mama."

Perlita lowered her voice. "I am grateful for the offer, Sylvia, but Isabel and I are not staying with you, and we won't do anything to put you into legal jeopardy."

"But Perlita—,"

"It's out of the question."

"You can't stay at home," Sylvia said. "They'll find you."

"Then we'll find someplace else to stay."

"Where?"

"I don't know."

Sylvia picked up her iPhone, punched in a number, held it up to her ear, and marched into the kitchen, where she continued her conversation out of earshot. She returned five minutes later and spoke to Perlita. "I have a safe place for you and Isabel to stay."

"Where?"

"You'll see when we get there. The fewer people who know about this, the better—including Rosita and Michael."

Agreed.

Rosie glanced out the window, then spoke to her mother. "Somebody may be outside. They'll follow your car."

"That's what I'm hoping for, Rosita. I want you to drive my

car to your house. Michael will drive your car to Marin using a different route. If somebody is watching us, they'll probably follow one of you."

"How will Mercy and Isabel get to their destination?"

"Somebody is coming to pick us up."

"You're planning to go with them?"

"Yes."

"Is there any way that I can talk you out of it?"

"No." Sylvia turned to Perlita. "I need you to turn off your phone."

"I won't be able to get in touch with my customers."

"The police and ICE will be able to track you if you leave it on." Sylvia reached into her pocket, pulled out a disposable "burner" phone, and handed it to Perlita. "From now on, I want you to use this."

Perlita put the phone into her pocket.

Sylvia stood up and put on her jacket. "We need to get ready to go. They're coming to pick us up in a few minutes."

16
"IT'S BETTER NOT TO KNOW"

At twelve-forty on Thursday morning, I pulled Rosie's Prius into her driveway and parked behind Sylvia's Civic. The lights were out inside the house. A cool breeze whipped through the trees. I got out of the car, looked around, and jogged up the five steps to the front door, which Rosie opened before I could insert my key.

"Anybody follow you?" she whispered.

"I don't think so. You?"

"Not as far as I could tell."

We went inside and sat down on the sofa, the lights still off. I looked down the hallway at Tommy's room, where I saw the light under the bottom of his door. "Still awake?"

"For now," Rosie said.

"Should we say something?"

"Better to let it go."

I deferred to her. "Did your mother make it home?"

"Yes. Perlita and her daughter made it to the safe house."

"Good." I held up my phone. "Have you seen the *Chronicle*'s website?"

"Not in the last hour."

"Edwards reported that Perlita is undocumented."

"It is what it is."

I gave my ex-wife, current boss, and best friend a knowing look. "Has your mother ever done something like this?"

"Wouldn't be surprised."

"Where did she learn about burner phones?"

"She's very resourceful."

"Do you know who she called?"

"No."

"Do you know who picked them up?"

"No."

"Do you know where they took Perlita?"

"It's better not to know."

Got it. "Did your mother just do something illegal?"

"It isn't illegal to have a cup of tea with your housekeeper."

"It could be construed as trying to hide an undocumented person."

"We aren't going to construe it that way."

"Did *we* do anything illegal?"

"Not as far as I know."

"If people find out that the mother of the Public Defender has been providing aid to an undocumented person, our lives will get very complicated."

"We'll deal with it."

"It could impact the election."

"We'll deal with that, too." She reached over and touched my cheek. "Are you staying tonight?"

"I'm going over to the apartment. I need to get clean clothes for the morning."

"Are you going to walk the stairs with Zvi?"

"Yes."

My friend, neighbor, and hero, Zvi Danenberg, was a retired science teacher at Mission High School who got up every morning at the crack of dawn and walked up and down the one hundred and thirty-nine steps connecting Magnolia Avenue in downtown Larkspur with the houses on the adjacent hill. The ninety-four-year-old climbed more than a million steps a year. In my never-ending and frequently futile quest to improve my conditioning, I joined him a couple of days a week.

Rosie smiled. "Give him my best."

* * *

I was awakened from an uneasy sleep by the sound of a high-pitched wail. I felt something on my chest and looked up into the wide green eyes of my neighbor's pearl-white cat.

"Morning, Wilma," I said. The twelve-pounder looked like an albino, but she was actually a Turkish Van. I glanced at my iPhone. Five-forty a.m. "You're up early."

She responded with a yawn. Then she curled up on my stomach, closed her eyes, and purred as she slept. I didn't have the heart to wake her.

Wilma lived in the apartment next door. When my neighbors became parents of twin boys, she started coming over to my place in the middle of the night in search of peace and quiet. She had impeccable manners, was a fine listener, and was excellent company.

I scratched her ears as I struggled to get my bearings in the bedroom of my cramped apartment behind the Larkspur fire station that was more suitable for a college student than a lawyer. The platform bed rested on cinder blocks. The nightstand came from IKEA. The framed photos on my dresser were dated. The first was Grace's high school graduation picture. The second was taken when Tommy was in third grade.

I was dozing off when I was startled by my phone. Wilma leapt off my stomach and darted out the window to the relative serenity of the apartment with the wailing babies. It took my fifty-eight-year-old eyes a moment to adjust before I was able to focus on Pete's name. I pressed the green button and held the phone to my ear. "Everything okay?"

"Fine, Mick. The investor in Cruz's restaurant, Jed Sanders, got back from Fiji last night. My sources tell me that he has coffee at Caffe Centro on South Park every morning around seven-thirty. His girlfriend, Christine Fong, is usually with him."

"I'll find them."

17
"IT'S A YOUNG MAN'S GAME"

"Mind if I join you?" I asked.

"Be my guest." The lanky man's voice bore the affectation of what my dad liked to call "East Coast Money."

I sat down across from Jed Sanders at the communal table at Caffe Centro. The aroma of coffee and pastries filled the cheerful breakfast and lunch spot in an earthquake-era building across the street from an oval-shaped park about halfway between Market Street and the ballpark. A once fashionable residential neighborhood during the Gold Rush, South Park devolved into an industrial zone frequented by drug dealers and the homeless. The area began to gentrify during the dot-com bubble in the nineties. By the early 2000s, it was smack-dab in the middle of San Francisco's tech hub. The park was now surrounded by new multi-million-dollar condos interspersed among refurbished buildings housing mobile gaming companies, fintech firms, and venture capitalists.

I pretended to look at my texts as I subtly took stock of Sanders. He was north of fifty, narrow face, ruddy complexion with a manicured stubble. His shoulder-length silver hair was pulled into a ponytail. A maroon shirt complemented a charcoal blazer with a burgundy pocket square. I couldn't have pulled off the grunge-chic look, but he carried it reasonably well.

A moment later, he was joined by a young woman with porcelain features, perfect makeup, and large brown eyes. In a single graceful motion, she sat down, placed a latte and avocado toast on the table, and continued her call using the hands-free mode on her phone. I recognized Christine Fong, the maître d' at El Conquistador, from a photo that Nady had found. She was half Sanders's age and height. They were a striking couple.

Fong ended her call, took a sip of coffee, and cut the avocado toast in half. Sanders set his phone on the table where he could see it, picked up his half of the toast, and took a bite.

"Good?" I asked.

"Yes."

"I'll try it next time." *Here goes.* "Jed Sanders, right?"

"Uh, yes." He picked up his phone.

"Seven Palms in Beverly Hills, right?"

"Right."

"One of the best meals of my life. Better than Spago. Better than The French Laundry. Better than Quince. Everything was perfect."

He lowered his phone. "Thank you."

I had never eaten at any of those restaurants. I extended a hand. "Mike Daley. I recognized you from *Food & Wine.*"

The only time I had ever seen a copy of *Food & Wine* was in the racks at the airport.

His grip was firm. "So nice to meet you, Mr. Daley."

"Mike."

"Jed." He pointed at Fong. "This is my business partner and companion, Christine Fong."

I shook her hand. "You were at Seven Palms, too, weren't you?"

"Yes."

I laid it on thick for a couple of minutes. They seemed to enjoy being recognized for running a restaurant that closed five years earlier.

"Why did you shut it down?" I asked. "It must have been doing well."

"It was." Sanders took a bite of toast. "Everything has to be perfect every night. If word gets out that you're slipping, you're done."

"The burnout rate must be high."

"It is. The hours are long. The demands are extraordinary. It's a young man's game."

"You weren't able to sell it?"

"Nobody wanted it. The rent was exorbitant. It was impossible to retain staff. It's better to shut down a few years early. You want to get out at the top of your game."

"Good advice." *And a nice humble-brag.* "How did you get started in the business?"

"In a roundabout way. I got a degree in forestry from Cal and quickly figured out that rangers didn't make a lot of money. To pay the bills, I took a job as a waiter for Alice. I discovered that I had an aptitude for cooking."

Alice, I surmised, was Alice Waters, founder of the legendary Chez Panisse in Berkeley.

Sanders explained that he also did stints at several other well-known Bay Area restaurants. He nonchalantly name-dropped Jeremiah Tower's Stars, Wolfgang Puck's Postrio, Nancy Oakes's Boulevard, Judy Rodgers's Zuni Café, and Thomas Keller's Bouchon.

I asked him how he ended up in L.A.

"I was looking to open my own restaurant when a space opened in Brentwood. I used the profits from the first restaurant to fund Seven Palms. It was hard running one restaurant. The second one almost killed me. We had a good run. Most restaurants close within a year. We kept ours going for a dozen."

I looked at Fong. "Did you work at both restaurants?"

"Just Seven Palms."

Sanders's voice filled with pride. "Christine started as a

cocktail server when she was still at UCLA. Within a year, I asked her to run the front of the house. Best decision I ever made."

It didn't seem like an opportune time to ask him if he started sleeping with a woman half his age around the same time. "Why did you come back to the Bay Area?"

"To be closer to family. Christine and I started a consulting firm. We also invest in promising young chefs." He glanced at his watch. "You'll have to excuse us. We need to go upstairs for a conference call about a potential new investment."

"I was hoping that I could prevail upon you for another minute of your time. I understand that you were involved with El Conquistador in the Mission."

"We were." The smile disappeared. "Carlos Cruz's death was a great tragedy."

"Yes, it was. I ate at El Conquistador." *A white lie, but short of a whopper.* "It was superb." *Time for the truth.* "I'm with the Public Defender's Office. We're representing Mercy Tejada. I'd like to ask you a few questions."

Sanders exchanged a glance with Fong. "We really need to get to work."

"It will be easier to chat for five minutes here than in court."

A hesitation. "We gave our statements to the police. We have nothing to hide."

Of course not. "I understand that you made a substantial investment in El Conquistador."

"We did."

"You must have done due diligence on Carlos Cruz."

"Of course. He was a talented chef. He showed 'once-in-a-generation' potential."

"Was he also a 'once-in-a-generation' businessman?"

"He was learning."

"From you?"

"And Christine." He glanced at his business partner and girlfriend, who responded with an icy glare. "I asked her to run the front of the house so that Carlos could focus on the kitchen." He forced a smile. "She's an exceptional manager."

"Was the restaurant profitable?"

"For the most part. The costs of running a business in San Francisco are exorbitant."

"I understand that Mr. Cruz's brother was the business manager."

"He was learning, too."

Not a ringing endorsement. I asked Fong whether she was pleased with the way things were running.

"Eventually. Every restaurant has growing pains."

"You knew my client?"

"Of course. I was very sad when Mercy was arrested for stabbing Carlos."

"Was she a good employee?"

"Most of the time. On a few occasions, I had to remind her of our high standards."

"Did she ever have an unsatisfactory performance review?"

"Not that I recall."

"We've been told that she and Mr. Cruz didn't always get along."

"That's accurate."

"We've also been told that Mr. Cruz was difficult to work with."

"At times."

Sanders interjected again. "He was a perfectionist."

Here goes. "Our client told us that he verbally and sexually abused her."

Sanders pushed out a sigh. "We received no formal

complaints from her."

"Did other employees complain?"

"A few. We took all such claims seriously. We turned them over to our lawyers who conducted full investigations. They did not find any wrongdoing by Mr. Cruz."

I looked at Fong. "You were working the night that Mr. Cruz died?"

"I was running the podium. Jed was eating in the dining room."

"Did you see anything out of the ordinary?"

"No."

My eyes darted to Sanders. "You?"

"Nothing."

Fong spoke up again. "Mercy and Carlos were arguing that night. I found out later that she claimed that he tried to kiss her."

"Did he?"

"I don't know. I didn't have time to ask him. Obviously, we would have taken any such claim very seriously."

Obviously. "What time did you leave?"

"Around eleven-twenty. As I recall, the only people still there were Carlos, his brother, a waitress, the dishwasher, and your client."

"I take it you didn't see Mercy or anybody else stab Carlos Cruz?"

"Correct."

I probed for a few more minutes. Their answers were consistent. Cruz was a gifted chef who could be temperamental. His brother was conscientious but inexperienced. The staff worked hard. Mercy had not reported any instances of alleged sexual harassment. Claims by other employees were immediately forwarded to their lawyers. Every employee was a

U.S. citizen or a legal resident. They couldn't understand what might have set Mercy off.

I looked at Fong. "Did Cruz ever behave inappropriately with you?"

She hesitated. "Define 'inappropriate.'"

"Was he ever unprofessional?"

"Occasionally. He was emotional. He yelled. Sometimes he swore. That's how he communicated. It isn't uncommon in the restaurant business."

"Did he ever make advances?"

"Just once." Her eyes lit up. "I explained to him that it couldn't happen again. It didn't."

Sanders added, "If it had, it would have been the end of El Conquistador and his career."

And your investment. "Were any of the other employees angry at him?"

"From time to time. Carlos was very demanding. El Conquistador was a high-pressure environment. People lost their tempers. It's the nature of the business."

I looked at Fong. "Is it possible that somebody was angry enough to kill him?"

"I don't know."

I turned back to Sanders. "What's his brother doing now?"

"Last I heard, he was working in real estate."

"Have you been able to re-let the space?"

"Not yet."

"That must be expensive."

"It is." He explained that he had formed a separate limited liability company to make the investment in El Conquistador. "We had to file for bankruptcy for that entity."

"It must have been painful."

"Not as painful as the night that Carlos died."

"Did you carry key-man life insurance?"

"Yes."

"How much?"

"A million dollars."

"That must have cushioned the financial blow."

"A little."

I handed him a card. "Thank you for your time."

"We have nothing to hide, Mr. Daley."

It was the second time that he'd mentioned it.

* * *

Rosie's tone was terse. "Anything useful from Sanders or Fong?"

"Not much." I pressed my iPhone to my ear as I walked west on Bryant on my way to the P.D.'s Office. It was difficult to hear her because of the roar of the I-80 Freeway a half-block north. I filled her in on the details.

"Any chance that Sanders and Fong will turn on each other?" she asked.

"Doubtful."

"Will they be strong witnesses?"

"Yes. They're attractive, articulate, and polished."

"I need you to meet me in the Mission at one-thirty. Cruz's brother agreed to talk to us at the El Conquistador space."

18

"HE WAS A BRILLIANT CHEF"

The young man with a shaved head, wisp of a beard, and slight paunch acknowledged us from a table in the back of the otherwise empty space that once housed El Conquistador. Alejandro Cruz was dressed in a powder blue oxford shirt and off-the-rack khaki slacks. He closed his laptop, stood, and smiled. "Over here."

As Rosie and I made our way across the narrow space, I tried to envision how El Conquistador looked on a busy night. The colorful murals were covered in dust. The kitchen equipment was gone—sold in the bankruptcy, I presumed. The tables were pushed against the wall, the graceful chairs stacked in the corner. The magic was gone.

We shook hands with Cruz and took seats across from him. Rosie flashed her best politician's smile. "Thank you for seeing us. We're sorry for your loss."

"Thank you. I want to see justice for my brother."

In response to my gentle probing, he filled in details of his biography. Graduated from Mission High and San Francisco State. An MBA from USF. Divorced. No kids. Carlos was his only sibling. His parents had run a taqueria. His mother had died of a brain hemorrhage when he was in college. His father died a few years later of complications from diabetes. He worked for a property management company.

"Why did you decide to go to work for Carlos?"

"He asked. He needed help on the business side, and he wanted to keep it in the family."

"What was he like?"

"He was a brilliant chef. Creative. Resourceful. Sensitive. He didn't have formal training, but he was obsessed with nutrition, ingredients, and technique. He studied history, botany, and traditional cooking methods. He elevated Mexican cuisine to an artistic level. That's why Jed Sanders agreed to invest in El Conquistador."

"How did you and your brother get along?"

"Fine."

"It must have been stressful working with him."

"At times. It's a stressful business."

"The press suggested that he had a big personality."

"He did."

"And he was difficult at times."

"He was."

"You never argued?"

"Occasionally. Carlos respected people who stood up for themselves."

"You were comfortable standing up to him?"

"When I had to."

"How did you like working with Jed Sanders?"

"Fine. He let Carlos run the restaurant."

"We understand that Sanders brought in a woman named Christine Fong to help with the front of the house."

"He wanted somebody with more experience in the restaurant business."

"And somebody to keep an eye on Carlos?"

"In part." He shrugged. "Carlos didn't spend a lot of time on budgets and spreadsheets. That was my job."

"And Fong's?"

"She helped."

"Your brother resented the fact that Sanders brought in his girlfriend to spy on him, didn't he?"

"He never mentioned it to me."

I find that hard to believe. "How did he and Fong get along?"

"Fine."

It was his default answer. "They didn't argue about budgets?"

"On occasion."

Rosie finally made her presence felt. "He thought that she was compromising his vision for the restaurant, didn't he?"

"Not really."

"She didn't respect him as a businessman, did she?"

"You'll have to ask her."

"Did you get along with her?"

"Well enough."

"Did you like her?"

"She did her job. I did mine."

"She told us that Carlos made inappropriate comments to her."

"She never mentioned it to me."

"On at least one occasion, he made an inappropriate advance."

"I don't know anything about it."

"We've been told by several people—including our client—that your brother made inappropriate advances to several people."

"There are always complaints by employees. We referred any issues to our lawyers, who investigated. They concluded that Carlos didn't do anything illegal."

Not exactly a denial. "You were at the restaurant on the night that Carlos died?" I asked.

"Yes." He confirmed that he left shortly before his brother. "I drove to my apartment on Guerrero Street. The police called after I got home."

"You went back to the restaurant?"

"I went to the hospital. By the time I got there, Carlos was gone."

Rosie lowered her voice. "That must have been horrible."

"It was."

"You knew Mercy?"

"Of course."

"Was she a good employee?"

"Yes."

"You knew that she was working her way through school and helping her mother support her baby sister, right?"

"Right."

"Did you ever see her argue with Carlos?"

"Almost every night." His expression hardened. "You know how it goes in stressful environments. Somebody says something. The other person takes it the wrong way and fires back. Soon both people are saying things that they shouldn't."

"Were they arguing on the night that he died?"

"Yes."

"About what?"

"Our dishwasher told me that Mercy said that Carlos tried to kiss her."

"Did he?"

"I don't know."

"You didn't ask him?"

"I didn't have time."

"Had she ever complained about similar behavior?"

"Not to me."

"You think she stabbed him?"

"Yes."

"What makes you think so?"

"She swore at him. She said that she was going to get him.

And I saw her take a knife out of the drawer in the kitchen shortly before Carlos left."

"It was a restaurant. Everybody uses knives."

He pointed at a hallway behind the kitchen. "She took it into the break room where our employees kept their personal stuff. When she returned, she didn't put it back in the drawer."

"She might have done so after you left."

"I don't think so."

"Did you see her take it outside?"

"No."

"So you didn't see her stab Carlos?"

"I had already left." He stood up. "Anything else?"

"Do you know if the D.A. plans to include you on their witness list for the trial?"

"Yes. And I am prepared to testify about what I just told you."

* * *

"Alejandro's testimony is going to be damaging," Rosie observed.

"At least we know that he's the witness who saw Mercy take the knife into the break room."

"If he's telling the truth."

We were standing on the corner of Seventeenth and Valencia at two-thirty on Thursday afternoon. The sun was out. Traffic was heavy. The aroma of fish tacos from El Toro Taqueria floated out to the busy street. Tech mothers were pushing babies in five-thousand-dollar strollers. The Latino mothers were pushing babies in more modest strollers.

"We'll need to discredit him on cross-exam," she said.

"It may not sit well with the jury to go after the brother of the deceased."

"We can't just roll over." She glanced at her watch. "Let's go for a walk around the corner and see if Juanita Morales is at home."

Morales had answered Mercy's calls for help and called nine-one-one.

"You think she'll talk to us?" I asked.

"I can be very persuasive."

19
"FIFTY YEARS"

The young man with the crew cut and the stars and stripes tattoo on his right arm looked at us through the patched screen door. "Yes?"

Rosie answered him. "I am Rosita Fernandez. This is my colleague, Michael Daley. We're with the Public Defender's Office. We'd like to speak to Juanita Morales."

"I am her grandson, Sergeant Ramon Encarnacion."

"Marines?"

"Army."

"Thank you for your service. We'd like to ask your grandmother a few questions about Mercedes Tejada."

"I'll see if she's available."

A potted geranium provided a little cheer as Rosie and I waited on the front porch of a weathered bungalow behind El Conquistador. Juanita Morales lived on Albion Street, the alley between Valencia and Guerrero, across from Duggan's Mortuary. I could see the cast iron fence surrounding the parking lot of Mission Police Station a half-block to the south.

A moment later, a gray-haired woman appeared next to her grandson. She gripped her cane and spoke to Rosie. "I'm Juanita Morales."

"Rosie Fernandez."

"I know. I voted for you. You're Sylvia's daughter."

"Yes, I am. How do you know Mama?"

"From church. I don't know her well."

"Have we met?"

"Briefly. You asked for my vote before the last election."

Rosie smiled. "It's nice to see you again."

Juanita smiled back. "Are you here to ask for my vote?"

"Yes. I am also here to ask for your help. Mind if we come inside for a few minutes?"

Her grandson touched her elbow. "You don't have to talk to them, Grandma."

"It's okay, Ramon. If there's a problem, I'll tell Ms. Fernandez's mother."

She escorted us into a living room with a drooping camelback sofa, two armchairs, and a coffee table covered by a half-completed jigsaw puzzle of the Grand Canyon. The aroma of salsa filled the cramped room. The walls were covered with family photos ranging from century-old black and whites to color pictures of young parents holding newborns.

Juanita took her seat on the sofa next to a basket holding a partially completed quilting project. Rosie sat down at the opposite end of the couch. I took a spot in one of the armchairs.

Her attentive grandson asked her if she was thirsty.

"Iced tea," she said. "Please bring some for Ms. Fernandez and Mr. Daley."

Rosie spoke up. "Rosie and Mike."

"Juanita."

Ramon disappeared into the kitchen and returned a moment later with a tray bearing four glasses of iced tea. He handed a glass to each of us, kept one for himself, and took a seat in the second chair. Sergeant Encarnacion was on duty.

Rosie pointed at a family portrait above the fireplace in which Juanita was surrounded by two dozen people. "When was that taken?"

"At my great-nephew's wedding last year. Four generations."

"That's wonderful. How many children do you have?"

Juanita beamed. "Five. Twelve grandchildren. Three great-grandchildren."

"You have a beautiful family." Rosie turned to Ramon. "I don't see you in the picture."

"I was on my second tour in Afghanistan. I'm going back next month."

Whenever I'm inclined to complain about my job, I try to remind myself that there are others who have it harder.

Rosie asked Juanita how long she'd lived in the house.

"Fifty years."

"My parents moved into the neighborhood around the same time. It's a nice community."

"It's changing." Juanita took a sip of iced tea. "You didn't come here to talk about gentrification."

"We understand that you were here on the night that Carlos Cruz died."

"I was."

"By yourself?"

"Yes. I've lived alone since my husband died almost twenty years ago, although it seems that one of my grandchildren or a great-niece or nephew is staying here most of the time. I'm sort of the Airbnb for our family." She flashed a sly smile. "If somebody is here keeping an eye on me, my children are less likely to try to get me to move into independent living."

Rosie returned her smile. "We've had similar discussions with my mother. Do you know Mercy?"

"No." She confirmed that she didn't know Perlita, either.

"You were familiar with El Conquistador?"

"Of course. I never ate there. Too expensive."

"Was the restaurant a good neighbor?"

"It was fine."

"Any problems?"

"Their valets took all of the parking spaces on our street."

"Did you know Carlos Cruz?"

"No."

"People have told us that he was difficult."

"I try not to judge people that I've never met."

"Do you know anybody who knew him?"

"Yes. They said he was a gifted chef."

"Was he a difficult person?"

"My friends try not to judge, either."

Fair enough.

Rosie leaned toward her. "Would you mind telling us what you saw that night?"

"I was working on a quilt when I heard noises outside. I went onto the porch to see what was going on. I heard a woman calling for help. I grabbed my phone and went across the street. Ms. Tejada was kneeling over Mr. Cruz. There was a lot of blood. She said that he had been stabbed and asked me to call nine-one-one, which I did."

"It must have been awful."

"It was."

"How was her demeanor?"

"Frantic. Her hands were covered with blood."

"Did you see a knife?"

"Yes. It was on the ground next to her. It was covered in blood, too."

"Just so we're clear, you didn't see her stab Carlos Cruz, did you?"

"No. I didn't see anyone stab him."

"Did you see anybody else in the alley?"

"No."

"Did she try to hide the knife or run?"

"No. She waited for the police and the ambulance. She was

cooperative."

Rosie lowered her voice. "Do you think she stabbed Carlos Cruz?"

"I don't know."

"Was she acting like a person who had just stabbed somebody?"

"She was acting like somebody who was trying to help."

* * *

At six-thirty the same evening, the co-head of the Felony Division marched into our conference room, put her laptop on the table, and took a seat across from Rosie, Nady, and me. At thirty-three, Rolanda Fernandez was a younger version of her Aunt Rosie in appearance, manner, and temperament. The woman whom Rosie and I used to babysit had the unenviable task of making sure that her ex-Uncle Mike fulfilled his administrative duties— the most difficult part of her job.

She cut right to it. "You going to get to reasonable doubt at Mercy's trial?"

Rosie answered her. "Maybe. How's your trial going?"

"Gang bangers who shoot up convenience stores don't get much sympathy from jurors. It's first-degree murder or bust."

"Chances of acquittal?"

"Slim.

"Keep fighting the good fight," Rosie said.

"It's what we do. Anything I can do to help on Mercy's case?"

"You know anybody who knew Carlos Cruz?"

"My dad."

Rolanda's father, Tony, was Rosie's older brother. He ran a produce market on Twenty-fourth around the corner from St. Peter's.

"How?" Rosie asked.

"He used to supply produce to El Conquistador."

20

"HE WANTED ONLY THE FRESHEST STUFF"

Tony Fernandez gave me a conspiratorial wink and handed me a can of Diet Dr Pepper. "For my favorite ex-brother-in-law."

He always kept a six-pack in the fridge behind the counter just for me. I popped open the can and took a sip. "To my favorite ex-brother-in-law."

Rosie feigned annoyance. "Mike's doctor doesn't want him drinking that stuff anymore."

Tony feigned contrition. "Only on special occasions."

"Thursday night isn't a special occasion. You're a bad influence." She took a deep breath of the cool air that smelled of fresh vegetables. "You appreciate the irony that he's drinking a soda full of artificial sweeteners in an organic produce market?"

"I do." Tony smiled triumphantly. "The first rule of retail is that you give customers what they want." Tony pecked his sister on the cheek. "I'll send Mike home with a bag of broccoli."

Rosie smiled. "Thank you, Antonio."

"You're welcome, Rosita. Mama okay?"

"Fine. So are the kids."

"Good. Is my favorite niece working on anything exciting over at Pixar?"

"Grace isn't allowed to talk about it. She signed a nondisclosure agreement."

"That's no fun."

"Working in the movie business isn't as glamorous as you might think."

"More glamorous than selling lettuce."

At seven-forty-five on Thursday night, Rosie, Tony, and I were standing near the register in his market at Twenty-fourth and Alabama. Over two decades, he had expanded into three adjoining storefronts on the commercial strip around the corner from St. Peter's.

"How's business?" I asked.

"Never been better."

Tony was a year younger and two inches shorter than I was, but he carried two-hundred and forty chiseled pounds on his frame. Except for his receding hairline and a mustache that was now more gray than black, the former Marine looked like he had just completed basic training. Widowed for almost a decade, he spent most of his time running the market, lifting weights at the Mission Y, and hanging out with Rolanda and her husband. He had a low-key relationship with a woman who ran a boutique on Valencia, but neither Tony nor his lady friend seemed inclined to commit to a more permanent arrangement.

"The rent isn't killing you?" I asked.

"I'm locked in for another ten years."

He was a savvy businessman who was attuned to the tastes and economic circumstances of his neighbors. He was also well-versed in the realities of running a business in the Mission. He quietly paid the obligatory "gratuities" to the gangs and the beat cops to keep his market on the "no hit" list. He viewed it as a cost of doing business.

"How are you dealing with the changing demographics of the neighborhood?" I asked.

He pointed to his left. "This side is high-end organic. The tech kids and the fancy restaurants on Valencia will pay anything for locally grown kale." He pointed to his right. "That's for the real people who live paycheck to paycheck and the mom-and-pop restaurants. It's good stuff, but it doesn't have the certified organic label, so it costs a lot less."

"Give the customers what they want."

"Exactly." He reached into a bin, pulled out a perfectly formed golden delicious apple, and handed it to me. "These just came in."

I took a bite. "Excellent. Organic?"

"Yes. You treating my daughter well?"

"Always."

"Rolanda is working on a tough case."

"Her clients killed four people at a 7-Eleven. They're bad guys."

"Any chance she can get them off?"

"Doubtful. The question is whether she can persuade the jury to go down to second-degree murder."

"Running a market isn't such a bad gig."

"Your customers are nicer than ours."

"For the most part."

I knew that Tony kept a nine-millimeter handgun in the drawer beneath the register—just in case. He had bought it legally and was trained to use it. In his two decades in the store, he had drawn it twice and never fired it.

His smile disappeared. "Rolanda said that you wanted to talk about Mercy Tejada."

"We do. You knew her?"

"I met her a couple of times at church." He confirmed that he also had a passing acquaintance with Mercy's mother. "How is Perlita?"

"Not bad under the circumstances." I wasn't inclined to give Tony any details about Perlita's whereabouts or his mother's involvement in her hastily planned disappearance.

Rosie had no similar reservations. "You probably know that Perlita is undocumented. She thought she was being followed by ICE, so arrangements were made for Perlita and her younger daughter to move to a safer place."

Tony nodded. "I know."

"Mama helped her."

"I know that, too."

"Has she done this before?"

"It's better not to know."

"Do you know where Perlita and her daughter are?"

"No. And if I did, I wouldn't tell you."

Rosie changed the subject. "Rolanda told us that Carlos Cruz used to shop here."

"For a while. I stopped selling him produce after he stopped paying me."

"We understand the issues of dealing with people who don't pay. You may recall that we used to run a two-person law firm."

"Three, if you count Rolanda."

"True. She was an excellent law clerk and is now an even better lawyer." Tony beamed when Rosie told him that she hoped Rolanda would run for Public Defender after she retired.

"You aren't planning to retire anytime soon, are you?"

"Not unless I lose the election."

"You're going to win."

"I hope so. You ever eat at El Conquistador?"

"Too rich for my blood. I'm just a humble lettuce peddler."

"What was Cruz like?"

"He was a world-class chef and a world-class dick. Loved the sound of his own voice. Thought he knew everything." He looked my way. "You worked at a big law firm. You know that type."

"I do."

"He wanted only the freshest stuff. He used to come over and pick it out himself. I put him in touch with a couple of my best suppliers. They bent over backwards for him. Then he stiffed them, too. He also hit on one of my suppliers."

"How did she react?"

"*He* didn't react well. He cut Cruz off right away."

"I'm seeing a pattern. Did you know anybody else who worked at the restaurant?"

"Cruz's brother, Alejandro, was the business manager. He's a decent guy. Carlos treated him like a busboy. The maître d', Christine Fong, was a pro. She didn't take any crap from him. Her boyfriend, Jed Sanders, bankrolled the restaurant. Another big ego. He once told me that Cruz was a disaster as a businessman. Reading between the lines, he was out of control."

"Drugs?"

"I wouldn't be surprised."

"Sexual harassment or other bad behavior?"

"If he hit on my supplier, he probably hit on people at the restaurant."

"Who else should we talk to for details?"

"Carlos's sous chef, Olmedo Rivera. Nice guy. Lived on Capp Street."

"Papers?"

"He was born here. He's a U.S. citizen."

"Anybody else?"

"A waitress named Carmen Dominguez used to live around the corner. She's undocumented, so she may be hard to find. I think she left town."

"Who might know where to find them?"

"Start with Gil Lopez. He knows everybody."

Father Guillermo Lopez was a priest at St. Peter's.

Tony turned to me and added, "If anybody knows how to talk to a priest, it's you."

21
"WE LIVE IN CHALLENGING TIMES"

I recited the familiar refrain. "Bless me, Father, for I have sinned."

"How long has it been since your last confession, Mike?"

"About a week, Gil."

"I didn't see you here."

"I usually go to Andy Shanahan at St. Patrick's in Larkspur."

"How's he doing?"

"Fine."

At seven o'clock the following morning, I was sitting in a musty confessional in the back of St. Peter's. I could see Father Guillermo Lopez's Roman nose and prematurely gray goatee. At thirty-six, he was one of the younger priests at the historic church. He had grown up around the corner and attended Saint Ignatius and USF before heading to the seminary. Smart, savvy, charismatic, and intensely political, he was primed to lead the community deep into the twenty-first century.

"Rosie okay?" he asked.

"Fine."

"Her mother?"

"Status quo."

"Good. Are your children going to church?"

"Not as often as I'd like. You do what you can, Gil."

"Understood. So, what do you have for me today?"

I went with my standard. "I had intimate relations with a woman who is not my wife."

"You're cheating on Rosie?"

"No, I'm sleeping with Rosie. You may recall that we're

divorced."

"You got a civil divorce, but your marriage wasn't annulled by the Church. As far as we're concerned, you're still married, so no harm, no foul. Anything else?"

"I told a judge that one of my clients was innocent. That was not entirely true."

"You knew that he was guilty?"

"Likely."

"I'm going to have to ding you for that one, Mike."

He let me off with a couple of Hail Marys.

The air was tinged with smoke from votive candles as we walked down the aisle of the modest church that was dedicated on July 4, 1886 and rebuilt twice after it was destroyed by fire. There was talk of tearing it down after it was damaged by a third fire in 1997, but the community rallied, and the Archdiocese came up with millions. The huge stained-glass window above the altar was restored to its original splendor, and the smaller ones along the sides were remade from scratch. St. Peter's would never match the grandeur of St. Mary's, but it reflected the working-class roots of its parish. Although I was now a member of St. Patrick's Parish, St. Peter's would always be my home.

I recited my Hail Marys. Then I looked up at the ceiling, where the words of Isaiah were inscribed: "I have loved, O Lord, the beauty of Thy house and the place where Thy glory dwelleth."

Gil was standing next to me. "Why did you come to see me, Mike?"

"I need to talk to you about Mercy Tejada."

He pointed at the doorway leading to the rectory. "I'll make you coffee."

* * *

"How long have you known Mercy and her mother?" I asked.

Father Lopez took a sip of watery Folgers. "Since I started working here. I knew Perlita's husband. His death was a great tragedy."

The dining room of the rectory reminded me of St. Anne's, where I spent three years as a junior priest: an oak table surrounded by a dozen wooden chairs; a credenza with stacked white plates; a Mr. Coffee machine. The walls were painted off-white. A simple wooden cross hung above the door. The only hint of the twenty-first century was a laptop on a butcherblock table next to a bookcase filled with religious texts.

I lowered my voice. "I trust that you are aware that Perlita and Isabel moved to a location where it will be harder for ICE to find them."

"I am."

"You're familiar with the process?"

"No comment."

"Do you know where they are?"

"No comment."

"Rosie's mother helped set it up. Rosie is concerned."

"We live in challenging times."

"Sylvia is eighty-five, Gil."

"Nobody is going to bother her, Mike."

"There are a lot of undocumented people in this community. How do you deal with it?"

"If you saw an injured child in front of Tony's market, wouldn't you try to help?"

"Of course."

"So would I." He touched his collar. "I leave the politics to others. For me, it's a moral issue. I focus on our parishioners. Perlita and her husband came here from Mexico because they couldn't feed themselves. They worked hard. They didn't take government money. They wanted the same things that everybody does: decent jobs, a place to live, and opportunities for their children."

"You sound like a politician."

"Sometimes it's unavoidable."

"A lot of people think undocumented people like Perlita should get in line behind those who have completed the legal hoops. Some say that they're taking opportunities away from 'real' Americans."

"I understand their point of view. I disagree with them, but I try not to be disagreeable. They're the Lord's children, too." He took another sip of coffee. "How is Mercy doing?"

"Not great."

"I'll try to visit her. Is she taking her insulin?"

"As far as we know. How well did you know her?"

"Well enough to know that she isn't capable of stabbing Carlos Cruz."

"Did she ever talk to you about El Conquistador?"

"She said the food was good, but it was a horrible place to work."

"Did she ever mention anything about sexual harassment by Cruz?"

"Not specifically. She told me that he was demanding and crude."

"Did Perlita ever talk to you about Mercy's job?"

"Yes. She said that Mercy hated her job and was looking forward to finding something better after she finished school."

"Did you ever meet Cruz?"

"A few times. His family didn't attend mass regularly." He said that he had met Cruz's parents before they died. "Fine people."

"What about his brother?"

"He struck me as fine young man."

"How did he and Carlos get along?"

He reflected for a moment. "They had different personalities. Carlos was creative and volatile. Alejandro was soft-spoken and meticulous."

"Sibling rivalry?"

"I have six brothers. It's inevitable."

"We're looking for a man named Olmedo Rivera who was the sous chef. He grew up on Capp Street."

"I've met him. As far as I know, he's still living in the neighborhood."

"We're also trying to find a woman named Carmen Dominguez, who was a waitress."

"Last I heard, she had left the area."

I handed him a card. "If you hear from her, please tell her that we'd like to talk to her."

* * *

I was walking down Twenty-fourth when Pete called. "What have you got, Mick?"

"Gil Lopez said that Olmedo Rivera is still working in the Mission."

"I'll find him."

"And he told me that Carmen Dominguez, the waitress, has disappeared."

"ICE is looking for her."

"You need to get to her first."

"Where are you heading now, Mick?"

"To the office. I need to check in with Rosie and Nady and deal with some lawyer stuff."

22
"THAT'S IT?"

"How was your campaign appearance?" I asked.

Rosie took off her glasses. "A small, but enthusiastic crowd. The hors d'oeuvres were mediocre. We raised almost twenty grand."

"Not bad for a Friday night."

Rosie, Nady, and I had gathered for a brief all-hands meeting at ten-forty-five on Friday night. Given Rosie's packed daytime schedule and her nightly campaign activities, we had to be flexible about finding time to prepare for Mercy's trial. I wanted to trade places with Luna, who was sleeping in the corner, a content smile on her face.

Rosie answered a couple of e-mails, then turned to Nady. "Thanks for staying late."

"Part of the program."

"Is Max okay?"

"He understands the drill. Besides, he's working, too."

Nady's fiancé of almost ten years was a junior partner at Story, Short & Thompson, a mega-firm at the top of Embarcadero Center that was the successor to Simpson & Gates, the mega-firm at the top of the Bank of America Building where I had spent five long years when I needed cash after Rosie and I got divorced. Max worked endless hours on interminable antitrust cases that were filed before he had started law school and wouldn't end until after his retirement.

Rosie spoke to her in a maternal tone. "You're going home after we're finished. If you don't dial it down a little, you're going to look like Mike in a few years."

"Uh, sure."

Rosie gave Nady her best imitation of her mother's "Don't mess with me" glare. "After this trial is over, I want you to take time off to get ready for your wedding."

"It's under control, Rosie."

"Your mother called me a couple of days ago. She wanted to be sure that you wouldn't be working over the holidays."

"I'll be in Hawaii with Max for our wedding."

"I'm going to hold you to that." Rosie smiled. "Don't mess with your mother. She's been planning this wedding since you left Uzbekistan."

Nady returned her smile.

"Did we get a preliminary witness list from DeSean Harper?" Rosie asked.

"Yes, and it's short. The first officer at the scene, Juanita Morales, Dr. Siu, Lieutenant Jacobsen, Inspector Lee, Sanders, Fong, and Cruz's brother."

"That's it?" Rosie asked.

"For now."

"We should include the other employees at the restaurant on our list. Where do we stand on pre-trial motions?"

"I'll have something for you to look at on Monday morning. We might want to reconsider our earlier discussion and ask the judge to allow the trial to be televised. It may be the only way that Perlita will be able to watch. If she shows up in court, she could be detained."

Rosie's face tightened. "We need to do what's best for our client, not her mother. I don't like televised trials. Everybody plays to the camera."

"Neither do I."

I interjected, "Neither does Judge Vanden Heuvel."

Rosie turned back to Nady. "Let's tell the judge that we don't want TV. Thanks for your help, Nady. I need to talk to Mike for a few minutes."

Nady woke up Luna and they headed down the hall.

Rosie checked her texts for a moment, then she turned to me. "Any word from Pete?"

"He's supposed to call me later tonight."

Her lips shrunk into a ball. "I'm not feeling good about this, Mike."

"Neither am I. Did you see Mercy?"

"Briefly. I'm worried. She's under an insane amount of stress, and she hasn't seen her mother since Perlita went underground."

"We can ask for a delay."

"No, we can't. She isn't going to hold up for another six months. And even if she did, she could be deported after the first of the year."

"Have you heard from Perlita?"

"I've left a couple of messages on her burner phone. You?"

"Nothing."

"I'll check with my mother."

My eyes locked onto hers. "You okay?"

"At the moment, a little too busy. Otherwise, fine."

"We've been through worse."

"We have." She gave me a thoughtful look. "Do you think we're getting too old for this?"

"No." *Well, maybe.* "Anything I can do to make it better?"

"Find me some hard evidence that somebody else stabbed Cruz."

My phone vibrated and Pete's name appeared on the display. I hit the green button and turned on the speaker. "Give me something good, Pete."

"How soon can you get down to the Mission?"

"Twenty minutes."

"Meet me at Pancho Villa. I found the sous chef, Olmedo Rivera."

23
"YOU GOTTA PAY THE BILLS"

It was almost midnight when the Lyft dropped me off next to the JC Decaux public toilet in the BART station plaza at Sixteenth and Mission. The smell of urine, marijuana, burritos, and Big Macs wafted through the area where drug dealers, hookers, homeless people, and tech workers mingled uneasily in front of a Wells Fargo with bars on its door. A Number 14 Mission bus idled across the street. A homeless man asked me for change. A man in a Warriors jersey offered me fentanyl. A woman in a halter top asked me if I was looking for a date.

Just another night in the Mission.

I headed west on Sixteenth past a new apartment building where the monthly rents cost more than my three years of law school, a liquor store that was still open, and a produce market that was closed. I stopped in front of Pancho Villa, a no-frills taqueria housed in a white stucco building with a terra cotta roof across the alley from the Bond Bar, a swank watering hole that replaced Esta Noche, a gay and transsexual bar that had been a safe zone for the LGBTQ community for three decades.

The security guard opened the door and let me inside. I was hit by a blast of hot air bearing the sweet smell of carne asada, guacamole, rice, beans, and salsa. It was five minutes before closing, but the restaurant was packed. An army of order-takers and cooks wearing white shirts with blue aprons were lined up behind the stainless-steel counter running the length of the room. Two cashiers pounded on their registers and kept the line moving. A row of Formica tables lined the wall beneath paintings from neighborhood artists.

I ordered a brick-sized super burrito with chicken, rice, black beans, guacamole, sour cream, lettuce, tomato, and mild salsa. I splurged on the "mojado" option, which included the "savory" sauce. I added a strawberry agua fresca and a churro and still got change from a twenty. *Not a bad deal.*

I carried the red plastic basket with my burrito to a table in the back corner, where Pete was picking at a Combination Platter #8: garlic prawns, steak tacos, an enchilada, and cebollitas asadas. My brother ate more than our teenage son, but never gained an ounce.

"You really going to finish that?" I asked.

"I was hungry, Mick."

I looked at my burrito. "If I eat this, I'll be up for three nights. Is Olmedo Rivera here?"

"He's the big guy who took your order."

I glanced at the baby-faced man built like an offensive tackle. "He looks younger than I thought."

"Thirty."

"How did he get to be the sous chef at a high-end restaurant like El Conquistador?"

"He was Cruz's friend—and occasional lover. They broke up a few months before Cruz died."

"How do you want to do this?"

"We wait."

"They're about to close."

"Eat slowly. After people clear out, we'll talk to him. You got any cash?"

I slid five twenties across the table.

"Any more?"

My burrito was getting expensive. I gave him another hundred.

* * *

Olmedo Rivera approached our table. "You guys almost finished?"

Pete smiled. "Almost. Sorry for keeping you late."

"No worries."

Rivera started to walk away, but Pete stopped him. "You used to work at El Conquistador, didn't you?"

"Yeah."

"It was really good." Pete held out a hand, which Rivera shook. "Pete Daley." He pointed to me. "This is my brother, Mike."

"Thanks for dinner," I said.

Pete finished his Coke Classic, put his plastic fork in the empty basket, and crumbled his paper napkins. "How did you end up working here?"

"You gotta pay the bills."

"I hear you." Pete stroked his chin. "I'm going to level with you, Olmedo. Mike is Mercy Tejada's lawyer. Can we buy you a beer and ask you a few questions?"

"I don't think that's a good idea."

Pete discreetly slipped him five twenties. "There's more where that came from."

"Meet me at Skylark in twenty minutes."

* * *

Rivera found us at a table against the back wall of Skylark, a dive bar a half block down the street. The red walls, cramped tables, and mahogany bar evoked the ambiance of a speakeasy. The drinks were strong. The DJ was blasting reggae music. The "Hunny Bunny" burlesque show had just concluded on the dance floor.

I was nursing a club soda. Pete was drinking a Red Stripe. Rivera ordered an El Chapo, a combination of mezcal, prickly pear liqueur, lime tamarind, and agave, served on the rocks with a cayenne salt rim. I would have passed out if I had taken a sip.

Pete flashed an appreciative smile. "I wasn't sure that you'd show."

Rivera's lips turned down. "The D.A. said I shouldn't talk to anybody."

"We're glad you're here. How long did you know Carlos Cruz?"

"Since we were kids. I used to help out at his parents' restaurant. We were friends."

Pete arched an eyebrow. "More than friends?"

"At times."

"Were you more than friends when you were working at El Conquistador?"

"For a while. It was hard working together and being together."

"Was it your decision to split up?"

"His. Life is complicated."

"Did you live together?"

"Briefly."

"What was he like?"

"A perfectionist. Moody. Depressed. Impossible when his meds were off."

"Prescription or recreational?"

"Both."

"Must have been a difficult working environment."

"It was."

"You were the sous chef?"

"Yes."

"What did that entail?"

"Doing everything that Carlos didn't want to do."

"Did you have any formal training?"

"No."

"You must have learned a lot from Carlos."

"We learned from each other."

"The *Chronicle* called him a genius."

His tone turned cynical. "Carlos convinced everybody that he had invented food."

"You must have had input in the menus and preparations."

"Some."

"For which you received little credit."

"Correct."

"That must have bothered you."

"A little."

Pete left it there. Rivera was getting antsy. We would wait until the trial to suggest that he was bothered enough to have killed his former lover. Pete glanced my way.

"Were you at the restaurant on the night that Carlos died?" I asked.

"Yeah."

"I take it that you didn't see our client or anybody else stab him?"

"Correct."

"Was Mercy a good employee?"

"She never gave me any trouble."

"How did she and Carlos get along?"

"Fine most of the time. Sometimes, they argued. Carlos was demanding. Mercy was opinionated."

"Were they fighting that night?"

"Yeah."

"Did she threaten him?"

"She swore at him and said that she would get him."

"Do you know why?"

"She said that Carlos tried to kiss her."

"Did he?"

"I don't know."

"Did you see her remove a knife from the kitchen shortly before Carlos was stabbed?"

"No."

"You knew Carlos's brother?"

"Alejandro is a good guy."

"How did he get along with Carlos?"

"Fine. Like all brothers, they argued every once in a while."

"About what?"

"Business."

"We talked to Jed Sanders. Did you get along with him?"

"Yeah."

"Did Carlos?"

"Most of the time. Sanders put a lot of money into the restaurant. He wanted to run it by the numbers. Carlos wasn't good at finance, so Sanders brought in his girlfriend, Christine Fong, to keep an eye on things. If we ordered an extra pound of flour, she got into Carlos's face."

"Were she and Carlos fighting on the night that he died?"

"I didn't see it."

"Did he ever say anything inappropriate to her?"

"No."

"Or touch her inappropriately?"

"No."

I shot a look at Pete, who finished his Red Stripe and placed three twenties on the table, which he covered with his hand. "We're looking for a waitress named Carmen Dominguez."

Rivera looked down at the cash. "She left town. ICE was looking for her."

Pete added two twenties to the pile. "Any idea where she went?"

"No."

"Who might know?"

Another glance at the money. "She was friends with the dishwasher at El Conquistador. His name is Junio Costa. He found a job at Tartine."

It was an upscale bakery near Mission Dolores.

Pete slid the five twenties across the table to Rivera. "Thanks, Olmedo."

He palmed the bills and headed to the door.

Pete glanced at his phone. "Tartine opens in seven hours."

"Costa won't have time to talk if we go first thing in the morning. I'll meet you there tomorrow night when it won't be as busy. Maybe I can persuade Rosie to join us."

His dour expression transformed into one of his infrequent grins. "Date night at a bakery, eh? You're a hopeless romantic, Mick. Between the burrito at Pancho's and a pastry at Tartine, you're going to gain twenty pounds."

24

"THEY WERE ALWAYS FIGHTING"

Rosie was sipping herbal tea. "Why don't we do this more often?"

"A murder trial. Running the P.D.'s Office. A re-election campaign. A kid in high school. Your eighty-five-year-old mother. We have a pretty full plate."

"Maybe you're right."

At seven-forty-five on Saturday evening, Rosie, Pete, and I were sitting at the communal table in Tartine, the popular bakery on the ground floor of a century-old apartment building at Eighteenth and Guerrero, about halfway between Pancho Villa and Mission Dolores. We wanted Pete to be present when we talked to Junio Costa so that we could call him as a witness if Costa refused to testify or disappeared. Otherwise, Rosie and I would be the only people who could testify as to what Costa had to say. You can't be a lawyer and a witness at the same trial.

The aroma of fresh bread, organic pastries, and handmade sandwiches filled the room. The industrial-chic décor featured exposed beams with whitewashed walls. The display case was filled with lemon meringue cakes, strawberry tarts, almond croissants, and banana cream pies. It had taken us almost an hour to make our way to the front of the line snaking out the door and around the corner. If we had come for breakfast, I would have ordered one of their legendary morning buns. Given the evening hour, I had ordered a spicy turkey sandwich with provolone and broccoli pesto. Rosie was eating the Niman Ranch smoked ham sandwich with Dijon mustard. I was saving my chocolate hazelnut tart for later. Pete was sipping coffee.

I lifted my mocha made with Valrhona chocolate and offered a toast to my boss. "To us."

"To us," Rosie said.

Pete looked at the counter, where four servers and two cashiers were processing orders. "Junio Costa is in the kitchen. We should wait until closing to approach him."

We nursed our drinks as the crowd thinned. We were the last people in the restaurant when a server with a streak of purple in her hair came up to us. "Almost finished?"

Rosie smiled. "Yes. Sorry to keep you late."

We went outside and sat at one of the tables on the sidewalk. The sun had gone down, and the foggy air was cool. Pedestrians hurried past us toward the restaurants on Valencia. A moment later, Costa came out the side door. He looked to be about twenty, with a stocky frame, facial hair that was more peach fuzz than beard, muscular arms, and a gold front tooth. His apron was soiled, his red bandana drenched. He leaned two black floor mats against the wall, grabbed a hose, and washed them down.

Rosie started to stand, but Pete stopped her. "Let him finish," he said.

Costa cleaned a half-dozen mats. As he was rolling up the hose, we approached him.

Rosie smiled. "Thank you for the wonderful dinner."

"You're welcome."

She extended a hand. "Rosie Fernandez. This is Mike Daley and his brother, Pete."

He spoke to us heavily accented English. "I have a Green Card."

"We aren't ICE."

"Police?"

"No. We aren't feds, either. I'm the San Francisco Public Defender. Mike is the head of our Felony Division. Pete is a private investigator. We're representing Mercy Tejada. We'd like to ask you a few questions."

His eyes darted from Rosie to me and back to Rosie. "I didn't see anything."

"Then it will be a very short conversation, Junio."

He glanced at his watch. "I need to get to my other job."

"It will just take a minute."

Another hesitation. He took off his apron. "Wait here."

He returned a moment later. He was dressed in a Giants' cap and a Warriors hoodie. He put his backpack on the table, but he didn't sit down.

Rosie got right to it. "You were the dishwasher at El Conquistador?"

"Yeah."

"You knew Mercy?"

"Yeah."

"You think she's a good person?"

"Yeah."

"Any reason to believe that she stabbed Carlos Cruz?"

A shrug. "I don't know."

"How well did you know Cruz?"

"He was my boss."

"People said that he was difficult."

"He yelled a lot."

"He hit on Mercy."

"Yeah."

"And others."

"Yeah."

"Did he ever hit on you?"

No answer.

"You can tell us, Junio."

"He asked me once about a three-way. I told him no."

In response to Rosie's gentle probes, he confirmed that Cruz's brother was intimidated by Carlos, Sanders was concerned about his investment, and Fong ran the front of the restaurant with an iron fist.

"We talked to Olmedo Rivera," Rosie said. "Good guy."

"Yeah."

"He and Cruz were going out."

"They split up."

"Rivera could have quit his job."

"He needed the money."

"Was Olmedo mad at Carlos on the night that he died?"

"Olmedo was mad at Carlos every night after they broke up."

"Mad enough to stab him?"

"I don't know."

"The police claim that Mercy took a knife into the break room."

"I didn't see it."

"Were Mercy and Cruz fighting that night?"

"They were always fighting. Carlos liked to yell at her."

"Because she wasn't working hard?"

"Because he could. He thought it was funny."

"She didn't think so."

"Neither did I. He told me that he wanted to sleep with her."

"She told us that Carlos tried to kiss her that night."

"She told me the same thing."

"Did she yell at him?"

"Yeah."

"Do you think she was angry enough to stab him?"

"I don't know."

"We may need you to testify."

"I'll think about it." He picked up his backpack and slung it over his shoulder.

Rosie held up a hand. "One more thing, Junio. We're looking for a woman named Carmen Dominguez."

"She left town."

"Is there anybody who might know where to find her?"

"Maria Garcia was the pastry chef. She and Carmen were friends."

"Any idea where we can find her?"

A shrug. Without another word, he started walking down Eighteenth.

Rosie looked at me. "He seemed reasonably forthcoming."

"Agreed. He's also a potential suspect. It would help if we had some evidence tying him to Cruz's death."

"That would be ideal, but it isn't essential to offer him to the jury as an alternative in a SODDI defense."

"You're prepared to throw him under the bus?"

"I'm prepared to throw anybody other than Mercy under the bus if I have to." I turned to Pete. "We need you to find Maria Garcia."

"I'm on it, Mick."

I turned back to Rosie. "You want to go to the office?"

"No, I want to see Mercy."

25

"TELL MAMA THAT I WANT TO SEE HER"

Mercy squeezed the armrests of the plastic chair in the consultation room in the bowels of the Glamour Slammer. "How's Mama?"

Rosie answered her. "Okay. So is Isabel."

"Where are they staying?"

"We don't know, but they're safe."

"Tell Mama that I want to see her."

"ICE is looking for her. If she comes here, they'll find her, and they may deport her. That wouldn't be good for her or Isabel."

"Will she be able to come to the trial?"

"Her call."

Mercy's eyes filled with tears.

The visitor area was quiet at nine-thirty on Saturday night. The action was down the hall in the intake area, where the usual weekend assortment of drunks, addicts, homeless, car thieves, shoplifters, and drug dealers were waiting to be processed. Visiting hours were over, but Rosie and I knew the night supervisor, who had arranged for us to see Mercy.

Rosie leaned forward. "Are you eating?"

"A little."

"Are you taking your insulin?"

"Yes."

"It's important."

"I know."

"Trial starts two weeks from Monday. We need you to be ready."

Mercy's voice was barely a whisper. "I will."

"We can request an extension, but your trial wouldn't start until after your Dreamer status ends."

"I want to do it now."

"Good." Rosie looked my way.

"We talked to Olmedo Rivera," I said. "He seems like a decent guy."

"He is."

"He said that he and Cruz were in a relationship."

"They were."

"Do you know why they broke up?"

"Carlos cheated on him."

"With whom?"

"Among others, Junio Costa."

"We talked to him, too. He said that he refused Cruz's advances."

"He lied."

"How do you know?"

"I caught them in the backroom of the restaurant drinking shots and doing coke. They weren't wearing clothes."

Got it. "How many times did you see them together?"

"Just once. Carlos was sleeping with other people."

"Who else?"

"Carmen Dominguez."

"We heard that she left town."

"I wouldn't be surprised. She's undocumented. She said that ICE was looking for her."

"Any idea where she is?"

"I don't know."

"Costa told us that she was friends with a woman named Maria Garcia, who was a pastry chef. Any idea where we might find her?"

"Last I heard, she was helping her brother, who runs a food truck in East Oakland. Supposedly, they have the best fish tacos in the East Bay."

"We'll find her. Was she sleeping with Cruz?"

"No."

"You sure?"

"Yes. For one, Maria didn't sleep around. For two, Maria doesn't sleep with men. And for three, she doesn't take any crap from anyone."

* * *

"Did you reach Pete?" Rosie asked.

"Yes," I said. "He's working with his sources in the East Bay to find Maria Garcia."

We were sitting in Rosie's office at ten-fifteen on Saturday night. We had just sent Nady and Luna home.

I packed my laptop. "You ready to go home?"

"Almost." She scrolled through her messages. "I'd like to make a quick stop on our way."

"Sure. Where?"

"Mama's house."

26

"WE KNOW WHO THEY ARE"

Rosie's brother took a sip of tea from a hand-painted mug that Rolanda had made for him when she was in second grade. "You still planning to start Mercy's trial on the twenty-eighth?"

"Yes," Rosie said. "We have no choice."

At eleven-ten on Saturday night, Tony, Sylvia, Rosie, and I were seated around Sylvia's dining room table. Rosie was drinking tea. I had a Corona. Sylvia's hands danced across her knitting. The TV in the living room was tuned to CNN, the sound muted.

Rosie looked at her mother. "Do you think Perlita will answer if we call her?"

"We can try."

Rosie pulled out her iPhone, but Sylvia stopped her. Sylvia reached into her knitting basket, took out a burner phone, and put it on the table. "Let's use this one."

"Fine, Mama."

Sylvia activated the speaker and punched in a number that she had memorized.

Perlita answered on the first ring. "Sylvia?"

"Yes. Rosita, Michael, and Tony are here."

"Hello."

Rosie spoke up. "We just visited Mercy. She's doing okay."

"Is she eating?"

"Yes. She's also taking her insulin."

"Good. I want to see her."

"And she wants to see you, but it wouldn't be a good idea right now."

"When?"

Rosie's lips turned down. "Not anytime soon."

"I want to go to the trial."

"We'll talk about it as it gets closer."

"I want to support my daughter."

Rosie took a deep breath. "You won't be able to support her if you're detained."

"We don't know for sure that ICE is looking for me."

Tony spoke up before Rosie could answer. "Yes, they are, Perlita."

"How do you know?'

"We know who they are. We watch them while they watch us."

The phone went silent.

Sylvia spoke up. "You need anything, Perlita?"

"We're okay for now."

"You'll give Isabel a hug for me?"

"Of course."

"Take care of yourself, mija. Rosita and Michael have everything under control."

"Thank you, Sylvia."

Sylvia ended the call and looked at Tony. "You're sure that ICE is looking for her?"

"Yes, Mama. Perlita should stay out of sight until things cool down."

Sylvia spoke to Rosie. "You *do* have this under control, right, Rosita?"

"Yes, Mama."

* * *

"Your mother was irritated," I observed.

Rosie corrected me. "She was pissed off."

True. "We're doing everything we can, Rosie."

"Mama gets frustrated when she can't control the narrative or the outcome."

"Reminds me of somebody else I know."

I was behind the wheel of Rosie's Prius. We were driving north on the Golden Gate Bridge at twelve-fifteen on Sunday morning. Traffic was light.

I glanced at Rosie, whose eyes reflected the lights from oncoming traffic. "You okay?"

"I'll be fine."

"You overwhelmed?"

Her tone turned more emphatic. "I'll be fine. Trial starts in two weeks. It'll be over in three. We'll get through it."

"And the election?"

"We'll get through that, too."

We drove in silence up the Waldo Grade and through the Robin Williams Tunnel. As we were making our way down the incline toward Sausalito, my phone vibrated, and Pete's name appeared on the display. I answered using the hands-free.

"You still up?" he asked.

"We're in the car heading home. Rosie is here."

"You got time for a little reconnaissance mission?"

"Yes."

"I'll pick you up in twenty minutes. I need you to stop at an ATM and get a couple hundred dollars in cash."

"Our out-of-pocket costs are starting to add up, Pete."

"High quality investigative work isn't cheap, Mick."

"I'll get the money. Where are we going?"

"East Oakland."

27
"FIVE TWENTIES FOR FIVE MINUTES"

At one o'clock on Sunday morning, Pete and I listened to the roar of trucks on the adjacent 880 Freeway as we walked up to the food truck parked in front of a beauty supply store in a strip mall on International Boulevard, East Oakland's main industrial drag. The faded yellow lettering read "El Conquistador."

"Catchy name," I said.

"Yeah, Mick." Pete tapped on the window.

A woman sporting a blue bandana spoke to us without opening the window. "Closed."

Pete flashed five twenties.

The window slid open. "What do you want?"

"We're looking for Maria Garcia."

"Who's asking?"

"Pete Daley. This is my brother, Mike, who is Mercy Tejada's lawyer. We'd like to ask you a couple of questions about Carlos Cruz."

"I don't know anything."

"Five twenties for five minutes."

"Meet me in the back."

* * *

"How long have you been working here?" Pete asked.

Maria Garcia was sitting at one of three metal picnic tables behind her brother's food truck. She spoke in unaccented American English. "About six months. My brother needed a hand, and I needed a job."

The moist air was filled with the aroma of carne asada, even though Maria and her brother, Jesus, had shut down the burners. Traffic was light on the six-lane thoroughfare paralleling the freeway. A decades-long effort to gentrify the grimy strip between the Fruitvale BART station and the Oakland Coliseum had been unsuccessful, and the stretch was one of Oakland's more dangerous areas.

Pete nodded at Maria's brother, a muscular man with a shaved head, a thick mustache, and a stud in his left ear. "How long have you owned this truck?"

"About a year."

"The name is the same as the restaurant where your sister used to work."

"It's a good name."

"How's business?"

"Not bad."

"You have a four-and-a-half-star rating on Yelp."

"Our food is good."

"You're open late."

"A lot of our customers work nights."

I turned to his sister. "Are you from around here?"

"Been here in East Oakland since our parents came up from Ecuador. It isn't always pretty, but it's home." Her eyes narrowed. "Before you ask, Jesus and I both have Green Cards."

"I wasn't going to ask. How long were you the pastry chef at El Conquistador?"

"A little over a year."

"Where did you learn to bake?"

"My cousins ran a bakery in El Cerrito."

"What was Cruz like?"

"He was an extraordinary chef and a total creep. He hit on everybody."

"Including you?"

"Twice. The first time, I explained to him that I wasn't interested in men in general, or him in particular. He didn't take the hint. The second time, I told him that I would cut off his dick if he did it again. He got the message."

"Good to hear."

A convoy of garbage trucks drove by us followed by an Oakland PD unit, lights flashing.

"Was Mercy a good employee?" I asked.

"Yes. She worked hard most of the time. She didn't take any crap from anyone."

"Including Cruz?"

"Especially Cruz."

"You think she was capable of killing him?"

"Everybody is capable of anything if you push them hard enough."

Not the answer I was hoping for. "You were at the restaurant on the night that Cruz died?"

"Yes." She said that she left a few minutes before eleven. "I didn't stab Carlos, and I didn't see anybody else—including Mercy—stab him."

"Mercy told us that Carlos tried to kiss her."

"He did. She told him to leave her alone."

"Did she threaten him?"

"She swore at him."

"Cruz's brother said he saw Mercy remove a knife from a drawer in the kitchen and take it into the break room."

"I didn't see it." She looked at her phone. "Your five minutes are up."

"One more thing. You knew a waitress named Carmen Dominguez, right?"

"Yes."

"We understand that Carlos treated her badly."

"He did."

"Why didn't she quit?"

"She needed the job."

"Any idea where we can find her?"

"I haven't seen her since Carlos died."

"Did she leave town?"

"I don't know."

"We heard that she was undocumented. Was ICE looking for her?"

"Could have been. Carmen didn't kill Carlos."

"Maybe she knows who did. Does she have any friends or family in the area?"

"She mentioned a cousin who lived near El Conquistador. He was in the auto parts business. I don't know his name."

* * *

"Can you find the cousin?" I asked.

Pete's right hand was on the steering wheel, eyes on the freeway. "Yeah." He looked into the rearview mirror. "We have company, Mick."

I turned around and looked out the back window. "Which one?"

"The black Explorer."

"ICE?"

"Could be. Hang on."

Pete hit the gas, cut across three lanes to the left, and then cut back across three lanes to the right. He faked getting onto the exit ramp leading to the Bay Bridge and then got off at the flyover to Berkeley. The SUV zigged and zagged with us until we got onto the exit ramp, then it peeled off.

My brother smiled triumphantly. "Convinced?"

"Yes. Why are they following us?"

"Maybe they think we'll lead them to an undocumented person."

"We might," I said.

"Then we need to be extra careful."

I looked out the window at the fog-shrouded Bay Bridge. "Trial starts two weeks from tomorrow."

"I'll find the cousin, Mick."

"This may not be so easy, Pete."

"Challenges make life interesting. And I know some people who deal in auto parts in the Mission."

28
"HE WANTS TO HAVE A FACE-TO-FACE"

Rosie looked up from her laptop. "Have you heard from Pete?"

"He's in the Mission looking for Carmen Dominguez's cousin."

The aroma of leftover pizza and Caesar salad floated through the conference room at eight-fifteen the following Wednesday night. Rosie, Nady, and I were sitting around the table and looking at the pre-trial motions that Nady had drafted.

I pointed at Luna, who was sleeping in the corner. "She has the right idea."

Nady smiled. "You'd get bored sleeping all day."

"Is Luna going to be in the wedding?"

"Unfortunately, no. It's complicated to bring a dog to Hawaii. She's going to be mad at us when we get home."

"She'll forgive you if you bring her treats. Any major changes in our motions?"

"No." She confirmed that we would still be asking for a gag order and no TV. "We don't want the D.A. to play this out on cable."

"Any basis to exclude the knife?"

"Doubtful."

"What's our narrative?"

"Mercy didn't stab Cruz."

"I like it. Simple." I looked over at Rosie. "Work for you?"

"It would be nice to have some hard evidence that somebody else did it."

"We take the evidence as it comes. You still thinking that

we'll go with a SODDI defense?"

"You got any better ideas?"

"No."

She turned to Nady. "Make sure that everybody who was at the restaurant that night is on our witness list."

"Already there. You planning to accuse everybody of murder?"

"If it's the only way to muddy the waters enough to get to reasonable doubt. Anything else from Harper?"

"Just a text. He wants to have a face-to-face tomorrow morning at his office."

"Tell him we'll be there."

* * *

I pressed my phone to my ear as I looked out the window of my office at nine-thirty on Wednesday night. "Where are you?"

Pete responded in a whisper. "Looking for Dominguez's cousin. I've talked to a couple of people who sell auto parts and various other products."

"Any solid leads?"

"On the cousin, no. On new shock absorbers, yes."

"I'll buy you new shocks if you find the cousin."

* * *

My phone vibrated as I was driving north on Van Ness on my way to the Golden Gate Bridge. I answered on the second ring. "What can I do for you, Jerry?"

The *Chronicle*'s finest responded with a smoker's hack. "Haven't talked to you in a few days, Mr. Daley. You still going to trial a week from Monday?"

"Yes."

"Any chance of a plea deal?"

"There's always a chance."

"I hear that you're meeting with the D.A. tomorrow."

"Who told you that?"

"A reliable source."

Harper wasn't prone to gossip, but his boss, Nicole Ward, was. "No comment."

"I talked to a couple of defense attorneys who said that your case looks shaky."

"It's a bad idea to handicap a trial on limited information."

"That's why I called you."

"We are very confident that our client will be exonerated."

"Can I quote you?"

"Yes. Anything else, Jerry?"

"I understand that you paid a visit to a woman named Maria Garcia last week."

"No comment."

"She and her brother were picked up by ICE earlier today."

Crap. "That's too bad."

"Any idea why?"

"No."

"She used to work at El Conquistador."

"I know."

"Were you planning to call her as a witness?"

Yes. "No comment."

"Did she have a Green Card?"

"I believe so."

"Seems ICE found an irregularity in her immigration status."

"That's too bad."

"And her brother's."

"That's too bad, too."

"Do you plan to do anything about it?"

"Nobody's asked us, Jerry."

I heard him wheeze. "Do you know how we can reach Perlita Tejada?"

"No comment."

"I'd like to interview her."

"You've already done enough damage by reporting that she's undocumented. If she shows up for an interview, ICE could detain her on the spot."

"We could do it by phone or Skype. She could call into my segment on *Mornings on Two* on Monday morning."

There was nothing to be gained by putting Perlita on TV. "I'm sorry, Jerry."

* * *

The light was on in Rosie's living room at eleven-thirty that same night. "Did you find out anything more about Garcia and her brother?" she asked.

"They're being held at the ICE office in San Francisco while their status is checked."

"Do they have Green Cards?"

"She said they did."

"Did ICE follow you there?"

"I'm not sure. Somebody was definitely following us on our way home. I hope we didn't lead ICE to them."

"You were just doing your jobs."

"It doesn't make it any easier." I told her about my conversation with Edwards. "I told him that we wouldn't let Perlita do an interview."

"That was the right call."

"She might be able to evoke some sympathy from the potential juror pool."

"Or we might be responsible for somebody else getting hauled in by ICE."

"True."

"You made the right call, Mike. Don't second-guess yourself."

29
"THERE ARE CONSEQUENCES FOR ILLEGALS"

At ten-fifteen the following morning, a Thursday, the District Attorney and front-running candidate for mayor adjusted the sleeve of her Hermes blouse, took a sip of Perrier from a crystal tumbler, and spoke to Rosie in a sugary voice. "So nice to see you."

My ex-wife played along. "So nice to see you, too."

Nicole Ward flashed a patronizing smile. "I hope your campaign is going well."

Rosie grinned right back. "Yours, too."

Ward and Rosie spent another five minutes exchanging fake smiles and phony pleasantries. Harper and I sat back and watched in bemused silence. Ward thought Rosie was a bleeding heart. Rosie thought Ward was an opportunistic lightweight.

Ward's mediagenic smile broadened. "We've taken the lead in the polls."

"That's great," Rosie said.

For Ward, maybe. For the citizens of San Francisco, maybe not.

We were sitting around the mahogany conference table that Ward had bought on her own dime to match the desk and bookcases that she had installed in her corner office in the D.A.'s new suite. The walls were lined with photos of Ward with political and social movers. They dwarfed the framed photos of her twin daughters next to her fifty-five-inch plasma TV.

Ward finally acknowledged my presence. "Good to see you, Michael."

"You, too, Nicole. I didn't know that you would be joining us this morning."

"DeSean thought it would be helpful."

His expression suggested otherwise.

Rosie's phony smile disappeared. "I saw you on TV yesterday."

Ward didn't realize that she was still grinning. "Only three weeks until election day."

"You were talking about our case. I didn't think it was an issue in the mayoral race."

"I have no control over the questions asked of me."

"You said that Mercy's mother is undocumented."

"It's a fact."

"It has no bearing on this case."

"Yes, it does."

"It will taint the potential juror pool."

"No, it won't." Ward's TV-ready smile finally disappeared. "If you want to request a change in venue and try this case in Bakersfield, that's fine with us. It will inconvenience everybody, and the chances that you'll get a better result are nil. In reality, you won't find a more sympathetic pool than here in San Francisco."

That much is probably true.

Rosie's eyes narrowed. "You put Perlita and her four-year-old daughter at risk."

"That wasn't my intent."

"Maybe not, but that was the real-world result."

"There are consequences for illegals."

"Putting their lives in danger serves no useful purpose."

"If Perlita's mother has been threatened, she should file a complaint with the police."

"If she does, there's a good chance that the cops will turn her over to ICE."

"There are consequences for illegals," she repeated.

Rosie turned and spoke to Harper. "You wanted to talk to us?"

Ward spoke up again before he could answer. "We wanted to spend a few minutes talking about logistics. Right, DeSean?"

"Right, Nicole."

I always found it demeaning that Ward treated her subordinates—including her Chief Assistant—like first-year associates at a big law firm. Then again, Harper had been dealing with Ward for years, and he understood her personality. He never betrayed his emotions in front of her. He was more forthcoming after a couple of glasses of wine at bar association gatherings.

He kept his voice even. "You're still planning to go to trial a week from Monday?"

"Yes," Rosie said.

"You going to ask for anything unusual in your motions?"

"Nothing out of the ordinary." She glanced at Ward. "No TV. No talking to the press."

Harper nodded. "Fine with us. Manslaughter instruction?"

"Still thinking about it. You?"

"Still thinking about it." Harper leaned back in his chair. "Any hints?"

"I could ask you the same question."

Harper's eyes darted from Rosie to Ward and then back to Rosie. "For what it's worth, Nicole and I are leaning toward requesting a manslaughter instruction."

Rosie nodded. "For what it's worth, so are we."

"So you're going to admit that she stabbed Cruz?"

"Absolutely not."

"Then you don't need a manslaughter instruction."

"If you're sure that Mercy stabbed Cruz, you don't need one, either. Why did you want to see us, DeSean?"

He looked at Ward. "Nicole has a proposition for you."

Ward tugged at her silk blouse that complemented her Prada skirt. The ensemble probably cost a couple of grand. "DeSean and I are willing to go down to second-degree murder if your client will plead guilty. We won't ask for any aggravating circumstances. Jail term will be at the low end of the scale."

"How low?"

"Fifteen years."

It was the minimum sentence, although there was no chance of parole. First-degree carried a minimum sentence of twenty-five years.

Rosie's stoic expression didn't change. "We won't recommend it to our client unless you go down to manslaughter."

"This isn't a manslaughter case, Rosie."

"You're right, Nicole. It isn't a murder case, either. You'll never get twelve people to convict beyond a reasonable doubt."

"This is our best and final offer. It will remain open only until nine o'clock tomorrow."

* * *

"How's your burger?" Rosie asked.

"Pretty good," I said. "Your club?"

"Not bad. Big John is going to be mad at us for patronizing another dive bar."

"He's been pals with the owners for years." I took a sip of iced tea. "Besides, you need to eat something other than a rubber chicken dinner every once in a while."

At eleven-forty the same morning, I was eating a Grand Slam Burger, and Rosie was devouring a Seals Stadium Club in the Double Play, a century-old watering hole at Sixteenth and

Bryant, a ten-minute walk from the D.A.'s Office. The strip mall across the street was built on the site of Seals Stadium, the longtime home of the old Seals Triple-A baseball team and, for a couple of glorious seasons while Candlestick Park was being built, the Giants. Except for the big-screen TVs and the ATM, the room looked the same as it did when my dad used to come here with Roosevelt Johnson for steak sandwiches. It was one of the few places left in San Francisco where UPS drivers, restaurant workers, auto mechanics, house painters, and tech entrepreneurs mingled amiably over burgers, fries, and beer. According to legend, Seals and Giants relief pitchers used to make their way across the street for a few pops between innings.

Rosie looked up at the TV, which was tuned to ESPN. "What do you think about Harper's plea deal?"

"I wouldn't take it unless he goes down to manslaughter."

"Neither would I. They seemed anxious to cut a deal."

"Either their case is squishy, or they understand that they're going up against an excellent lawyer representing a sympathetic client. We're also three weeks from election day."

"You think Ward is making a political calculation?"

"Everything in her life is a political calculation. She wants a conviction or a deal by election day. A not-guilty verdict won't please her bloodthirsty constituency."

"Then she should go down to manslaughter."

"She'll be accused of going soft."

Rosie finished her sandwich. "We have a legal obligation to present the deal to Mercy."

"Let's see what she has to say."

30
"NO"

Mercy's answer was succinct. "No."

"Do you want to sleep on it?" Rosie asked.

"No. I'm not going to plead guilty to a crime that I didn't commit."

"We'll inform the D.A."

At one-forty-five the same afternoon, Mercy, Rosie, and I were in the consultation room in the Glamour Slammer. Mercy's eyes were red, her manner withdrawn. It appeared that she had accepted the reality that she was going on trial for murder and there was a reasonable possibility that she might be convicted.

Rosie kept her tone even. "Are you taking your insulin?"

"Yes."

"It looks like you've lost weight."

"I haven't been hungry."

"Do you need to see a doctor?"

"No."

Rosie explained that we would submit pre-trial motions on Monday morning. "Do you have any questions?"

"No."

"We'll need you to be ready to start trial a week from Monday."

"I will."

Rosie reached over and took her hand. "We haven't made any final decisions, but we may need you to testify."

Mercy clutched her tissue. "I don't know."

"We would ask you just a few questions. We'll need a forceful denial, and then we would get you off the stand."

"I'll think about it."

"Anything else?"

"I want to see Mama."

"We talked about it, Mercy. This isn't a good time."

"I want her to be at the trial."

"It's risky for her to be out in public."

"Nobody knows who she is."

"Yes, they do. Her picture has been on the news. It's been reported that she's undocumented. If she shows up in court, there's a good chance that ICE will be waiting for her."

Mercy didn't respond.

Rosie squeezed her hand. "We'll come see you over the weekend."

* * *

"She's coming apart," Rosie said. "One of us needs to check on her every day."

"Agreed."

We were walking through the sheriff's department parking lot between the Hall of Justice and the Glamour Slammer. The fog was rolling in, and the wind was whipping down the freeway off-ramp, causing my eyes to water.

"I'm not sure that it's a good idea to have her testify," I said.

"Let's see how she's doing as we get closer to trial."

"It would be nice if she could see her mother."

"That's an unnecessary risk."

True.

"Have you heard from Pete?" she asked.

"He's in the Mission looking for Carmen Dominguez's cousin."

"What about Maria Garcia and her brother?"

"Still detained by ICE. My sources tell me that there is no

timetable for processing their cases."

"Not good."

"You got a campaign event tonight?"

"Yes, but first I want to talk to Nady."

31
"PEOPLE ALWAYS OPT FOR SELF-PRESERVATION"

Nady's lips formed a tight ball as she stared at her laptop. "No plea deal?"

Rosie answered her. "Correct. We've informed Harper."

"On we go."

Rosie, Nady, and I were meeting in the conference room at the P.D.'s Office at six-thirty the same evening, a Thursday. The office was busy—it generally didn't slow down until after eight. The hubbub had no impact on Luna, who was sleeping in the corner, paws up, snoring.

"She'll get up when she's hungry," Nady observed.

I studied the checklist on my laptop. "Did you get an updated witness list from Harper?"

"Nothing has changed."

"How many trial days has he asked for?"

"Three."

"We should try to keep our defense short. If everything goes exceptionally well, we won't need to put on any defense witnesses. We'll try to persuade the jury at closing argument that the D.A. didn't prove its case beyond a reasonable doubt."

Rosie looked up. "That would take some, uh, cojones, but it probably won't be enough. At the very least, we'll need our forensics expert to testify." She looked at me. "I trust that he's prepared to opine that Cruz's blood flew upward when Mercy removed the knife."

"He is."

"Good."

"You're still planning a SODDI defense?" Nady asked.

"For now," Rosie said. "Our witness list should include Jed Sanders and Christine Fong, along with Cruz's brother, the sous chef, the dishwasher, and Maria Garcia."

"She won't be available if she's still detained by ICE."

"Hopefully, she'll be released before the trial starts."

"You think you can get somebody to confess?"

"Probably not, but I might be able to get one or more of them to throw somebody else under the bus. When push comes to shove, people always opt for self-preservation."

"Do you have a favorite?"

"Doesn't matter."

"Do you have any hard evidence proving that one of them stabbed Cruz?"

"I don't need it."

"That isn't an ideal scenario," I observed.

"We work with what we have, Mike."

We spent another hour going over our trial exhibits. I agreed to spend some additional time preparing our blood spatter expert. We discussed the possibility of retaining a jury consultant but decided that it would be too costly. Rosie had excellent instincts about jurors—I trusted her more than the so-called experts.

Finally, Rosie turned to me. "It would make our lives easier if Pete could find some solid evidence that somebody else stabbed Cruz."

"I'm going to see him tonight."

* * *

Big John smiled broadly as he approached our booth in the back of Dunleavy's. "Why the long faces, lads?"

"Long week," I said.

Pete took a sip of bitter coffee. "*Really* long week."

Dunleavy's was quiet at eleven-thirty on Friday night. A

couple of off-duty firefighters were shooting pool. Two cops were finishing their fish and chips before they resumed the graveyard shift. A half-dozen tech kids were staring at their laptops. Big John's business had gone up substantially when he installed free Wi-Fi.

My uncle gave me a knowing look. "No Rosie tonight?"

"Campaign appearance."

"My fish and chips are better than the stuff they serve at political events. She's going to win the election, Mikey."

"I know."

Pete looked up from his phone. "You got any good news, Mick?"

"Maria Garcia and her brother were released by ICE. Turns out that they had valid Green Cards."

"Great. Will she testify?"

"I don't know."

Big John pulled up a chair and sat down next to my brother. "You all right, Petey?"

"Yup."

"My darlin' great-niece okay?"

"Fine, Big John."

"And your lovely wife?"

"She's okay, too."

"You kids getting along these days?"

"For the most part. Donna is unhappy about my erratic hours."

Pete's wife understood the demands of his job, but her tolerance was tested when he was unable to attend their daughter's school events—especially when he was working for his older brother.

Big John put a hand on his shoulder. "Maybe you could come work for me."

"Working the night shift wouldn't be great, either."

"You can take the day shift. It's quieter."

"I don't think so, Big John." He looked at me. "And I need to help my big brother."

"You can take a day off this weekend," I said.

"Not if you want me to find Carmen Dominguez."

Big John pretended to wipe a non-existent spill with his dish towel. "You got this case under control, Mikey?"

"Yes."

"You don't sound as confident as you usually do."

"It's going to be close."

"How does Rosie feel about it?"

"She'll feel better when Pete finds somebody who can alibi our client or point the finger at somebody else."

He looked at Pete. "You gonna be able to do that, Petey?"

"I hope so, Big John." He stood up and put on his bomber jacket.

"Take the rest of the night off," I said to him.

"I'm going to the Mission. Trial starts a week from Monday."

"You want company?"

"No."

32
"SHE LEFT TOWN"

"How long have you been here?" I asked.

Pete was sitting in the driver's seat of his Crown Vic, his face covered in stubble. "On and off since I saw you on Friday night."

At ten-thirty on Sunday night, he was parked in the lot for Duggan's Funeral Home behind the empty storefront that used to house El Conquistador. His head remained still, but his eyes were moving.

"Why are you here?" I asked.

"To buy shocks. Did you bring cash like I asked you?"

"A thousand dollars."

"Good."

"Seems a little pricey."

"We may need to give my new mechanic a gratuity."

"Who's your new mechanic?"

"Carmen Dominguez's cousin."

"You got a name?"

"Yoan Uribe. Thirty-two. Single. Green Card. In the daytime, he works for Terminix. At night he makes extra money by selling auto parts. I didn't ask where he gets them."

"Doesn't matter, Pete. Have you talked to him?"

"Text."

"Burner phone?"

"Of course."

"What time are you supposed to meet him?"

"Eleven." His eyes darted toward a stocky man making his way toward us through the alley. "Right on time. Let me do the talking, Mick."

* * *

"Yoan?" Pete asked.

"Yeah. Pete?"

"Yeah. This is my brother, Mike."

We shook hands. His palm was calloused, his grip strong. He motioned us to follow him through the side door leading into a one-car garage in the back of an apartment building across the alley from El Conquistador. When he flipped on the light, I saw that the garage was filled with auto parts, laptops, iPads, and cell phones. He presented Pete with a set of shocks and held out a hand.

Pete pressed five hundred dollars in cash into his palm. "Thanks, Yoan. You got any of the new iPhones?"

"Soon." He started making his way toward the door, but Pete stopped him.

"You know Carmen Dominguez?"

His mustache twitched. "Maybe."

"We'd like to talk to her."

"She left town."

Pete pointed at me. "My brother is a lawyer. He's representing Mercy Tejada."

Uribe didn't say anything.

Pete kept talking. "Mercy worked with Carmen at El Conquistador. Mike is looking for people who were at the restaurant on the night that Carlos Cruz died."

"Carmen didn't kill him."

"I know."

"Then why do you want to talk to her?"

I finally spoke up. "Maybe she knows who did."

"From what I've seen on the news, your client did." He took another step toward the door, but I stopped him. "Can you give us her phone number?"

"I don't have it."

I didn't believe him. "Can you get a message to her?"

"Maybe."

I slid ten twenties into his palm. "There's more if you help us find her."

"What do you want me to tell her?"

"We know that Cruz treated her badly. I know a lawyer who represents victims of sexual harassment. I would be happy to introduce Carmen to her. She should file a lawsuit right away. It could be worth some real money for her, Yoan."

"Let me see what I can do."

* * *

"You think we'll hear back from him?" I asked.

"Maybe," Pete said. "You think she has a case?"

"Probably. She has nothing to lose by filing."

We were back in Pete's car at eleven-thirty the same night.

"You think Yoan knows where she is?" I asked.

"Yeah."

"Any chance you can tap his phone or texts?"

"No."

"Can you keep an eye on him?"

"I already have somebody watching him."

My phone vibrated. Rosie's name appeared on the display. I pressed the green button.

"Are you still with Pete?" she asked.

"Yes." I explained that we had located Carmen Dominguez's cousin.

"Good. What about Dominguez?"

"Not yet."

"Bad. How soon can you get over to Mama's house?"

"Ten minutes."

"We need to talk."

33
"THERE HAS TO BE A WAY"

It was after midnight when Rosie met me at the front door of her mother's house. "Is your mom okay?" I asked.

"Fine."

"What's going on?"

"Things are getting a little complicated."

I hung up my coat and followed her into the dining room, where Sylvia was sitting at the head of the table, her fingers working furiously on her knitting.

"Good to see you, Michael," she said.

My eyes moved from Sylvia to Father Lopez, who was next to her. "Didn't know you were here, Gil."

"I talked to Perlita a little while ago."

"Are she and Isabel okay?"

"Yes." He waited a beat. "Perlita wants to see Mercy."

"We've talked about this, Gil. It isn't a good idea."

"There has to be a way."

"If she goes to visit Mercy, there's a good chance that somebody will alert ICE."

"What if I go with her?"

"Unless you can out-wrestle the ICE officers, you won't be able to prevent them from detaining her. They might also arrest you for providing aid to an undocumented person."

"They won't arrest a priest."

"I've seen stranger things."

"She's desperate, Mike."

"I understand, Gil."

"What if you and Rosie came with us?"

"Doesn't matter."

"I take it that you would have the same concerns if Perlita attends the trial?"

"I'm afraid so."

He pushed out a sigh. "Can she watch it on TV?"

"Probably not. We're going to ask the judge not to televise it. We think the prosecution will do the same. This judge doesn't like having cameras in her courtroom."

"Any chance that I can persuade you to change your mind?"

"We don't think it would be in Mercy's best interests."

"Can you ask for a closed-circuit hookup so that only Perlita can watch the trial?"

"We can ask, but the chances that the judge will approve it are slim."

"Is it okay if I come to the trial?"

"We were hoping that you would be there."

* * *

Sylvia's chin was resting in her hand. "Can I come to the trial?"

"Of course," Rosie said. "Mercy will find it very supportive to see you there."

"Can I bring my knitting?"

"Yes."

Sylvia took a sip of tea. "Are you angry at me for getting you involved in this case?"

"Of course not, Mama. We're just doing our job."

* * *

"You think Pete will find Dominguez?" Rosie asked.

"If anybody can find her, he will."

We were driving north on 101 through Mill Valley at one-thirty on Monday morning. The windshield was covered with mist. I was behind the wheel. Rosie was in the passenger seat. I was listening to the news on KCBS. Rosie was checking messages.

She lowered her phone. "Nady will file our pre-trial motions when she gets in."

"Good."

"Is our spatter expert ready?"

"Yes."

"What's our narrative?"

"Mercy didn't stab Cruz," I said.

"Short and sweet. That's good. What else?"

"We need to give the jury some options." I ran down the list: Jed Sanders and Christine Fong. Cruz's brother. Olmedo Rivera. Junio Costa. Maria Garcia. "You probably won't be able to get anybody to confess, but you might be able to cast enough shade on people other than Mercy to get the jury to reasonable doubt."

"Even on manslaughter?"

"If we can convince them that Mercy didn't stab Cruz, they have to acquit on manslaughter."

"True." She exhaled heavily. "I wish we had more."

"So do I."

Her phone vibrated. She hit the green button, put the phone to her ear, listened intently for a moment, and repeated the word "Yes" several times. She ended the call and looked at me. "We aren't going to be able to call Maria Garcia as a witness."

"ICE let her go."

"She's dead, Mike."

"What the hell happened?"

"My source at Oakland PD said that she and her brother were shot and killed during an armed robbery at the food truck a few hours ago."

Hell. "Did they catch the guy who did it?"

"He's dead, too. Maria's brother shot him."

"Any chance he had anything to do with our case?"

"Doubtful. My source said that he was a small-timer who had been hitting businesses on International Boulevard for the last couple of months."

"I'll text Pete and let him know."

We drove the rest of the way home in silence.

34

"IT'S THE HUMANE THING"

Judge Kathleen Vanden Heuvel removed her glasses. "Any additions to your papers?"

"Nothing from me," Rosie said.

"I don't have anything," Harper said.

At three-thirty in the afternoon on Wednesday, October twenty-third, Judge Vanden Heuvel had summoned us to her chambers in Department Fourteen on the second floor of the Hall. Unlike our D.A.'s fancy new digs, Judge Vanden Heuvel believed that civil servants—including judges—should be responsible stewards of taxpayer money and conduct business in modest quarters. Her laptop sat on a metal desk. The folding chairs where Harper, Rosie, and I sat could have been purchased at Scandinavian Designs. Her only personal items were framed photos of her parents, sister, and several nieces and nephews.

At sixty-seven, Judge Vanden Heuvel had been on the bench for about five years. The native of Wisconsin and graduate of the law school at Berkeley had successful stints as an Alameda County prosecutor, a white-collar defense attorney, and, most recently, a law professor. She had been nominated by Governor Jerry Brown to fill the vacancy created when her sister, Louise, had retired. She was a thoughtful jurist who read filings carefully, studied case law, and respected precedent. With a smoky voice and a dignified demeanor, she commanded her chambers and her courtroom without raising her voice.

She tugged at her shoulder-length blonde hair which complemented her sky-blue eyes. Her right hand shook slightly—a subtle sign of early-stage Parkinson's. She spoke to Harper. "Any chance you and Ms. Fernandez might be able to work out a plea bargain before Monday?"

"We have nothing on the table at this time."

Her head didn't move as her eyes shifted to Rosie. "I understand that Mr. Harper offered a deal for second-degree."

"Our client declined."

The judge's eyes moved back to Harper. "Are you still willing to accept a plea for second-degree?"

"No, Your Honor."

The judge's right eyebrow rose slightly.

Harper added, "Instructions from the D.A."

"Fine." She put on her reading glasses and looked at her computer. "We're set to start trial on Monday at ten a.m. I trust that you have exchanged witness lists?"

We nodded.

Rosie cleared her throat. "Maria Garcia will not be available to testify. Unfortunately, she was killed in an armed robbery on Sunday night."

"I'm sorry. Any other issues before we turn to pre-trial motions?"

"No."

"You asked me to exclude the knife found on the ground next to your client because of alleged chain-of-custody issues. I have reviewed the evidence and I have decided that there is no legitimate basis to exclude it."

This was expected.

"I am granting your motion prohibiting either side from talking to the press. It will serve no useful purpose to try this case in the media."

This was also expected.

Rosie glanced at Harper, then turned back to the judge. "I

trust your ruling includes our District Attorney?"

"It applies to everybody at the D.A.'s Office." She looked at Harper. "To avoid any misunderstandings, please explain to Ms. Ward that my ruling covers statements in all private and public settings, including press interviews and campaign appearances—live and on TV."

"Yes, Your Honor."

Out of the corner of my eye, I caught a slight grin on Rosie's face.

The judge spent another fifteen minutes walking us through other evidentiary issues. Then she turned to the question of televising the trial. "As you know, I am generally resistant to TV coverage, and this case is no exception. The prosecution and the defense have agreed with my views, so there will be no TV cameras in court."

Rosie spoke up. "Your Honor, we would like you to consider the possibility of having one camera in the courtroom to provide a closed-circuit feed to Mercy Tejada's mother."

"She can't come to court?"

"No."

"Health reasons?"

"No, Your Honor. It has been reported in the press and by the D.A. that she's undocumented. If she comes to court, there is a substantial chance that she will be detained."

Harper hadn't expected this. "This is highly unusual, Your Honor."

Yes, it is.

Rosie spoke again. "We will pay for the cost of the setup and the cameraperson."

Harper shook his head. "We have no way of controlling access to the video. As a result, it would defeat the purpose of your ruling against broadcasting the trial."

"We will accept responsibility for keeping the video private, and we understand that we would be held in contempt if it is disseminated beyond Ms. Tejada's mother."

Harper wasn't buying. "There is no legal authority for allowing a private video feed."

"It's the humane thing," Rosie said.

"I'm all in favor of humanity, but such an arrangement isn't necessary to guarantee the defendant's right to a fair and impartial trial."

Rosie and Harper volleyed for a few minutes until the judge stopped them with an upraised hand. "I am sympathetic to Ms. Tejada's mother, but I am not aware of any statute or case law authorizing a closed-circuit broadcast to just one person. As a result, while I would like to be compassionate, I am not going to authorize a private broadcast of this trial."

"But Your Honor—," Rosie said.

"I've ruled, Ms. Fernandez. You and Mr. Daley and/or one or more of your subordinates can report on the trial to the defendant's mother."

"It isn't the same, Your Honor."

"It's the best that I can do." Judge Vanden Heuvel glanced at her computer. "There is one more issue. I see that the prosecution and the defense have requested a manslaughter instruction to the jury. I wanted to inform you that I will not make a final determination on that question until after each side has completed its presentation to the jury."

It was the right call.

"I'll see all of you at ten o'clock on Monday morning."

35
"WE HAVE A SITUATION"

"Did you really think Judge Vanden Heuvel would allow a closed-circuit hookup to Perlita?" Nady asked.

"No," Rosie said. "But it didn't hurt to ask."

Rosie, Nady, and I were in Rosie's office at five-forty-five on Wednesday evening. Unlike my early days as a Deputy P.D., there were no legal pads on the table or poster-sized exhibits on the floor. Except for brief interludes to check our phones, our eyes were focused on our laptops, our fingers glued to our keyboards. I could see the final remnants of sunlight through Rosie's window. When you're preparing for trial, you lose track of time, except for the clock in your head counting down the days, hours, and minutes until the start of jury selection.

I looked at Nady. "Is our diagram of El Conquistador ready?"

"It's in the conference room."

"Good." While most of our exhibits were computer-generated, Rosie and I liked to have a drawing of the crime scene to show the jury. "Did you go over and see Mercy today?"

"Yes. She's getting nervous."

This was "Nady-speak" for "She's a basket case." "Is she eating?"

"A little."

"Taking her insulin?"

"She said that she was."

"How do you think she'll hold up in court?"

Nady wiggled her fingers. "We'll see."

Rosie looked up from her laptop. "I want you to sit with us at the defense table. Mercy feels comfortable with you."

"Of course," Nady said.

I asked Rosie if her mother was still planning to come to the trial.

"Yes. So is Father Lopez. We'll arrange for them to sit behind Mercy."

We spent another hour going over our juror questionnaire, Rosie's opening statement, the anticipated order of the prosecution's witnesses, and strategies for rebutting Harper's case. Over the years, you develop a feel for the rhythm of trial work. It's also critical to remember that you're playing to an audience of twelve jurors plus four alternates. While it's nice to win your case in the court of public opinion, the only people who matter are in the box.

It was almost seven o'clock when Rosie closed her laptop. "My campaign appearance in North Beach started twenty minutes ago."

"You need to go."

"It won't get serious until everybody is on their second glass of wine."

Nady headed back to her office. I was taking a final sip of room-temperature coffee when my phone rang. Father Lopez's name appeared on the display.

I pressed the green button and held the phone to my ear. "Hi, Gil. I'm here with Rosie."

His voice was tense. "Can you come down to St. Peter's right away?"

"Sure. What's going on?"

"I'll explain when you get here. We have a situation."

36
"THIS IS GOD'S HOUSE"

"What exactly did Gil say?" Rosie asked.

"He would explain when we got to St. Peter's."

We were driving south on Potrero Avenue past San Francisco General. Rosie was behind the wheel of her Prius. She was a more aggressive driver than I was, and she was weaving through evening traffic.

"Do you have time for this?" I asked. "Your campaign event has already started."

"One of my proxies will handle it until I get there."

"Does this make me your proxy at the P.D.'s Office?"

"As a matter of fact, it does."

Her phone rang and her brother's name appeared on the display. She answered it using the hands-free mode. "You okay, Tony?"

"Fine, Rosita. Have you talked to Mama today?"

"Not since this morning."

"I just tried to call her, but she didn't answer."

"I'll give her a call."

"Where are you?"

"Near SF General. Gil Lopez asked us to come down to St. Peter's. He didn't say why."

"The cops have blocked the street in front of the rectory. Somebody said it had something to do with Mercy's case."

"We'll be there in five minutes."

Rosie ended the call and turned right onto Twenty-fourth. We inched forward three blocks to the corner of Twenty-fourth and Florida. Tony's market was on the north side of the street.

The rectory of St. Peter's was on the south side.

Rosie's eyes narrowed. "What the hell?"

Two police cars were parked in front of the rectory, lights flashing. Two unmarked black SUVs were parked behind them. The law enforcement presence looked out of place in front of the modest three-story building with a faded mural depicting civil rights leaders.

I looked over at Rosie. "ICE?"

"Probably."

Even more jarring was the fact that the rectory was surrounded by about a hundred people, arms interlocked, singing "We Shall Overcome." They were led by Father Ernesto Cortez, an eighty-year-old priest who had presided at St. Peter's for more than a half-century.

Rosie's mother was standing next to him.

* * *

Rosie's tone was even. "What are you doing here, Mama?"

"I'm a member of our parish's emergency response committee."

"How did you get here?"

"I walked."

"You have two artificial hips and two artificial knees."

"It's only three blocks."

"It's cold."

"It's invigorating. And it's a beautiful evening, Rosita."

I didn't want to minimize the gravity of the circumstances, but I found myself grinning. Rosie had won almost every argument we'd ever had, but I had never seen her win one with Sylvia.

Rosie pushed out a frustrated sigh. "How long are you planning to be out here?"

Sylvia glanced at her watch. "The next shift starts in an hour.

Tony will drive me home."

"You promise to go home?"

"Yes, Rosita."

Realizing that it would be impossible to change her mother's mind, Rosie turned to Father Cortez, who was standing face-to-face with two clean-shaven men with matching ICE windbreakers. A second priest was recording the standoff on his iPhone.

Father Cortez's tone was polite, but resolute, as he addressed the ICE officers. "I can't let you inside, Doug."

The older ICE guy answered him in a professional tone. "Please, Father. Let's not make this more difficult than it has to be."

"Please inform your superiors that Father Cortez politely asked you to stand down."

"We can't do that, Father."

"Yes, you can." He looked at his colleague who was recording. "This is God's house. You were baptized here. So were your parents. You don't want to be on every news outlet and social media post showing you barreling over an eighty-year-old priest and storming one of the oldest churches in San Francisco, do you?"

The officer frowned. "I'll talk to my boss."

"Thank you, my son. Peace be with you."

"And you, too, Father." He and his partner retreated to their SUV for further instructions.

Father Cortez looked at Rosie and me. "Good to see you."

"Good to see you, too," Rosie said.

"You'll forgive me if I can't shake hands. Our protest consultant said that we're not supposed to unlock our arms until we're sure that the situation is over."

Rosie grinned. "You really have a protest consultant?"

"Of course. Back in the sixties, we had to figure this out ourselves. Nowadays, there are consultants for everything. Fortunately, ours is a member of the parish who works *pro bono*."

"Anybody I know?"

"Luisa Cervantes."

"I understand that her treatments are going well."

"They are. Her doctor wouldn't allow her to stand outside in the cold, but we're keeping her posted on Facetime."

Modern technology has many productive uses.

Rosie pointed at the police cars. "You're prepared to be arrested?"

"Absolutely." He gave her a knowing look. "It's been a few years."

"I would be grateful if you could try to keep Mama out of jail."

"I'll do the best that I can." Father Cortez's jowls wiggled as he grinned. "I understand that she has an excellent defense attorney."

"She does." Rosie pointed at the locked doors leading into the rectory. "I take it that Perlita and Isabel are inside?"

"Yes."

"And this isn't the first time you've provided sanctuary?"

"It isn't."

"Gil Lopez wanted to see us."

"I know." He and Sylvia lifted their interlocked hands so that Rosie and I could pass between them. "He's waiting for you inside."

37

"WE ANSWER TO A HIGHER LAW"

Father Lopez took a sip of tea. "Thank you for coming over so quickly."

Rosie and I eyed each other. "You're welcome, Gil," I said.

We were sitting in the dining room of the rectory where I had met with him a couple of weeks earlier. It was seven-thirty p.m. The sun had gone down, and the streetlight outside cast an eerie illumination through the window that was protected by iron bars.

"Why did you want to see us?" I asked.

"I wanted to talk to a lawyer."

"The Archdiocese has an army of lawyers."

"A criminal defense lawyer."

"Are the cops outside planning to arrest you?"

"Not as far as I know."

"Do they have any reason to arrest you?"

"I don't think so."

Rosie had heard enough. "Why are dozens of your parishioners—including my mother—surrounding this building?"

"It's our emergency procedure when it appears that one of our parishioners may be detained."

"Perlita?"

"Yes."

"Let's start from the beginning."

He picked up a burner phone and punched in a number. "Can you join us?"

Perlita and Isabel emerged from the kitchen. Perlita gave

her daughter an iPad and asked her to keep herself occupied, then she joined us at the table.

Gil templed his fingers in front of his face and spoke softly. "I have a confession."

There's a switch. Don't react. Listen.

"Contrary to your excellent advice, I took Perlita to see Mercy earlier today."

Crap.

"Perlita wanted to see her daughter, and Mercy wanted to see her mother. It seemed like the right thing to do, but it was a mistake."

And now you see the consequences.

"We got inside without being noticed. We talked to Mercy for about fifteen minutes, and then we came back here. ICE showed up fifteen minutes later."

"If they have a valid search warrant," I said, "we have no legal authority to prevent them from coming inside."

"This isn't the first time this issue has come up, and we have an understanding with them. They won't set foot inside our church without permission."

"That 'understanding' has no legal force."

"That's why we have people surrounding the building. We've instructed them to remain calm, be polite, and not resist if ICE decides to come inside. We're filming everything. If ICE moves in, we'll put video on social media. That'll be a bad look."

"You're relying on their fear of embarrassment?"

"We're relying on their good character and Christian values."

"We can't guarantee that they won't change their minds."

"We're pretty sure that the powers that be won't allow it—at least for now. The head of the ICE office in San Francisco used to be an altar boy for Father Cortez."

A fortuitous coincidence. I looked at Perlita. "You've been here the entire time?"

"Yes. Father Lopez said that Isabel and I can stay here until Mercy's trial is over."

I looked at Gil. "You have room?"

"Some of the priests are doubling up."

"Do you have other guests here at the inn?"

"No comment."

Rosie made her presence felt again. "What's your plan if ICE comes inside?"

"We'll figure it out. Between you and the lawyers for the Archdiocese, we have an excellent legal team."

"Does the Archdiocese know that you have people staying here?"

"They do now."

"And they're okay with it?"

"For now."

"You understand that what you're doing may be technically illegal?"

"We like to believe that we answer to a higher law."

"How much longer are your people available to surround the building?"

"As long as we need them."

"Then I need a favor. I want you and Father Cortez to find a replacement for my mother. It isn't healthy for an eighty-five-year-old with artificial hips and knees to be out in the cold."

"Will do. Our community is very supportive. Even the tech kids help us."

"Makes me proud to be a native of the Mission, Gil."

"Me, too, Rosie."

"My dad always said that we should never forget how lucky we are to live in San Francisco."

38
"THE CHURCH ALWAYS WINS"

"Your mother wasn't happy about going home," I said.

Rosie nodded. "She likes to be in the middle of the action. She's determined to stay relevant. And she doesn't want to admit that she's slowing down."

"My mother was the same way."

"I remember."

"Do you think we're going to be the same way?"

"Absolutely."

Rosie was behind the wheel as we drove north on Van Ness on our way to her campaign appearance in North Beach. Traffic was heavy on the perpetually busy thoroughfare where a seemingly endless construction project to install bus and bike lanes was in its second decade.

I looked at the illuminated dome of City Hall. "Your mother said that she's planning to go back to St. Peter's tomorrow to man the barricades."

"Gil promised to talk her out of it. If he can't do it, I'll try."

"What are the odds?"

"I haven't been able to talk Mama out of anything in fifty-four years."

"Did you know that Gil was housing undocumented people at St. Peter's?"

"I wasn't surprised."

Not exactly the answer to my question. "I take it that your mother knew?"

"I'm sure."

"It's, uh, illegal."

"It is what it is, Mike. If you were still a priest, would you house undocumented people?"

"Yes.

"Would you have taken Perlita to see Mercy?"

"No."

"Too risky?"

"Too cautious. I'm a chicken."

"How do you think your former masters at the Archdiocese would have reacted if you decided to house undocumented people at St. Anne's?"

"Poorly. They're big on following rules—especially the ones that they make up themselves. I always got dinged in my reviews for coloring outside the lines."

"What if the Church's rules conflict with the State of California's rules?"

I smiled. "The Church always wins."

She reached over and squeezed my hand. "You've always said that you weren't a good priest, but I'll bet that wasn't true."

"Maybe." I decided to become a priest when I was looking for answers after my brother Tommy died. After a couple of unhappy years as a junior priest, I decided that it wasn't for me. "It wasn't a good fit."

"I think things worked out pretty well. If you had stayed at the Church, we probably never would have met, and Grace and Tommy wouldn't have been born."

"I think things worked out pretty well, too."

* * *

Rosie finished her club soda and put her empty glass on the bar. "Ready to go home?"

"I'll meet you in front in a couple of minutes," I said.

I pushed my way through the bar of the San Francisco Italian Athletic Club, which was housed in an off-white building with red trim across from Washington Square. The Stars and Stripes and the Italian flag had flown on parallel poles on the roof since 1917. The ground floor had a banquet room with wood-carved ceilings and ornamental chandeliers. The gym upstairs had a low ceiling with a miniature basketball court. If you wanted to do Pilates or cross-fit, you needed to go to the upscale Bay Club on the opposite side of Telegraph Hill.

I inhaled the aroma of prime rib, spaghetti, and perspiration as I inched past older club members who were tossing back Manhattans, gesturing with unlit cigars, and playing liar's dice. The younger generation sipped Chardonnay and stared at their phones. Rosie had given a campaign speech during the spumoni dessert course of the monthly prime rib dinner. North Beach had changed a lot since 1917, but it was still a political necessity for candidates to press the flesh at the IAC.

I felt a tap on my shoulder and heard a familiar sing-song voice shouting above the din. "As I live and breathe. Michael J. Daley, Esquire."

I turned around, smiled, and looked into the eyes of an impeccably dressed man leaning against the bar and sipping chianti. "As I live and breathe. Nick 'the Dick' Hanson."

"How the hell are you, Mike?"

"Couldn't be better. How about you, Nick?"

"Couldn't be better."

"I didn't know that you were a member of the club."

"Indeed I am."

"You aren't Italian, Nick."

"Never have been." The diminutive ninety-five-year-old adjusted the fresh red rose in the lapel of his three-piece Brioni suit that matched the color of his one-piece toupee. "They made me an honorary Italian sixty years ago."

I played along. "How does that work?"

"You pay the initiation fee to the club and you buy a couple of rounds for the Board." He grinned triumphantly. "You know how things work in San Francisco. It's always been a 'pay-to-play' town."

Indeed it has.

Nick "the Dick" Hanson was one of my hometown's last larger-than-life characters. The nonagenarian P.I. had been running the Hanson Investigative Agency in North Beach for three-quarters of a century. He had started as a one-person shop in a room above what is now the Condor Club on Broadway. Nowadays, he headed a high-tech operation employing dozens of his children, grandchildren, and great-grandchildren. In his spare time, he wrote mystery novels that were thinly veiled embellishments of his more colorful cases. His books appeared regularly on best-seller lists, and Danny DeVito was playing Nick in a wildly successful Netflix series.

"Did you run the Statuto this year?" I asked.

"Nah. I bummed up my knee running the Bay to Breakers."

The IAC's annual 8K race was first run through North Beach in 1919. It commemorated the Italian Constitution (the Statuto Albertino), and it raised funds for charity. It was more bacchanalia than athletic event. The post-race brunch featured all-you-can-drink mimosas.

He took a sip of chianti. "I saw Rosie, but I didn't see you at the Triple-I last week."

"I had to be in court."

The San Francisco Irish-Israeli-Italian Society, affectionately known as the "Triple-I,", was hatched in the fifties by George Reilly, a member of the Board of Supervisors who twice ran for mayor (and lost), Nate Cohn, a theatrical trial lawyer whose clients included Frank Sinatra, Melvin Belli, Duke Ellington, and the Birdman of Alcatraz, and Charlie Barca, a fun-loving police captain. The "Society" had no dues, no website, and almost no organization, and its members didn't need to be Irish, Jewish, or Italian. For its first fifty years, its secretary was the late John Shimmon, who was of Lebanese descent. Its sole purpose was organizing boisterous luncheons at the IAC on St. Patrick's Day, Israeli Independence Day, and Columbus Day, where politicians, cops, lawyers, labor leaders, business execs, and other hangers-on rubbed elbows for old-fashioned civic bonhomie and consumed copious amounts of Italian wine. I used to accompany my dad and Big John to the festivities every year.

Nick finished his wine. "My new book is coming out next week."

"I'll look forward to reading it. Rosie and I have been binge-watching the Netflix series."

"That's great. By the way, she gave a good speech. Everybody thinks she's going to win the election."

"We're confident."

"I saw that you're handling Mercy Tejada's trial. You think it's a good idea to represent a Dreamer right before the election?"

"We don't make staffing decisions based on political considerations."

"Very admirable. A lot of people aren't happy about it."

"We live in a complicated world, Nick."

"Indeed we do."

I decided to play a hunch. "Did your firm have any involvement in the investigation of Carlos Cruz's death?"

"Briefly. My grandson, Rick, and I talked to some people in the Mission."

"May I ask who hired you?"

"Jed Sanders and Christine Fong. We've done work for them

in the past."

"We've met them. Why did they hire you?"

"They were concerned about legal exposure after Cruz died. Seems Cruz was either sleeping with or hitting on everybody who worked at the restaurant."

"So we've discovered." I walked him through the names on our witness list, all of whom he recognized. "Should we talk to anybody else?"

"Look for a guy named Mauricio Vera. He lived in an apartment behind El Conquistador. He was in his garage working on his car on the night that Cruz was killed."

"Did you have any reason to believe that he had anything to do with Cruz's death?"

"No."

"But?"

"He told us that he heard an argument outside around the time that Cruz was killed. I'm not sure if it will make any difference in your defense, but it can't hurt to talk to him."

"We will."

"Give my best to Rosie and Pete." He looked over my shoulder, recognized a familiar face, and smiled. "Gotta run, Mike."

He pushed his way past me before I had a chance to thank him.

* * *

"What took so long?" Rosie asked.

We were driving west on Bay Street toward the Golden Gate Bridge.

"I ran into Nick Hanson," I said.

"I saw him earlier tonight. I don't understand why he doesn't retire. His grandkids run the agency, and he owns millions of dollars worth of real estate in North Beach."

"He's tried several times. He gets bored. He likes to be in the middle of the action."

"Just like Mama."

"Jed Sanders and Christine Fong hired Nick and his grandson to poke around after Cruz died. He said that we should talk to a guy named Mauricio Vera."

"I trust that you've asked Pete to find him?"

I couldn't resist. "Indeed I did."

39
"NO PROMISES"

I was sitting in the passenger seat of Pete's car at four o'clock on Friday afternoon—three days before Mercy's trial was set to begin. He pointed at a muscular young man in a hard hat, overalls, and heavy boots who was lugging a four-by-four across a construction site at the corner of Eighteenth and Mission.

"Mauricio Vera," he said. "Twenty-seven. Born in El Salvador. Came here looking for work. No kids. Sends money to his girlfriend in El Salvador when he can."

"U.S. citizen?"

"Trying to get a Green Card. He's probably on a watch list for ICE."

"Criminal record?"

"A couple of parking tickets. At the moment, he's living in an SRO across the alley from El Conquistador."

It was the acronym for a "single room occupancy" hotel, which was San Francisco-speak for a flophouse.

He added, "He won't be living there much longer. Somebody bought the property and is going to tear it down and build million-dollar condos."

"How soon does he get off work?"

"Five minutes."

＊ ＊ ＊

Maurico Vera took a bite of his carne asada burrito. His work shirt and jeans were covered in dust as he eyed us warily and spoke in lightly accented English. "Thanks for dinner."

Pete took a sip of his Pacifico. "You're welcome."

We were sitting at a picnic table in La Taqueria, a pint-sized burrito joint at Twenty-fifth and Mission that was a perennial on the *Chronicle*'s list of best Mexican places. What it lacked in ambiance, it made up for in the freshness of its burritos. Jammed between Dianda's Italian Bakery and Elsy's Salvadoran restaurant, you waited in line at the counter, placed your order, and hoped a spot would open at one of the tables. It was cash-only and always packed.

Pete took another drink of beer. "Is it easier for you in Spanish?"

"English is fine."

"Okay." Pete and I were fluent in both. "Mike works for the Public Defender's Office. He's representing Mercy Tejada. I'm helping him. Her trial starts Monday. Do you know her?"

"No."

"She's a nice person."

"I'll take your word for it."

"How long have you lived here?"

"Almost two years." He confirmed that he was from El Salvador. "My girlfriend is still down there. I'd like her to come up here, but it's hard."

"Are your parents still down there?"

"My mother died when I was a baby. My dad was killed in the drug wars."

"I'm sorry. Was he a police officer?"

"He was a lawyer who defended people accused of hauling drugs. The cops didn't distinguish between the drug runners and their lawyers."

"He must have been very brave. Did you ever think about becoming a lawyer?"

"Yeah."

"But?"

"After I saw what happened to my dad, I decided to get out of the country."

I finally spoke up. "Have you been back?"

"No. I'm trying to get a Green Card so I can stay."

"Our office can help you."

"That would be great."

"I'll have one of my colleagues contact you. In the meantime, I was hoping that you could help us. I understand that you live across the alley from El Conquistador."

"For now. The building where I live has been sold."

"We might be able to help you find a new place."

"That would be great, too."

"You were living there on the night that Carlos Cruz died?"

"Yes."

"You were at home when it happened?"

His eyes narrowed. "Who told you?"

"Nick Hanson. You know—the little P.I. on Netflix. You talked to him, right?"

"Yeah."

"Nick said that you told him that you were working on your car that night."

"I was."

"Was the garage door open?"

"No. I didn't see anything."

"Did you hear anything?"

He waited a beat. "Arguing."

"What exactly did you hear?"

"The first voice said something like, 'I can't believe you did this to me.' The other guy said, 'No.' I think he repeated it two or three times."

"Did you talk to the police?"

"Yes. They knocked on my door the next day."

"You didn't report it sooner?"

"I didn't know that Cruz had been killed until they told me."

"You didn't see the police cars and the ambulance?"

"We see them in the Mission every night."

"Did you hear anything more from the cops?"

"No."

"They didn't ask you to sign a statement or be available to testify?"

"No."

Either the cops never told Harper about Vera's statement, or Harper decided that it wasn't important.

Pete slid five twenties across the table. "Was one of the voices that you heard Cruz's?"

Vera deftly pocketed the bills. "I don't know. I never met him."

"Were both voices male?"

"I think so."

"You sure?"

"Pretty sure."

Absolutely sure would be better. I placed five more twenties on the table. "We need you to testify at Mercy's trial."

His eyes darted from the money to me and then back to the money. "Not a good idea."

"You strike me as a person who wants to do the right thing and tell the truth."

He nodded.

"Your testimony will help Mercy."

"It could get me deported."

"I will personally defend you if you're detained by ICE."

"I can't do it."

"I won't let anything bad happen to you, Mauricio."

"Right." He finished his burrito, gulped down his beer, and

crushed his napkin. "It's too risky. Besides, I can't afford to give up even a half-day of work."

"How much are they paying you at the construction site?" I asked.

He hesitated. "Twenty-five an hour."

It was probably less. "We'll pay you fifty an hour to testify."

Another hesitation. "Let me think about it."

"That's fine." I handed him a card. "You'll call me if you think of anything else?"

"Sure."

"You got a phone?"

"I know that it sounds paranoid, but I buy a new burner every couple of days."

"It's smart to be paranoid."

Pete handed him a new burner. "You can contact us on this one."

"Thanks." He put the phone into his pocket. "No promises."

"Understood."

40

"IT GETS US A LITTLE CLOSER TO REASONABLE DOUBT"

"Will Vera testify?" Rosie asked.

"I'm not sure," I said.

Friday had turned into Saturday, and then into Sunday. On Saturday, Rosie and I had taken a break to watch Tommy and the Redwood Giants pull out a last-second win over Marin Catholic. On Sunday morning, we attended mass at St. Peter's with Perlita and Isabel along with Rosie's mother and brother. The service was piped outside to the people surrounding the rectory. Father Lopez delivered a sermon on the importance of tolerance, love, grace, and charity. Putting his words into action, he delivered coffee and doughnuts to the ICE guys outside. Rosie and I spent Sunday afternoon at the Glamour Slammer with Mercy. She was anxious, but more determined than the last time we had seen her.

At eight-thirty on Sunday night, I was standing in the corner of Rosie's office, where Luna had graciously accepted a treat. Ever the optimist, she sat, rolled over, and shook my hand in a futile attempt to extract another Milk-Bone from my empty pockets.

"Sorry to disappoint you," I said to her.

Nady answered for her. "She'll get over it. She always does."

I returned to my seat at the table, where Rosie, Nady, Pete, and I were in the middle of last-minute preparations.

Already in trial mode, Rosie's eyes burned with intensity. "How does Vera help us?"

"He heard two voices outside—both male," I said.

"You said that he wasn't sure if the second voice was a man."

"We just need to suggest it. It won't be a big leap for the jury to fill the gap and conclude that the killer was a man. We'll also ask Inspector Lee why the interview with Vera wasn't included in the police reports."

"Because it wouldn't have helped their case," Rosie said.

"Exactly."

"It isn't an exoneration."

"It gets us a little closer to reasonable doubt."

Rosie looked over at Nady. "Add him to our witness list."

"Already done."

Rosie turned to Pete. "Can you find him again?"

"Yes. He has a daily construction gig at Eighteenth and Mission."

"What if he gets something better or he decides to bolt?"

Pete flashed a knowing grin. "I'm tracking him."

"How?"

"I gave him a new burner phone to contact us. As long as it's on, I'll know where he is."

"What if he turns it off?"

"Then we'll have to rely on the guy I hired to follow him."

I love my brother.

Rosie nodded with admiration. "Any sign of Carmen Dominguez?"

"Working on it," Pete said. "I need to get back down to the Mission to talk to a couple of my operatives."

"We're running out of time."

"You'll be doing jury selection for at least a couple of days."

"We'll need her by the end of the week."

"Plenty of time." Without another word, he headed out the door.

Rosie looked at me. "We need to prepare as if Dominguez won't be available."

"Agreed, but we should also be ready if Pete finds her. He's very resourceful." I turned to Nady. "You went over and saw Mercy again tonight?"

"Yes. She's as ready as she's going to be."

"You think she can handle testifying?"

Nady considered her answer. "If we absolutely need her."

We spent the next two hours going over our jury selection questionnaires, Rosie's opening statement, our trial exhibits, and our defense strategy. It was almost eleven o'clock when Rosie finally turned off her laptop. "I think we've settled on a narrative. The prosecution doesn't have enough evidence to prove beyond a reasonable doubt that Mercy stabbed Cruz."

"I like it," I said. "It will be easy for the jury to follow."

Rosie looked over at Luna, who was sleeping peacefully in the corner. "It's nice that somebody isn't losing any sleep over this trial." She turned to Nady. "You should take her home. She's going to have a busy week."

"I will."

I spoke up again. "You ready to head home?"

Rosie nodded. "I want to stop at Mama's house on our way."

41
"YOU DO WHAT YOU CAN"

Sylvia's lips were pursed as she focused on her knitting. "You're all set for tomorrow?"

"Yes, Mama," Rosie said.

"You saw Mercy earlier today?"

"Mike and I were there this afternoon. Nady saw her this evening. She's doing a little better."

"Is she ready for trial?"

"Yes, Mama."

"I'll let her mother know."

Sylvia, Tony, Rosie, and I were sitting at Sylvia's dining room table at eleven-thirty on Sunday night. The aroma of chicken filled the room. It was quiet outside.

"Did you go over to St. Peter's again tonight?" Rosie asked.

Sylvia nodded.

"You promised, Mama."

"I stayed inside with Perlita and Isabel. They have plenty of people outside. It's turned into a block party. People have brought lawn chairs. A couple of bands were playing. They hooked up a big screen TV so people could watch the World Series."

"Sounds a bit bizarre."

"People adapt, Rosita."

"The feds are still there?"

"Yes."

"Any indication that they're going inside?"

"No."

"Maybe everybody could go home."

Sylvia shook her head. "The ICE people could change their minds."

"Father Lopez told us that they have an understanding with the ICE guys that they won't go inside without telling him first."

Sylvia stopped knitting. "He believed them?"

"He's betting on their moral character."

"He's more trusting than I am. And you?"

Rosie's mouth turned up. "He has more faith in human nature than I do."

"That's why he's a priest and you're a lawyer, dear."

Rosie touched her mother's hand. "Are you coming to court tomorrow?"

"Yes." She looked at Tony. "You're still available to give me a ride?"

"Of course, Mama."

"Thank you." She turned back to Rosie. "Father Lopez will be there as well. He's arranged for several other priests to hold down the fort at St. Peter's."

"Mercy will be pleased to see you."

"You do what you can. Are you still planning to do campaign appearances in the evenings?"

"A few."

"It's a lot, Rosita."

"The election is a week from Tuesday. After the trial and the election are over, Mike and I are going to take a little break."

"Sounds like a good idea." Sylvia finally put down her knitting. "Rosita?"

"Yes, Mama?"

"I appreciate everything that you and Michael are doing for Mercy."

"We're just doing our jobs, Mama."

"You're going to get an acquittal, right?"

"I think so, Mama. We'll do our best."

"I'll see you in court."

* * *

"You ready for trial?" I asked.

"Of course," Rosie said. "You?"

"Yes."

At one-twenty a.m., we were in Rosie's bed, wide awake. We never slept much on the eve of trial. It was unseasonably warm, so the window was open. The only illumination came from a streetlamp outside. Tommy was asleep down the hall.

"Something bothering you?" she asked.

"You sounded more confident with Nady than your mother."

"It's important to show confidence to your subordinates. I never try to BS Mama."

"How do you really think this trial is going to go?"

"We have a decent chance to get to reasonable doubt, but it's going to be an uphill climb."

"Sounds about right."

Her eyes lit up. "We're in agreement?"

"Seems like it."

"There's a first time for everything." Her tone turned thoughtful. "It's been a while since we've tried a case together."

"Feels like old times."

"Those were good times, Mike. Sometimes I miss being young, ambitious, and energetic."

"We may not be so young anymore, but we're still pretty ambitious and very energetic."

"I guess so."

"When we first met almost twenty-five years ago, did you ever imagine that you would be P.D. and we would have two great kids?"

"I thought it was in the realm of possibility."

I leaned over and kissed her. "We're going to win this case, Rosie. And you're going to win the election."

"Yeah."

"And then we're going to take a little time off."

"Sounds like a good plan. Are you going to get up early and walk the steps with Zvi?"

"Yes."

"You aren't going to get much sleep."

"It's overrated. Besides, we never get any sleep the night before trial."

She grinned. "Are you suggesting that we ought to do our customary pre-trial ritual?"

"It's worked well in the past."

"The sacrifices that we make for our clients." She kissed me. "Let's see how energetic you really are."

42
"ALL RISE"

At nine-fifteen on Monday morning, Rosie, Nady, and I lugged our laptops, trial bags, and exhibits through the throng of reporters on the front steps of the Hall. The sun was shining. A cool breeze hit our faces.

News is distributed electronically nowadays, but we were reminded that it is still gathered the old-fashioned way: by reporters shouting questions.

"Ms. Fernandez? Does your client plan to cut a plea deal?"

"Ms. Fernandez? Is it true that your client will be deported when the trial is over?"

"Ms. Fernandez? Will this case have any bearing on your chances for re-election?"

"Ms. Fernandez? Ms. Fernandez? Ms. Fernandez?"

When we reached the top of the stairs, Rosie stopped, turned around, and faced the nearest camera. "We are pleased to have the opportunity to defend Mercy Tejada in court. We are confident that she will be exonerated."

* * *

"Good to go?" Rosie asked.

Mercy's voice was a hoarse whisper. "Yes."

"Remain calm and don't be afraid to look the judge and the jurors in the eye."

Mercy was sitting between Rosie and me at the defense table in Judge Vanden Heuvel's stuffy courtroom. Nady was to Rosie's left. Mercy was wearing a white blouse with a navy skirt that Perlita had provided. Rosie's mother and Father Lopez were sitting behind us. Nicole Ward was sitting behind Harper. She was busy working the press. I figured that she would depart when jury selection started. Andy Erickson sat next to Harper at the prosecution table along with Inspector Lee, who was the only witness permitted in court prior to his testimony. Erickson was the Assistant D.A. assigned to assist Harper. Jerry Edwards was in the third row of the gallery. The other seats were divided about equally between members of the media and courthouse regulars.

I felt a rush of adrenaline as the bailiff recited the traditional call to order. "All rise."

Here we go.

A fan pushed around heavy air bearing the odor of mildew. Judge Vanden Heuvel emerged from her chambers, surveyed her domain, and walked deliberately to her chair with the assistance of a cane. She turned on her computer, put on her reading glasses, glanced at her docket, and raised her right hand. "Please be seated."

She never used a gavel.

She turned on her microphone and addressed the bailiff in a soft, but commanding tone. "We're on the record. Please call our case."

"The People versus Mercedes Margarita Tejada."

"Counsel will state their names for the record."

"DeSean Harper and Andrew Erickson for the People."

"Rosita Fernandez, Michael Daley, and Nadezhda Nikonova for the defense."

"Let's pick a jury."

* * *

Two days later, at one o'clock on Wednesday afternoon, our twelve jurors and four alternates were seated in the uncomfortable chairs in the box. They had just returned from lunch, and they appeared to be well-nourished and reasonably attentive. Judge Vanden Heuvel ran a tight courtroom, so the process had gone more rapidly than usual. Most trial attorneys (including yours truly) believe that cases are won and lost during jury selection. To the people in the gallery, however, the process of asking the same questions to a seemingly endless parade of potential jurors is decidedly dull. As a result, by mid-morning on Tuesday, our crowd had thinned, although Sylvia and Father Lopez had remained in their seats. When we finished jury selection, the gallery had filled up again.

The conventional wisdom says that you should try to pick jurors who are uninformed and easily manipulated. In this case, however, Rosie and I had sought educated women, who (we hoped) would understand the concept of reasonable doubt and be more inclined to give Mercy the benefit of the doubt. Fortunately, the pool of potential jurors in San Francisco is generally more educated than in many other places. Our panel included nine women, eight of whom were college educated, and six of whom were people of color. Two of the four alternates were also female, and one of the male alternates was a naturalized citizen born in Mexico. We were hoping that the female jurors who worked for Google and Facebook would be sympathetic.

Judge Vanden Heuvel addressed the jurors in a reassuring tone. She thanked them for their service and invited them to notify the bailiff if they had concerns. Then she read the standard instructions. "Do not talk about this case to anyone or among each other until deliberations begin. Do not do any research on your own or as a group. Do not use a dictionary or other reference materials, investigate the facts or law, conduct any experiments, or visit the scene of the events to be described at this trial. Do not look at anything involving this case in the press, on TV, or online."

She said it nicely, but she meant it.

She added the admonition that was unnecessary when I became a Deputy Public Defender but was now essential. "Finally, do not post anything on Facebook, Twitter, Instagram, Snapchat, WhatsApp, or other social media. If you tweet or text about this case, it will cost you."

The jurors nodded.

The judge looked at Harper. "Do you wish to make an opening statement?"

"Yes, Your Honor." He stood, buttoned his charcoal suit jacket, strode to the lectern, placed a single note card in front of him, and spoke directly to the jury. "My name is DeSean Harper. I am the Chief Assistant District Attorney of San Francisco. I am grateful for your service, and I appreciate your time and attention."

He pointed at a poster-sized photo of a smiling Cruz. "Carlos Cruz was a gifted chef, successful restaurateur, and generous contributor to the Mission District where he was born. His parents were naturalized citizens who worked long hours to create opportunities for Carlos and his brother. Against overwhelming odds and as a result of his extraordinary talent and hard work, Carlos became an award-winning chef." He pushed out a melodramatic sigh. "And now Carlos is dead. It is an unspeakable tragedy."

He pointed at Mercy. "We will demonstrate beyond a reasonable doubt that the defendant, Mercedes Tejada, stabbed Carlos on a Saturday morning in October of last year."

He lowered his arm. "Carlos was only thirty-two. His family and friends are devastated. We cannot bring him back, but we can bring his murderer to justice."

I was reluctant to interrupt so early in his opening, but I

needed to make a point. "Objection as to the use of the term 'murderer.' Argumentative."

"Sustained. The jury will disregard Mr. Harper's use of that term."

Sure they would.

Harper continued as if I hadn't objected. "I am asking you to fulfill your civic duty. It's your job to listen carefully, weigh the evidence, and find justice for Carlos."

He moved closer to the jury. "Carlos was killed just after midnight on Saturday, October twenty-seventh of last year. He had just completed a shift at his award-winning restaurant, El Conquistador. He supervised a staff of a dozen people, including the defendant."

His word choice was deliberate. He would always call Cruz by his first name to humanize him. He would refer to Mercy only as "the defendant."

"Carlos gave the defendant a job while she attended City College. He paid her well and let her work flexible hours. She was frequently late and had performance and attitude issues. Nevertheless, Carlos believed in her. His faith and trust were not reciprocated."

And she refused to sleep with him.

"On the night of October twenty-sixth, the defendant was in a bad mood and spent much of the evening arguing with Carlos. Her attitude made it difficult for her colleagues to do their jobs. Nevertheless, they completed the dinner service and everybody—including Carlos—pitched in to wash the dishes and prepare for the following day."

Harper's tone was somber. "Carlos left the restaurant at twelve-thirty a.m. The defendant followed him shortly thereafter. She stabbed Carlos in the alley. A witness arrived a moment later and saw a bloody knife on the ground next to the defendant. So did the first officer at the scene. The Medical Examiner determined that Carlos died of a stab wound. Our DNA expert confirmed that the blood on the knife matched Carlos's. The only fingerprints on the knife were those of the defendant."

Harper shot a disdainful glance at Rosie. "The defense is going to try to muddy the water by suggesting that somebody other than the defendant stabbed Carlos. That's their job. It's also why it is critical that you evaluate the evidence carefully and do yours."

Harper moved in front of the jury box. "Another witness will testify the defendant removed a knife from a drawer in the kitchen and took it into the break room. It was part of a matching set. The same knife was found next to Carlos's body."

Harper's lips turned down. "Coincidence? I don't think so."

Mercy turned to me, jaws clenched. "Can you do anything?" she whispered.

"Stay calm."

Harper walked back to the podium, where he spent five minutes expounding upon the "overwhelming evidence" that Mercy had stabbed Cruz. "During this trial, you are going to hear a lot about 'reasonable doubt.' It's an important legal concept. But there's something even more important: common sense. It's your job to evaluate the evidence, deliberate carefully, and use your common sense. I promise that I will provide more than enough evidence to find the defendant guilty of first-degree murder."

He returned to the prosecution table and sat down.

Judge Vanden Heuvel looked at Rosie. "Opening statement, Ms. Fernandez?"

"Yes, Your Honor."

She could have deferred until after Harper had completed

the prosecution's case, but she wanted to connect with the jurors right away.

She walked to the lectern and worked without notes. "My name is Rosie Fernandez. I am the San Francisco Public Defender. Contrary to what Mr. Harper just told you, my client, Mercy Tejada, has been wrongly accused of a crime that she did not commit. It's your job to see that justice is served and to correct this egregious mistake."

Rosie was already in full command of the courtroom. All eyes in the jury box were locked onto hers.

Rosie moved in front of the jurors. "Mercy Tejada is a kind and generous soul who graduated at the top of her class at Mission High and was attending City College with the intention of transferring to State to study nursing. Prior to this case, she had never been arrested. In fact, she had never been in trouble. She worked at El Conquistador to pay her tuition and to help her mother—a single parent—pay the rent and take care of Mercy's four-year-old sister, Isabel. Mercy's contributions were essential after her father died tragically in an accident a few years ago. She worked grueling hours at El Conquistador and was a dedicated employee."

Rosie made eye contact with the jurors in the first row. "If you have ever worked at a restaurant—which I have—you know that it's demanding. Carlos Cruz got the publicity, but Mercy and the staff made El Conquistador a world-class dining experience."

The juror who worked at Google was paying attention—or doing an excellent job of pretending to do so—but it didn't mean that she was buying everything that Rosie was selling.

Rosie was still talking. "Mercy left the restaurant a few minutes after Carlos did. When she got outside, she found him on the ground, a knife protruding from his stomach. She did what you and I would have done: she tried to help him. She removed the knife, tried to stop the bleeding, and called for help. A neighbor arrived within a minute and called nine-one-one. The police and the ambulance showed up shortly thereafter. It was too late to save Carlos Cruz. It was, in fact, a great tragedy."

Rosie took a deep breath. "Mr. Harper asked you to use your common sense. So will I. If you had just stabbed somebody, would you have called for help? Would you have tried to stop the bleeding? Would you have stayed until the police arrived? Would you have left the bloody knife on the ground knowing that your fingerprints were on it?"

"Objection," Harper said. "Argumentative. I would ask you to instruct Ms. Fernandez to stick to the facts in her opening."

Judge Vanden Heuvel turned to the jury. "An opening statement should not be treated as fact. It merely constitutes a roadmap of what the anticipated evidence will show."

The judge knew that the jurors weren't going to forget what they had just heard. Harper was trying to break up Rosie's flow.

Rosie flashed a caustic grin at Harper, nodded politely at the judge, and picked up where she had left off. "Just because they found a knife next to Mercy doesn't prove that she stabbed Carlos Cruz. Bottom line: Mr. Harper cannot prove beyond a reasonable doubt his unsubstantiated contention that she did. As a result, using your common sense, you cannot vote to convict Mercy of first-degree murder."

There was no reaction from the jurors as Rosie walked back to the defense table.

I leaned over and whispered, "That was good."

Rosie didn't look at me when she whispered, "It was fine."

The judge spoke to Harper. "Please call your first witness."

"The People call Juanita Morales."

43

"THERE WAS A BLOODY KNIFE"

Harper approached the witness box and stopped a respectful distance from the rail. "Where were you in the early morning of Saturday, October twenty-seventh of last year?"

Juanita Morales sat up straight, hands folded in her lap. Dressed in an off-white blouse and a hand-knitted scarf, she looked like a kindergarten teacher. "In my living room."

"Your house is across the alley from the back door of El Conquistador?"

"Yes."

"You heard shouting outside at approximately twelve-thirty-six a.m.?"

"Objection," Rosie said. "Please instruct Mr. Harper not to lead the witness on direct."

"I'll rephrase," Harper said. "Did you hear anything outside?"

"Someone was calling for help."

"What did you do?"

"I went to see what was going on. A young woman was kneeling over a man who had been stabbed."

"Is that woman in court today?"

"Yes. The defendant, Ms. Tejada."

"Did you see anything else?"

"There was a bloody knife on the ground next to her."

Harper had what he needed: a body and a weapon. "No further questions."

"Cross-exam, Ms. Fernandez?"

"Yes, Your Honor. May we approach the witness?"

"You may."

Rosie walked across the courtroom and stopped a few feet in front of the box. "Ms. Morales, I think it's very commendable that you went out to help."

"Thank you."

"You didn't see Mercy stab the decedent, did you?"

"No."

"You didn't see anybody else stab the decedent either, did you?"

"No."

"When Mercy was kneeling over the decedent, she was trying to help him, wasn't she?"

"It looked like it to me."

"And she asked you to call nine-one-one, didn't she?"

"Yes."

"She was very upset, wasn't she?"

"Yes."

"But she didn't try to run away, did she?"

"No."

"In fact, she continued to help the decedent and waited for the police to arrive, didn't she? And she cooperated with them, right?"

"Yes."

"That must have struck you as a bit odd, didn't it?"

"I don't understand."

"If Mercy had stabbed the decedent as Mr. Harper has suggested, don't you think that she would have tried to run?"

"Objection," Harper said. "Calls for speculation."

Yes, it does.

"Sustained."

Rosie had made her point. "No further questions."

* * *

Harper stood at the lectern. "Please state your name and occupation for the record."

The young cop adjusted the star on his pressed patrol uniform. "David Dito. I have been a police officer at Mission Station for three years."

"You've received several commendations and you train younger officers?"

"I have and I do."

Dito was, in fact, a solid cop from a multi-generation SFPD family. His uncle, Phil Dito, was my S.I. classmate who had also worked with Pete at Mission Station.

Harper asked the judge for permission to approach the witness, which the judge granted. He walked to the front of the box. "You were on duty at twelve-thirty-eight a.m. on Saturday, October twenty-seventh of last year?"

"Yes. I was at Mission Station. My partner and I were preparing to go out on patrol in our vehicle when we received a nine-one-one call about an emergency behind El Conquistador, approximately a half-block north of our location. We drove to the scene immediately."

"Couldn't you have just walked?"

"Standard procedure. We didn't know if we would have to pursue a suspect by car."

"What did you know about the situation?"

"Someone had been stabbed. The nine-one-one dispatcher had requested an ambulance."

It was a textbook direct exam. Harper was asking short questions, and Dito was providing precise answers.

"What time did you arrive?"

"Twelve-forty-one a.m."

"What did you find?"

Dito pointed at Mercy. "The defendant, Ms. Tejada, was

kneeling over the victim, Carlos Cruz. There was a bloody knife on the ground next to her."

Harper walked to the evidence cart and picked up the Messermeister, which had been tagged and placed inside a plastic evidence bag. He introduced it into evidence and held it up for everybody to see. Then he handed it to Dito. "Is this the knife?"

"Yes. It's a Messermeister Meridian Elite Stealth chef's knife. They cost about two hundred and fifty dollars each. We subsequently determined that it was one of a matching set of six. We found the other five knives in a drawer in the kitchen."

Another building block: Harper had introduced the alleged murder weapon.

"What did you do next?" he asked Dito.

"I called for backup, administered first aid, and asked my partner to escort the defendant to our squad car. Additional officers and the ambulance arrived within minutes. The officers began the process of securing the scene while I assisted the EMTs."

"No further questions, Your Honor."

"Cross-exam, Ms. Fernandez?"

"Yes, Your Honor. May we approach the witness?"

"Yes."

Rosie moved directly in front of Dito. "You didn't see Mercy stab the decedent, did you?"

"No."

"Ms. Morales didn't see Mercy stab the decedent either, did she?"

"No."

"In fact, you were unable to find any witnesses who saw Mercy stab the decedent, right?"

"Right."

"So you have no personal knowledge and no eyewitness accounts of who stabbed Carlos Cruz, correct?"

"Correct."

It was an obvious point, but Rosie wanted to remind the jury that this was a circumstantial case.

Rosie kept pushing. "Officer Dito, you spoke to Mercy when you arrived, didn't you?"

"Yes."

"She didn't confess to stabbing the decedent, did she?"

"No."

"She told you that she had removed the knife from the decedent's stomach and tried to stop the bleeding, didn't she?"

"Yes."

"And she was very upset, wasn't she?"

"Yes."

"How many times have you been called to a scene where somebody was deceased or seriously injured?"

"I can't give you an exact number."

"Ballpark estimate. Five? Ten? Twenty?"

"I'd say about a dozen."

"How many times have you seen the victim of a stabbing?"

"Including this situation, twice."

"In the other case, was anyone still in the immediate vicinity when you arrived?"

"Yes."

"I'll bet he was upset, wasn't he?"

"Yes."

"So it's fair to say that Mercy's demeanor wasn't unusual in the circumstances, right?"

"Objection," Harper said. "Calls for speculation as to what was going on inside the defendant's head."

Rosie shook her head. "I am not asking the witness to read

Mercy's mind. I'm simply asking him to describe her demeanor."

Harper tried again. "She's asking Officer Dito to speculate as to how somebody should act in these circumstances. That isn't within his area of expertise."

"He's a police officer," Rosie said.

"He isn't a psychologist."

The judge frowned. "I'm going to overrule the objection."

Dito remained calm. "Based upon my limited experience, I would say that the defendant's demeanor was not unusual in the circumstances."

Rosie walked back to the lectern. "Officer Dito, did Mercy attempt to run away?"

"No."

"You must have found that odd, didn't you?"

"Objection," Harper said. "Calls for speculation."

"I'm simply asking Officer Dito to tell us about his own reaction to the situation."

"Overruled."

Dito appeared slightly flustered. "Could you repeat the question?"

"Yes. You found it odd that Ms. Tejada didn't attempt to flee, didn't you?"

"No."

"You didn't think it was curious that she waited for the police?"

"Happens all the time, Ms. Fernandez."

"No, it doesn't, Officer Dito."

"Objection. There wasn't a question."

"Withdrawn," Rosie said. "Officer Dito, if you had just stabbed somebody, you wouldn't have stuck around until the cops arrived, would you?"

"Objection. Speculation."

"Sustained."

"And you wouldn't have helped the person you had just stabbed, would you?"

"Objection. More speculation."

"Sustained."

"You would have tried to run, wouldn't you?"

"Objection. Even more speculation."

"Sustained. Please, Ms. Fernandez."

"And you certainly wouldn't have left a bloody knife on the ground next to you where the police would have found it, right?"

"Objection. Even more speculation."

"Withdrawn," Rosie said. "No further questions, Your Honor."

"Redirect, Mr. Harper?"

"No, Your Honor."

"Please call your next witness."

"The People call Dr. Joy Siu."

44

"IT'S BASED UPON THE LAW OF GRAVITY"

Dr. Siu sat in the witness box sporting a charcoal pantsuit in lieu of her customary white lab coat. "I am the Chief Medical Examiner of the City and County of San Francisco."

Harper was at the lectern. "How long have you held that position?"

"Almost four years. Prior to that time, I was a full professor and Chair of the M.D. Ph.D. Program in anatomic pathology at UCSF."

Harper got as far as her undergrad degree at Princeton and her medical degree and Ph.D. at Johns Hopkins before Rosie cut him off. "Your Honor, we will stipulate that Dr. Siu is a nationally recognized authority in the field of anatomic pathology."

"Thank you, Ms. Fernandez."

Harper appeared disappointed that he wouldn't be able to dazzle the jury with her C.V. He presented the autopsy report to Dr. Siu as if he was handing her the stone tablets. "Could you please identify this document?"

"It's the autopsy report that I prepared for Carlos Cruz."

"Were you able to determine a cause of death?"

"Mr. Cruz died of a single stab wound that caused substantial injuries to his stomach, colon, and gall bladder. This resulted in massive internal bleeding. He was pronounced dead at San Francisco General at one-twenty-four a.m."

Another building block: cause of death.

Harper handed the Messermeister to her. "You're familiar with this weapon?"

"Object to the characterization of this knife as a weapon," Rosie said. "Foundation."

"I'll rephrase," Harper said. He turned back to Siu. "You're familiar with this knife?"

"Yes. It's a Messermeister Meridian Elite Stealth chef's knife."

"You're aware that Officer David Dito found this knife on the ground next to the defendant, who was kneeling over Carlos Cruz's body when Officer Dito arrived?"

"Yes."

"And that it was later determined that Carlos's blood was on this knife?"

"Objection. Assumes facts not in evidence."

"I'll rephrase. Did you find blood on this knife?"

"Yes."

"Did you authorize a DNA test?"

"Yes. The DNA on the knife matched Mr. Cruz's DNA. The test did not find anybody else's blood."

"Dr. Siu, in your best medical judgment, was this knife used to stab Carlos Cruz?"

"Yes." Siu turned to the jury. "The wound was consistent in size, shape, and depth with one that was likely to have been administered by the Messermeister."

"Did you find lacerations on Mr. Cruz's hands or other evidence of defensive wounds?"

"No."

"What did you conclude?"

"It was likely that Mr. Cruz knew his attacker."

"No further questions."

"Cross-exam, Ms. Fernandez?"

"Mr. Daley will be handling cross."

Rosie and I decided that I should make an early appearance

and play the role of bad cop.

I stood, buttoned my suit jacket, and moved to the front of the box, where I picked up the Messermeister. "The analysis of a stab wound is different than a gunshot wound, isn't it?"

"Yes."

"Unlike a gunshot where you can match the spent shells to a particular firearm, you have no way of knowing for sure whether a stab wound was generated by a particular knife, right?"

"You can take very precise measurements of the wound and the knife and match them up with a substantial degree of certainty."

"But not one hundred percent, right?"

"Right."

"So, you have no way of determining with any degree of certainty that the stab wound to the decedent was caused by this knife, do you?"

"As I said, the wound was consistent in size and shape with one that could have been administered by the Messermeister."

"But you can't match up the knife precisely, right?"

"Objection. Asked and answered."

"Sustained."

It was the best that I could do. "In performing the autopsy, you ordered standard toxicology tests, didn't you?"

"Objection," Harper said. "This issue was not addressed during direct."

"It's addressed in the autopsy report," I said.

"Overruled."

Siu looked at her unopened report as if to remind herself of its contents. "I ordered toxicology tests."

"The decedent had cocaine and alcohol in his system, correct?"

"Correct."

I shot a suggestive glance at the jury but didn't ask for elaboration. I turned back to Siu. "You testified that you found no evidence of defensive wounds, right?"

"Right."

"But you would acknowledge that the attacker could have surprised the decedent, right?"

"There was very little room between Mr. Cruz and his car, so there was no way that his attacker could have sneaked up from behind. As a result, while it is theoretically possible that Mr. Cruz was surprised, it seems highly unlikely."

"It's also possible that the decedent was distracted before he was stabbed, isn't it?"

"I suppose that's theoretically possible, too."

Theoretical possibilities are the best that we can do for now. "No further questions."

* * *

Lieutenant Katherine Jacobsen's badge gleamed as she stood adjacent to an enlarged photo of Mercy's sweatshirt displayed on the monitor next to the witness box. She used a Cross pen as a pointer. "This area is heavily caked with blood. We believe that the defendant pressed this part of her sweatshirt against Mr. Cruz's wound."

Harper was at the lectern. "And the area above it?"

Jacobsen drew an imaginary circle. "These droplets form a so-called 'projected pattern,' usually caused by arterial damage during a beating or stabbing. In such circumstances, the victim's blood flies in a projected fashion, causing the drops to land on the attacker's clothing."

"You're aware that the defendant has claimed that the blood got onto her clothing when she removed the knife?"

"I am."

"In your expert opinion, do you find it credible?"

"No. The defendant said that she found Mr. Cruz lying on the ground with a knife protruding from his stomach, which she removed by pulling upward. In such circumstances, the victim's blood could not have flown upward to create the projected pattern."

"Is that based upon your knowledge of anatomy?"

"No, it's based upon the law of gravity."

"In your expert opinion, how do you think the projected pattern was formed?"

"When the defendant stabbed Mr. Cruz."

"No further questions."

"Cross-exam?"

"Yes, Your Honor." I moved to the lectern. "Lieutenant Jacobsen, you analyzed the blood on the Messermeister knife, didn't you?"

"Yes."

"And you testified that you found Mercy's prints on the knife?"

"Correct."

"Right hand or left hand?"

"Right."

"You're aware that Ms. Tejada is left-handed?"

"Yes."

"You must have found it curious that a left-handed person used their right hand to stab somebody, didn't you?"

"Either hand would have been strong enough to have administered the fatal stab wound."

"But you didn't find it the least bit curious?"

"Objection," Harper said. "Asked and answered."

"Sustained."

I had planted the seed. "Lieutenant, you are aware that Mr.

Cruz wasn't pronounced dead until one-twenty-four a.m., correct?"

"Correct."

"So he was still alive when Mercy found him in the alley, right?"

"Not necessarily."

"But legally, he was still alive, right?"

"Right."

"Which means that his heart was still beating."

"We don't know that for sure, either."

"He couldn't have been alive if his heart wasn't beating, right?"

Harper started to stand, then reconsidered.

Jacobsen responded with any icy glare. "I suppose, Mr. Daley."

"If his heart was still beating, his blood must have been circulating, correct?"

"Correct."

"Blood flows through our bodies at a rate of approximately four miles per hour, doesn't it?"

"Approximately."

"It is therefore possible that the force of the blood pumping through the decedent's body may have caused it to spatter upward and create the 'projected pattern' when Mercy removed the knife, isn't it?"

"That's highly unlikely, Mr. Daley."

"But not impossible, right, Lieutenant?"

"In my thirty-plus years of working on these matters, I have never seen such a scenario."

"Perhaps this is the first time. No further questions."

"Please call your next witness, Mr. Harper."

"The People call Olmedo Rivera."

45

"THEY WERE FIGHTING ALL NIGHT"

Cruz's onetime lover was sitting ramrod straight in the box. "My name is Olmedo Rivera. I was the sous chef at El Conquistador."

Harper stood a few feet from him. "What did your job entail?"

Rivera was sweating through an ill-fitting double-breasted suit jacket. "Food preparation, management of the kitchen staff, and implementation of Carlos's vision."

At two-thirty on Wednesday afternoon, the jury was dialed in to the baby-faced young man whose obvious discomfort evoked sympathetic expressions.

Harper's tone was conversational. "You must have known him very well."

"I did." Rivera gulped water from a paper cup. "We went to school together. I worked at his parents' restaurant. Carlos asked me to help when he bought his first food truck. Eventually, he asked me to be the sous chef at El Conquistador."

Rosie and I had no grounds to interrupt as Harper led Rivera through a carefully scripted timeline of his lifelong relationship with Cruz. While it had no direct relevance to Cruz's death, it allowed Rivera to build empathy with the jury.

"Do you have any formal training as a chef?" Harper asked.

"I learned everything from Carlos."

"How long did you work at El Conquistador?"

"From the day it opened until the day it closed."

"You were working on the night that Carlos was killed?"

"Yes."

Harper pointed at the life-size photo of Cruz that he had positioned on an easel next to the box. "It must have been very difficult for you to lose such a close friend."

"It was."

"Would it be fair to say that El Conquistador was Carlos's baby?"

"I like to think that it was my baby, too."

This was obviously rehearsed—and effective.

"Was the restaurant crowded on the evening of October twenty-sixth of last year?"

"It was always crowded."

"Was Carlos in good spirits?"

"For Carlos. He was never satisfied. He wanted everything to be perfect every night."

"Are you saying that he wasn't easy to work for?"

"He was intense. You have to obsessed to be successful in the restaurant business."

Harper responded with an exaggerated nod. "You also knew the defendant?"

"Of course."

"Was she a good employee?"

"At times, her attention to detail on preparation, table set-up, and customer experience were lacking. She thought that it was okay to be 'just good enough.'"

"Did Carlos talk to her about it?"

"He did. She became defensive and angry." Rivera glared at Mercy. "Carlos tried to help her. He let her work flexible hours to attend college. He let her go home early to take care of her baby sister. He went out of his way to mentor her, but she didn't appreciate it."

"How was the defendant's mood on the night that Carlos died?"

"Angry. I asked her to bring up a bottle of wine from the basement, and she said that she was too busy. A few minutes later, I found her sending texts in the break room. I told her that she needed to work harder. She glared at me and didn't answer."

"How were she and Carlos getting along?"

"They were fighting all night."

"About what?"

"She said that Carlos had tried to kiss her."

"Did he?"

"I didn't see anything. At one point, she told him that she would get him for the way that he had treated her."

"Those were her exact words?"

"As close as I can remember."

"You thought she was serious about harming him?"

"Objection," Rosie said. "Calls for speculation."

"Overruled."

Rivera glared at Mercy. "I don't know what was going through her mind that night."

"No further questions."

"Cross-exam, Ms. Fernandez?"

"Yes, Your Honor." Rosie moved to the front of the box. "You didn't see Mercy stab the decedent, did you?"

"No."

"And you didn't see her take a knife out the back door of the restaurant, did you?"

"I left before she did."

"Which means that you didn't see it, right?"

"Right."

"You testified that the decedent was extremely difficult to work with, didn't you?"

"At times."

"And he yelled at his employees, including Mercy and you, didn't he?"

"Yes."

"So it wasn't unusual for the decedent and Mercy to have been arguing, was it? In fact, it was no different than any other night at El Conquistador, right?"

"That's fair."

Rosie walked to the lectern. "Mr. Rivera, in addition to your long-time friendship and business relationship with Mr. Cruz, you also had a personal relationship, didn't you?"

"Objection. Ms. Fernandez is asking about matters not addressed during direct."

Rosie feigned disdain. "Your Honor, Mr. Harper questioned this witness about his relationship with the decedent. We should be able to follow up on the same subject."

"Overruled."

Rosie's eyes swung back to Rivera. "You and Carlos Cruz were lovers, weren't you?"

"Yes."

"You lived together for a period of time, but Mr. Cruz broke up with you, didn't he?"

"Yes."

"And you were unhappy about it, weren't you?"

"It was difficult."

"And acrimonious. You thought that he treated you badly, didn't you?"

"At times."

Harper got to his feet. "This line of questioning is irrelevant to the matters at hand and is very painful for Mr. Rivera."

Judge Vanden Heuvel spoke to Rosie. "Please get to the point, Ms. Fernandez."

"Yes, Your Honor." She turned to Rivera. "You're still bitter about it, aren't you?"

"Yes."

"And you were angry at Carlos that night, weren't you?"

"At times."

"You were angry enough to stab him, weren't you?"

"No."

"No further questions."

* * *

Junio Costa clutched a flimsy paper cup. "I was the dishwasher at El Conquistador."

Harper was at the lectern. "You were at work on the night that Carlos Cruz died?"

Costa looked ill at ease in a black sport jacket with baggy gray slacks. "Yes."

The temperature had risen to about eighty-five degrees in Judge Vanden Heuvel's courtroom. Sensing that the jury was getting antsy, Harper led Costa through a brisk description of the events on the night that Cruz died. The young dishwasher's delivery was stilted, but effective. Harper had coached him to emphasize the fact that Mercy had been in a bad mood and had been fighting with Cruz for much of the evening.

Harper moved in front of the box. "You heard the defendant arguing with Carlos that night, didn't you?"

"Yes."

"Do you know why?"

"She said that Carlos tried to kiss her."

"What else did she say?"

"She said that she would 'get him.'"

"No further questions."

Rosie was on her way to the front of the box before Harper sat down. She froze Costa with an icy glare. "Did Mr. Cruz ever hit on you?"

"Excuse me?"

"You testified that Ms. Tejada and the decedent were arguing because Mr. Cruz tried to kiss her. My question is whether he ever tried to kiss you or made advances to you?"

A hesitation. "Uh, no."

"Not even once?"

"No."

Mercy leaned over and whispered, "He's lying."

Rosie was in Costa's face. "You said that Mercy was angry because the decedent tried to kiss her, right?"

"Right."

"If Carlos Cruz tried to hit on you, you would have been angry, too, right?"

"Yes."

"But it doesn't mean that you would have killed him, right?"

"Objection. Speculation."

"Overruled."

Costa held up a hand. "Right."

Rosie's eyes narrowed. "You didn't see Mercy attack the decedent, did you?"

"No."

"And you would acknowledge that he was difficult to work for, wouldn't you?"

"At times."

"And you complained about him to your co-workers at times, didn't you?"

"Sometimes."

"And I'll bet that you argued with him on the night that he died, right?"

"Maybe."

"Maybe you were so mad that you stabbed him that night, right?"

"No."

"So just because Mercy argued with Carlos doesn't mean that she stabbed him, right?"

"Objection. Speculation."

"Sustained."

Rosie took a deep breath. "Are you married, Mr. Costa?"

"No."

"Girlfriend?"

"No."

"Boyfriend?"

"Yes."

"Do you and your boyfriend ever argue?"

"Sometimes."

"But you would acknowledge that just because you argue doesn't mean that you would turn around and stab him, right?"

"Right."

"And you would also agree that if your boyfriend was stabbed, it would be unfair to accuse you of his murder just because you had an argument earlier that day, right?"

"Objection," Harper said. "Speculation."

"Sustained."

"No further questions, Your Honor."

Judge Vanden Heuvel looked at the clock. "Let's take a fifteen-minute recess."

46
"HE WAS A GIFTED CHEF"

Mercy's fists were clenched. "Maybe we should have taken the plea bargain."

Rosie tried to sound reassuring. "It's always difficult during the prosecution's case."

It was hotter in the consultation room than in court. The pressure of trial, the stifling heat, and the cumulative effect of a year of unforgiving stress were taking a toll on Mercy. Rosie always said that you should never second-guess yourself once trial starts, but I was beginning to think that we were asking more from a nineteen-year-old than she had to give.

Mercy exhaled heavily. "We're getting killed."

"It's only the first day of testimony, Mercy."

* * *

Christine Fong's demeanor was professional, her attire businesslike, her tone confident. "I was the maître d', and I managed the front of the house at El Conquistador. The primary investor asked me to step in after the restaurant had been open for about six months."

Harper was standing in front of the box. "Jed Sanders?"

"Correct. He wanted an experienced manager." She confirmed that she had worked for Sanders in a similar capacity at one of his restaurants in Los Angeles.

"You must have known Carlos Cruz very well."

"I did. He was a gifted chef."

"Was he a good businessman?"

"He was smart, motivated, and savvy."

Very diplomatic.

"On the other hand," she added, "he had a lot to learn."

Not so diplomatic.

Harper nodded. "You were mentoring him on business issues?"

"Yes."

"Was he good to work with?"

"He was a passionate perfectionist."

"How did you get along with him?"

"Fine."

"Some of his employees described him as difficult."

"He never asked anybody to do anything that he hadn't done himself. Staff turnover was comparable to similar establishments."

"You also know the defendant?"

"I interacted with her every day."

"Was she a good employee?"

Fong looked over at Mercy. "She's very bright. Carlos and I believed that she had a lot of potential. Unfortunately, she didn't always perform with great enthusiasm."

"You pointed this out to her?"

"That was part of my job. She didn't handle criticism well. She became defensive."

"How did she get along with Carlos?"

"Reasonably well most of the time. Carlos gave her every opportunity to succeed."

Especially when he was hitting on her.

Harper glanced at the photo of Cruz. "You were there on the night that he was killed?"

"Yes. It was a devastating loss."

"Did you see Carlos and the defendant interact that night?"

"They were arguing."

"Do you know why?"

"Ms. Tejada claimed that Carlos had tried to kiss her."

"Did you see anything?"

"No."

"Did you hear the defendant say anything that might have been construed as a threat?"

"Objection," Rosie said. "Calls for speculation."

"On the contrary," Harper said, "I am simply asking for Ms. Fong's observations about the back-and-forth between Mr. Cruz and the defendant."

"Overruled."

Fong sat up taller. "Ms. Tejada told the defendant that she would 'get him.'"

"No further questions."

"Your witness, Ms. Fernandez."

Rosie strode to the front of the box. "You received multiple complaints that the decedent made inappropriate sexual advances toward employees, didn't you?"

"In each case, our lawyers conducted a full investigation and found no credible evidence of illegal behavior. We counseled Carlos to use better judgment to avoid future misunderstandings."

Misunderstandings. Right.

Rosie moved in closer. "Did you investigate Mercy's accusation that the decedent had tried to kiss her?"

"There wasn't time that night."

"What about afterward?"

Fong shrugged. "There was no point, Ms. Fernandez. Carlos was dead."

"You were at the restaurant on the night that he died?"

"Yes."

"You didn't see Mercy stab the decedent, did you?"

"No."

"And you didn't see anybody else stab him, right?"

"Right."

"So you have no knowledge of who stabbed Mr. Cruz, do you?"

"Correct."

"No further questions."

* * *

Sanders was up next. He had ditched the grunge look in favor of Brooks Brothers. "I ran two award-winning restaurants in Los Angeles. About ten years ago, I closed them and started a consulting firm with Ms. Fong to invest in promising young chefs."

Harper was standing at the lectern. "You invested in Carlos Cruz?"

"He was a gifted chef."

He and his girlfriend had rehearsed their lines.

He added, "Carlos was a once-in-a-generation talent."

"Sort of the LeBron James of fine cuisine?"

A little hyperbolic for my taste.

Sanders nodded. "You could say that."

Judge Vanden Heuvel maintained her stoic demeanor, but a couple of the jurors were yawning. The retired engineer from Genentech was fading. The young man from Twitter looked as if he couldn't wait to get outside and turn on his phone. The woman from Google was fanning herself with her notepad.

"Were you involved in day-to-day operations at the restaurant?" Harper asked.

"We always insist on having substantial input on everything: menu, design, budget, kitchen, and staffing. When you make a considerable investment, you want to make sure that you give it the best chance to succeed."

"You were at the restaurant on the night that Carlos died?"

"Yes. The dining room was full. The energy was positive."

"You knew the defendant?"

"She struck me as bright and ambitious."

"Did you see any interactions between Mr. Cruz and the defendant?"

"They had harsh words. Ms. Tejada claimed that Carlos tried to kiss her."

"Did you see him do so?"

"No."

"Were you able to verify her accusation?"

"No."

"Did Ms. Tejada threaten him?"

"Yes." He glared at Mercy. "My recollection is that she told him that she would 'make him pay.'"

"No further questions."

Rosie headed straight to the front of the box. "You were aware that Carlos Cruz had been accused of sexual harassment on multiple occasions, right?"

"Yes. We took such accusations very seriously. Our lawyers found no evidence of any illegal conduct."

"You brought in Ms. Fong to keep an eye on Mr. Cruz after he was accused of sexual harassment, didn't you?"

"I brought her in because she is an experienced and competent manager."

"You also have a personal relationship with her, don't you?"

"We've been seeing each other for several years."

"And you were trying to protect your investment, weren't you?"

"That's just good business, Ms. Fernandez."

"You set up a separate limited liability company to own the restaurant, didn't you?"

"It's standard practice to limit potential legal and financial exposure."

"You filed for bankruptcy for that entity, didn't you?"

"We had no choice."

"So you lost your entire investment?"

"Most of it."

"You carried a key-man life insurance on Mr. Cruz, didn't you?"

"Also standard business practice."

"How much?"

"A million dollars."

"That must have cushioned the financial blow."

"It helped, but I can assure you that the last thing I wanted to do was collect on our key-man policy."

"Sounds like you had a million reasons."

"Objection," Harper said. "There wasn't a question there."

"Withdrawn. You didn't see Mercy stab the decedent, did you?"

"No."

"And you didn't see her take a knife out of the restaurant, did you?"

"No."

"So you have no first-hand knowledge of who stabbed the decedent, do you?"

"No."

"In fact, it's possible that you or even Ms. Fong may have stabbed him, isn't it?"

"Objection. Speculation."

"Sustained."

"No further questions."

* * *

Rosie, Nady, and I were in the consultation room at four-forty on Wednesday afternoon. After court had adjourned, we spent a few minutes with Mercy before she was escorted back to the Glamour Slammer. She had alternated between panic and resignation.

The door opened. A deputy let Rosie's mother and Father Lopez inside.

Sylvia spoke first. "We are going back to St. Peter's to update Perlita."

"Thanks," Rosie said. "I need you to explain to her that the D.A. usually does well early in the process."

"I'll do the best that I can."

I looked at Father Lopez. "Any update on our friends from ICE?"

"They're still in their van in front of the rectory. There's no indication that they're preparing to move in, and they've promised to give me a heads-up before they do."

"You trust them?"

"I believe that it was President Reagan who coined the expression, 'trust but verify.'"

47

"THINGS ALWAYS LOOK BETTER IN THE MORNING"

"Did you talk to your mother?" I asked.

"Briefly," Rosie said. "Perlita isn't holding up very well. She's under an ungodly amount of stress."

I could only offer a weak cliché. "You do the best that you can."

Her office was quiet at eight-forty-five on Wednesday night. Nady was staring at her laptop, a sleeping Luna curled up at her feet. A few Deputy P.D.s were scattered in the hallways, and the ever-reliable Terrence "The Terminator" was still at his desk.

Rosie looked at Nady. "Do you think the jury was buying what Harper was selling?"

"For now." The corner of Nady's mouth turned up. "You're a better salesman."

"Thank you. Who do you think they'll put up first tomorrow?"

"Cruz's brother. You're going to have to go after him. Then he'll put up Inspector Lee to tie their case together."

"We'll need to be ready to start our defense tomorrow."

"Unless you can persuade the judge to drop the charges before we put on a defense."

"I'm not *that* good of a salesman."

* * *

It was almost midnight when Rosie finally powered down her laptop. "Do you think we can get the jury to reasonable doubt?" she asked me.

"Yes." *Well, probably.*

"Harper is a good lawyer."

"So are you."

"I'm not feeling great about it, Mike."

Neither am I. "Things always look better in the morning."

The co-head of the Felony Division strolled into Rosie's office. Rolanda forced a smile. "I'm not getting a wildly happy vibe in here."

"First day of the D.A.'s case," Rosie said. "You know how it goes. How's your trial?"

Rolanda's lips turned down in a perfect imitation of her aunt. "Not bad. We're starting closing arguments tomorrow. We may get the case to the jury by the end of the day."

"You going to get to reasonable doubt?"

"I'm not feeling great about it, Rosie."

"Things always look better in the morning."

Rolanda smiled. "My dad told me that you had a pretty good day in court."

"He wasn't there. Who did he talk to?"

"Grandma. He saw her at St. Peter's."

"What did Grandma tell him?"

"That your opening was very good, and your cross-exams were solid."

"Grandma was less enthusiastic about my performance when we talked after court."

"Grandma says nicer things about you when you aren't around. I've never understood why she does that."

"You'll understand better when you and Zach have kids of your own."

* * *

My phone vibrated as I was driving across the Golden Gate Bridge. Pete's name appeared on the display. "You promised me something useful," I said.

"When are you going to start the defense?" he asked.

"Could be as soon as tomorrow."

"Try to slow-walk things. I may have a line on the waitress, Carmen Dominguez."

48
"HE WAS MY BROTHER"

Judge Vanden Heuvel's courtroom was slightly cooler when we reconvened at ten o'clock the following morning, a Thursday. It seemed fitting that we were working on Halloween. In what passed for a hint of whimsy in the otherwise grim surroundings, the court reporter had put a miniature pumpkin on her desk.

Harper had switched from a charcoal to a navy suit. He stood at the lectern. "What is your relationship to Carlos Cruz?"

Alejandro Cruz was wearing a gray suit with a conservative tie. "He was my brother."

"I'm sorry for your loss. Your occupation?"

"I am currently in the real estate business. Before that, I was the general manager of El Conquistador restaurant, where I was responsible for accounting, finance, budgets, personnel, leasing, insurance, and dealing with our investor."

"Sounds like you had a lot of responsibility."

"I did. We were running a high-end restaurant with a very small staff. It was like working for a startup where everybody has to pitch in. At times, I would help in the kitchen, clear tables, or do the dishes."

"The restaurant was doing well?"

"It was very successful."

"Did you enjoy working with your brother?"

"Very much. Carlos always wanted to open his own restaurant. El Conquistador was a dream come true. I was happy to be a part of it."

Cruz was laying it on a little thick.

Harper moved closer. "You were working on the evening that your brother was killed?"

"Yes. I spent most of the night in my office. I was in the kitchen, too, but I tried to stay out of Carlos's way when he was cooking."

"Was your brother in a good mood that night?"

"Yes. He was happiest in the kitchen."

"You knew the defendant?"

"I interacted with her almost every day."

"Was she a good employee?"

"For the most part. At times, she didn't always take as much initiative as we would have liked. We spoke to her about it. She didn't handle constructive criticism well."

"You didn't terminate her."

"Carlos was big on second chances."

Mercy leaned over and whispered, "He's full of crap."

I nodded.

Harper turned to the matter at hand. "Did you see your brother interact with the defendant that night?"

"Yes. Ms. Tejada was angry at Carlos. According to our dishwasher, she said that Carlos tried to kiss her."

"Did he?"

"I don't know."

"Did you talk to her about it?"

"I didn't have time."

"Did you ask your brother about it?"

"Yes. He told me that Ms. Tejada was having a bad night."

"You left it there?"

"It was busy."

"Were you in the kitchen at approximately eleven-forty-five that night?"

"Yes. I was helping with setup for the next day."

"Was the defendant helping, too?"

"Yes."

"How was her demeanor?"

"Agitated."

"Did she say anything to Carlos?"

"She said that she would 'get him.'"

"Those were her exact words?"

"As I recall, yes."

Mercy leaned over again. "That's another lie," she whispered.

I held up a hand.

"Did you notice anything else that night?" Harper asked.

"I saw her remove a Messermeister chef's knife from a drawer and take it into the break room where our staff stored their personal belongings."

"People must have taken knives out of drawers all the time."

"They did, but it seemed odd."

"Did you see her come back into the kitchen?"

"Yes."

"Did she have the knife in her possession?"

"No."

"Were you concerned?"

"I didn't think about it until I found out that Carlos had been stabbed by a Messermeister."

"You're sure it was the same knife?"

"It was from a set of six, one of which was missing the next day."

"No further questions."

"Ms. Fernandez?"

Rosie walked to the evidence cart, picked up the Messermeister, and handed it to Cruz. "Is this the knife that you claim that Ms. Tejada removed from the kitchen?"

"It's the same kind of knife. I presume that it's the same one the police found on the ground next to her."

"You didn't see her stab your brother, did you?"

"No."

"You didn't see anyone stab anybody, did you?"

"No."

"And you didn't see her take the knife outside, did you?'

"No."

"Were you in the kitchen the entire time that Mercy was at the restaurant?"

"No."

"So it's possible that she could have returned the knife to the drawer when you weren't looking or you weren't there, right?"

His tone turned grudging. "Right."

Rosie nodded at the juror from Google, who nodded back. Rosie moved a step closer to Cruz. "There were a lot of people working that night, correct?"

"Correct."

"Several of whom didn't always get along with your brother, right?"

"At times."

"And several of whom had lodged sexual harassment claims against him, right?"

"Right."

"All of which were whitewashed by your lawyers, right?"

"Objection to the use of the term 'whitewash,'" Harper said.

"I'll rephrase," Rosie said. "Your lawyers determined that your brother had not technically violated the law, correct?"

"Correct."

"But you would acknowledge that just because there may not have been a technical legal violation does not necessarily mean that your brother was innocent, right?"

His expression turned smug. "I'm not a lawyer."

"Please answer the question, Mr. Cruz."

"The fact that our attorneys at a high-priced firm found no evidence of illegal activity does not necessarily mean that they exonerated my brother."

"And you would also acknowledge that there were still some hard feelings between your brother and several staff members?"

"Yes."

"And the investor, Mr. Sanders?"

"Yes."

"And the manager, Ms. Fong?"

"Yes.

"And you?"

"Not really."

"And you would also agree that those people also had access to the knife, right?"

"I suppose."

"And it is therefore possible that any number of people other than Ms. Tejada could have removed the knife from the drawer and stabbed your brother, isn't it?"

"Objection. Speculation."

"Sustained."

"In fact, it's possible that you could have stabbed your brother, right?"

"Objection. Speculation."

"Sustained."

"No further questions."

"Redirect, Mr. Harper?"

"No, Your Honor."

"Any additional witnesses?"

"Just one, Your Honor. The People call Inspector Kenneth Lee."

49
"NOTHING FURTHER"

Inspector Lee sat in the box, arms at his sides. A cup of water was on the ledge next to him, but he wouldn't touch it. Nervous witnesses drink water. Experienced homicide cops never get thirsty.

At ten-twenty on Thursday morning, Harper had orchestrated a crisp direct exam in which Lee had brought together the major elements of their case. Mercy worked at the restaurant. She and Cruz had a history of acrimony, and they had argued on the night that he died. Lee repeated Alejandro's testimony that Mercy had taken a knife into the break room and returned without it. The first officer at the scene found a knife next to Mercy. The blood on the knife matched Cruz's. The only fingerprints were Mercy's.

Rosie objected frequently and, as far as I could tell, fruitlessly.

Harper addressed Lee from the lectern. "Inspector, could you please summarize what happened at El Conquistador?"

"Of course, Mr. Harper." Lee spoke directly to the jury. "It was a typically busy night at El Conquistador. The defendant and Carlos Cruz had a history of conflict, even though Carlos had given the defendant a job, allowed her flexibility in her schedule, and overlooked her less-than-stellar performance. She and the defendant had a heated argument that night."

I glanced at the jury. All eyes were focused on Lee.

"The defendant removed a Messermeister knife from a drawer in the kitchen and took it into the employee break room. She did not have the knife in her possession when she returned.

It was from a set of six, one of which was not in the drawer the following morning. The knife used to stab Carlos Cruz was, in fact, a Messermeister.

"Carlos Cruz was the next-to-last person to leave the restaurant. The defendant followed him a moment later. She stabbed Carlos with the Messermeister, which was covered in Carlos's blood. The only fingerprints on the knife were those of the defendant."

Lee turned his eyes from the jury to Harper, who obliged by teeing up the final question.

"What did you conclude, Inspector?"

"That the defendant, Mercedes Tejada, with premeditation and intent, followed Carlos out of the restaurant and stabbed him with intent to kill. Carlos died a short time later."

"No further questions."

"Cross-exam, Ms. Fernandez?"

"Yes, Your Honor." She walked to the lectern and stood perfectly still. "Inspector, Mr. Cruz's brother told you that Mercy removed a knife from a drawer in the kitchen and took it into the employee break room, correct?"

"Correct."

"And he said that he didn't see her bring it back into the kitchen, correct?"

"Correct."

"But you would acknowledge that Mr. Cruz wasn't in the kitchen the entire time after Mercy allegedly took the knife until the moment that she left the restaurant. It is therefore possible that Mercy returned the knife to the drawer when Mr. Cruz wasn't there, right?"

"It's possible."

"Nobody else saw Mercy remove the knife from the drawer, right?"

"Right."

"Perhaps that's because she didn't take it in the first place."

"Alejandro said that she did."

"You have no way of knowing that he was telling the truth."

"I had no reason to disbelieve him."

Rosie feigned disbelief. "He's the only person who saw Mercy take the knife, right?"

"Right."

"Which conveniently filled a huge gap in your narrative, didn't it?"

"Objection," Harper said. "Argumentative."

"Sustained."

Rosie moved in front of Lee. "Mercy was at the scene when you arrived, wasn't she?"

"Yes."

"And she tried to assist the decedent, didn't she?"

"Yes."

"And she called out for help, correct?"

"Correct."

"And when Juanita Morales arrived a few minutes later, Mercy instructed her to call nine-one-one, didn't she?"

"Yes."

"Mercy made no attempt to flee, right?"

"Right."

"And she continued to assist Mr. Cruz until the police and the EMTs arrived, didn't she?"

"Yes."

"It must have struck you as odd that she attempted to help the man that she had allegedly just stabbed, didn't it?"

"I thought it was good that she tried to help."

"And it also must have struck you as even stranger that she didn't try to run, didn't it?"

"I don't know what was going through her mind."

"If you had just stabbed somebody, would you have stuck around until the cops arrived?"

"Objection. Asks for speculation."

"Sustained."

Rosie walked over to the evidence cart, picked up the Messermeister, and held it up. "This is the knife that you believe was used to stab Mr. Cruz, right?"

"It's the knife that I believe *your client* used to stab Mr. Cruz."

"But you don't know for sure that she did, do you?"

"I believe the evidence supports the conclusion that she did."

"You testified that the forensic expert found Mr. Cruz's blood on this knife, right?"

"Right."

"But you would acknowledge that it doesn't prove that Mercy stabbed him, right?"

"Not by itself."

"In fact, you found no witnesses who saw Mercy or anybody else stab Mr. Cruz, right?"

"Right."

"You also testified that Mercy's fingerprints were found on this knife, right?"

"Right."

"Which proves that she held the knife, but it doesn't prove that she used the knife to stab Mr. Cruz, does it?"

"I believe that she did."

"But it's also possible that Mercy got her prints on the knife when she removed it from Mr. Cruz's stomach, right?"

"Objection. Speculation."

"Overruled."

Lee answered with a grudging, "It's possible."

"They found fingerprints only from Mercy's right hand on this knife, right?"

"Right."

"You're aware that Mercy is left-handed, correct?"

A hesitation. "Correct."

"It must have struck you as odd that she used her lesser hand to swing this knife, right?"

"It is what it is, Ms. Fernandez."

Rosie gave the jury a moment to absorb Lee's answer. "Ms. Morales testified that she saw the knife on the ground next to Mercy, didn't she?"

"Yes."

"And Officer Dito also saw the knife on the ground, right?"

"Right."

"You would agree that just because there was a knife on the ground doesn't prove that Mercy used it to stab Mr. Cruz, right?"

"Not in and of itself. However, with the other evidence, we concluded that she did."

Rosie flashed a sarcastic grin. "And that's also a very convenient fact that supports your version of the story, isn't it?"

"Objection. Argumentative."

"Sustained."

Rosie looked at the knife. "Inspector, you didn't find any evidence that Mercy tried to move this knife, did you?"

"No."

"Or hide it?"

"No."

"If you had just stabbed someone, would you have left the knife on the ground in plain view knowing that the police were about to arrive?"

"Objection. Speculation."

"Sustained."

Rosie walked back to the lectern. "Let's be honest, Inspector. You didn't seriously consider anyone other than Ms. Tejada as a suspect, did you?"

"We considered everyone at the restaurant until we were able to rule them out."

"No further questions."

"Cross-exam, Mr. Harper?"

"No, Your Honor."

"Any additional witnesses?"

"Nothing further, Your Honor. The People rest."

"I trust you'd like to make a motion, Ms. Fernandez?"

"Yes, Your Honor. The defense moves that all charges against Ms. Tejada be dismissed on grounds that the prosecution has failed to prove its case beyond a reasonable doubt."

"Denied." She looked at her watch. "We'll recess for lunch. Since it's Halloween, I would like to end our proceedings a little early so that everybody can go home and take their kids trick-or-treating. Please be ready to call your first witness at one o'clock sharp."

50

"SOMETIMES YOU HAVE TO STAND UP FOR WHAT'S RIGHT"

Mercy ignored her uneaten turkey sandwich. "That wasn't so bad, right?"

"Right," Rosie said.

"You said that if things went well enough, we wouldn't have to call any witnesses."

Rosie rested her hands on the table in the consultation room. "It isn't enough. We want to give ourselves the best chance of persuading one or more of the jurors to get to reasonable doubt. We'll want to put up our blood spatter expert to refute Lieutenant Jacobsen's testimony. Then we'll want to call some of the other people who were at the restaurant to give the jury some alternatives."

Mercy fidgeted with her sandwich wrapper. "And if that isn't enough?"

"We may need you to testify."

* * *

"You really think we should put Mercy on the stand?" I asked.

Rosie shook her head. "Ideally, no, but we need her to be ready."

We had stayed in the consultation room while a deputy escorted Mercy to the bathroom. The mood was gloomy. Nady picked at her sandwich.

There was a knock. I opened the door and saw Rosie's mother and Father Lopez. I assured the deputy that they were legitimate visitors and closed the door behind them.

Rosie spoke up. "Everything okay, Mama?"

"Yes, Rosita."

"We need to get back into court in a few minutes."

Father Lopez spoke up. "My source at ICE informed me that the powers-that-be are talking about coming in tonight and detaining Perlita."

"Peacefully, I hope?"

"That seems to be the plan. We've spread the word around the neighborhood that there may be trouble, and people are responding. About a thousand people are surrounding the rectory, with more on the way. I've encouraged everybody to remain peaceful, but things could get out of hand. I'm going back to church to try to keep everybody calm."

Sylvia's eyes narrowed. "I'm going with him to stay with Perlita."

Rosie eyed her mother. "Is there any way that I can talk you out of it?"

"No."

"I don't want you to get you hurt, Mama. And I don't want you to get arrested, either."

"I'm not going to throw myself in front of the ICE officers, Rosita. I'm just going to sit with Perlita and Isabel."

"I don't like it, Mama."

"Sometimes you have to stand up for what's right."

Rosie walked over and kissed her mother. "You'll be careful?"

"Always, Rosita."

Rosie turned to Father Lopez. "You'll take Mama back to St. Peter's?"

"I have a driver waiting downstairs."

"We'll come over when we're finished in court."

51
"IT COULD HAVE"

I stood at the lectern. "Would you please state your name for the record?"

"Dr. Lloyd Russell."

"You're a medical doctor?"

"I have a Ph.D. in criminology. My area of expertise is blood spatter patterns."

I had met Lloyd Russell in Berkeley thirty years earlier, when he was my criminology professor. At eighty-eight, the relentlessly upbeat academic had a cherubic face, dancing blue eyes, and the wisp of a beard that gave him an air of gravitas. Though he had moved to emeritus status, he still kept an office on campus and taught a graduate seminar every spring. His credentials were impeccable, with a B.S. from Harvard, master's from Stanford, and Ph.D. from Cal. The championship bridge player, scratch golfer, and avid skier always showed up in court in a corduroy sport jacket with leather elbow patches, a checkered shirt, and a polka-dot tie to bolster his bona fides as an academic. Outside of court, he preferred Armani suits. Juries loved him.

I started walking him through his C.V. We got as far as his time at Stanford before Harper stopped us.

"Your Honor," he said, "we will stipulate that Dr. Russell is a noted authority on evidentiary issues with a specialty in blood spatter."

Russell spoke in a disarming voice. "I prefer the term, 'world-class expert.'"

Harper surrendered. "So stipulated."

"Thank you, Mr. Harper."

The juror from Google seemed pleased.

I pressed a button on my laptop and a photo of Mercy's sweatshirt appeared on the flat screen. "You analyzed the spatter pattern on Ms. Tejada's sweatshirt?"

"I did, Mr. Daley." He turned to the judge. "May I leave the box to point out certain items to the jury?"

"You may."

He walked purposefully to the TV. He removed the wire-rimmed glasses that he always brought with him to court—even though his eyesight was twenty-twenty—and used them to gesture. "This area in the middle of the chest has a contiguous stain indicating that this garment was used to try to stem the bleeding from an open wound."

"That would be consistent with Ms. Tejada having used her sweatshirt to try to stop the bleeding after the decedent had been stabbed?"

"It would."

"There are also some smaller drops above the thicker stain, aren't there?"

"Yes, Mr. Daley." He again used his glasses to point. "There are about a dozen droplets in this area."

I glanced at the jury. Every eye was focused on the engaging professor. I tossed him another softball. "Would you mind describing in layman's terms the nature of those droplets?"

"They form what is known as a 'projected pattern,' which is generally caused by blood flying across an open space and landing on clothing in small droplets."

"What types of injuries generally cause such a pattern?"

"It is most often associated with a blow to the head by a blunt object, which causes the skin to tear."

"But that's not what happened in this case, correct?"

"Correct. There is no evidence of any such blunt trauma, and the decedent did not suffer any abrasions to his skull. Dr. Siu's autopsy report concluded that the decedent died of a stab wound to his stomach."

"Is this pattern consistent with such a stab wound?"

"Yes, it is." He put his glasses into his breast pocket. "However, it also could have been caused when the knife was removed from the decedent's stomach."

"Even if the decedent was lying on the ground?"

"Yes. If the decedent's heart was still beating, it could have caused blood to spatter in the direction of the person who removed the knife."

"So if the decedent was lying on his back with a knife protruding from his stomach, and Ms. Tejada attempted to help him by removing the knife, you're saying that the blood could have flown up and caused a so-called 'projected pattern' on her sweatshirt?"

"Yes, Mr. Daley."

"Doesn't that defy the law of gravity?"

"Not if his heart was still beating."

"No further questions."

"Cross-exam, Mr. Harper?"

"Just a couple of questions." Harper stood at the prosecution table. "Dr. Russell, you've consulted on hundreds of cases over the years, haven't you?"

"Yes."

"How many involved the so-called 'projected pattern?'"

"Dozens."

"Of those, how many involved a situation where the blood was projected upward?"

"A couple."

"You know Lieutenant Katherine Jacobsen, don't you?"

"Yes. She's an excellent spatter expert whose work I respect."

"Lieutenant Jacobsen concluded that the blood couldn't have flown upward."

"I respect her opinion, but I respectfully disagree with her."

"You've known Mr. Daley for a long time, haven't you?"

"More than thirty years."

"And you would therefore be inclined to help him, wouldn't you?"

"I would never let my personal relationships color my professional judgment."

Good answer.

"How much is the Public Defender's Office paying you to appear today?"

"Nothing."

"You're working *pro bono*?"

"I've reached the point in my career where I don't need the money, and I'm more interested in justice being served."

"No further questions, Your Honor."

* * *

"That was good," Rosie said.

"He's a gem," I replied.

We were sitting in the consultation room during the mid-afternoon break. Mercy's eyes were a little brighter. She took a bite of her sandwich—it was the first thing that she had eaten since the trial started.

"Is it enough?" I asked.

"Not quite," Rosie said. "I want to give the jury some options."

52

"IT WAS MORE THAN INAPPROPRIATE"

Rosie stood in front of the box. "You were working on the night that Carlos Cruz died?"

Olmedo Rivera took a drink of water. "Yes."

"In addition to being the sous chef at El Conquistador, you and the decedent had a personal relationship, didn't you?"

"Yes."

"Which ended on bad terms, right?"

"Yes."

"You were upset about it, weren't you?"

His lips turned down. "Life goes on."

"Carlos Cruz was on your case that night, wasn't he?"

"Yes."

"In fact, he was always on your case, wasn't he?"

"He was a perfectionist."

"And you finally got tired of it, didn't you? And as you were leaving the restaurant, you grabbed a knife and waited for him outside, didn't you?"

"No."

"And when he came outside, you and Mr. Cruz had words, right?"

"No."

"You lost your composure and you stabbed him, didn't you?"

"Objection," Harper said. "There isn't a shred of foundation for any of this."

"Overruled."

The sous chef finished his water and crushed the paper cup. "I didn't stab Carlos. We didn't always get along, but I cared for him."

"No further questions."

* * *

Costa was up next.

Rosie walked right up to the front of the box. "You were working at El Conquistador on the night that Carlos Cruz died, weren't you?"

The young dishwasher took a gulp of water. "Yes."

"He was hard on you, wasn't he?"

"He was hard on everybody."

"He made inappropriate advances toward you, didn't he?"

"No."

"He tried to sexually assault you, didn't he?"

Costa poured himself another cup of water but didn't answer.

"He did, didn't he?"

Another hesitation. "I guess. Yeah."

"That's horrible, Mr. Costa. And he threatened to fire you if you didn't have sex with him, didn't he?"

"Objection," Harper said. "Relevance."

Rosie feigned indignation. "I'll tie this all together in a moment, Your Honor." She hadn't taken her eyes off Costa. "Carlos Cruz told you that he would have you deported if you didn't give in to his sexual advances, didn't he?"

"No."

"You're under oath, Mr. Costa."

Costa's lips formed a straight line across his face. "Yes."

"And he was especially demanding on the night that he died, wasn't he?"

"No."

"And you'd finally had enough, so you grabbed a knife from the kitchen and waited for him outside, didn't you?"

"No."

"And when he came outside, you got into an argument and you stabbed him, didn't you?"

"No."

"You'll feel better if you tell the truth, Mr. Costa."

"Objection. Ms. Fernandez's entire strategy seems to be firing off specious accusations at everybody who was at the restaurant that night."

That's the whole idea of the SODDI defense.

"Sustained."

"No further questions."

* * *

Rosie glared at Christine Fong. "You didn't like Carlos Cruz, did you?"

"Our relationship was purely professional."

"You didn't answer my question. You didn't like him, did you?"

"Not especially."

"Because he was running your boyfriend's restaurant into the ground, wasn't he?"

"He wasn't an experienced businessman."

"But he was an experienced sexual predator, wasn't he?"

"Our lawyers investigated several complaints and concluded that he hadn't engaged in any illegal activity."

Rosie put her hand on the rail. "He hit on you, didn't he?"

"No."

"He tried, didn't he?"

"No."

"Come on, Ms. Fong. He hit on everybody else. Surely he must have hit on you."

"Objection. Asked and answered."

"Sustained."

Rosie lowered her voice. "You didn't like him because he tried to lay his hands on you, didn't he?"

"No."

"Never?"

Fong took a deep breath. "Once or twice."

"And you rejected him, didn't you?"

"Of course. I told him that if he ever tried to touch me again, we would shut down the restaurant."

"But that didn't stop him, did it?"

Another pause. "No."

"He hit on you again on the night that he was killed, didn't he?"

Fong's eyes filled with unvarnished rage. "Yes."

"And you rejected him again, didn't you?"

"Yes."

"And you told him that if he ever tried it again, you would not only close the restaurant, but make him pay, right?"

"Words to that effect."

"You took a knife from the kitchen and you waited outside, didn't you?"

"No."

"And you stabbed him, didn't you?"

"Absolutely not."

"Carlos Cruz was a serial sexual predator, wasn't he?"

"Yes."

"And you'd finally had enough, right?"

Fong folded her arms tightly. "No."

"No further questions."

* * *

Rosie stood directly in front of Sanders. "You invested millions in El Conquistador, didn't you?"

"Yes."

"The restaurant did very well for a while, didn't it?"

"Yes."

"And then Mr. Cruz's reckless behavior resulted in substantial cost overruns, didn't it?'

"It was an issue."

"And you started losing money, didn't you?"

"It was an issue," he repeated.

"He had big alcohol and substance problems, didn't he?"

"It was another issue."

"So you brought in your girlfriend to keep an eye on him, didn't you?"

"The restaurant needed more professional management."

"You never liked Carlos Cruz, did you?"

"Our relationship was professional."

"And you never really trusted him, did you?"

"If I hadn't, I wouldn't have funded his restaurant."

"You knew that he was a sexual predator, didn't you?"

"There were complaints. Our lawyers dealt with them."

"He hit on everybody who worked at the restaurant, didn't he?"

"Not everybody."

"Including your girlfriend, right?"

Sanders pushed out a sigh. "Once or twice."

"Why didn't you shut him down?"

"I warned Carlos about his behavior. He promised to use better judgment."

"Better judgment?" Rosie let out a mocking laugh. "He hit on your girlfriend again on the night that he was killed, didn't he?"

"Yes."

"He finally crossed the line, didn't he?"

"It was unacceptable."

"You let him put his hands on everybody else, but you finally decided that it was unacceptable when he put his hands on Ms. Fong?"

"It was inappropriate."

"It was more than inappropriate. It was illegal. So you took matters into your own hands that night, didn't you?"

"No."

"You also had a key-man life insurance policy on Mr. Cruz, right? You knew that if he died, you could recoup a million dollars of your investment, didn't you?"

"That's ridiculous."

"You grabbed a knife. You waited outside. And you stabbed him, didn't you?"

"No."

"And Ms. Tejada came along and tried to help Mr. Cruz, didn't she? And you let her take the blame, didn't you?"

"Absolutely not, Ms. Fernandez."

"You'll feel better if you start telling the truth, Mr. Sanders."

"Objection. There wasn't a question there."

"Withdrawn. No further questions."

"Cross-exam, Mr. Harper?"

"No, Your Honor."

"Any additional witnesses, Ms. Fernandez?"

Rosie turned around and locked eyes with Mercy. "Just one, Your Honor."

53
"THEY'LL RESPECT YOU"

Rosie spoke to Mercy in the maternal tone that she usually reserved for her mother and our daughter. "How are you holding up?"

Mercy's eyes darted from Nady to me before they settled on Rosie's. "Fine."

"You want something to drink?"

"No."

The consultation room was hot at three-thirty on Thursday afternoon. A long day in court had taken a toll on Mercy, but she seemed to be catching a second wind.

Nady looked at her phone, opened a text, and excused herself. "I need to deal with this. I'll meet you back in court."

Rosie kept her tone even. "Do you think you're up for testifying?"

Mercy swallowed. "I don't know."

"It will be just the way we prepared. I will ask you only one question: whether you stabbed Cruz. I want a definitive one-word answer: no." Rosie reached over and touched her hand. "You can do it, Mercy."

"What about cross-exam? What if Harper comes after me?"

"He won't."

"How do you know?"

"He already has what he needs. He'll lose the jury if he pushes too hard."

Mercy considered for an interminable moment. "I'm not sure, Rosie."

"I'll protect you. Think about everything that you and your

mother have accomplished. All of the hard work and late nights. I want you to stand up for yourself like you always have."

"What if the jury doesn't believe me?"

"They will. More important, they'll respect you."

Mercy's expression turned resolute. "Okay."

* * *

Rosie stood in front of the box where Mercy was sitting, arms at her sides, tears in her eyes. "Mercy, did you stab Carlos Cruz?"

"No, Ms. Fernandez."

"No further questions."

"Mr. Harper?"

"May we approach the witness?"

"You may."

I felt my heart pounding as Harper walked to the front of the box. "Mr. Cruz made sexual advances to you on several occasions, didn't he, Ms. Tejada?"

Mercy glanced at Rosie, who nodded. "Yes."

"But you didn't report them, did you?"

"I was afraid."

"And you didn't quit, did you?"

"I needed the money."

"Carlos Cruz put his hands on you again on the night that he died, didn't he?"

"Yes."

"And he tried to kiss you again, didn't he?"

"Yes."

"And you'd finally had enough, right? So you took a knife from the kitchen and went outside and confronted him, didn't you?"

"No."

"And you argued, didn't you?"

"No."

"And he mocked you like always, didn't he?"

"No."

"And you lost your temper, didn't you?"

"No."

"And you stabbed him, didn't you?"

"No."

Harper took a step back. "Everybody in this courtroom feels badly that you were a victim of sexual harassment, but it didn't give you the right to stab Carlos Cruz."

"Objection," Rosie said. "There wasn't a question there."

"Withdrawn. No further questions."

"Redirect, Ms. Fernandez?"

"No, Your Honor."

"Did you wish to call any additional witnesses?"

Before Rosie could answer, the door opened and Nady came inside. She walked down the aisle and joined us at the defense table.

"Ask for a recess," she whispered.

"What's going on?"

"I can't talk about it here. Meet me in the stairwell down the hall."

54
"IT WAS THE RIGHT THING TO DO"

Rosie and I pushed our way through the crowded corridor and opened the door to the stairwell, where we found Nady and Pete.

My brother got right to it. "Mauricio Vera is prepared to testify that he heard two guys arguing behind El Conquistador."

"That would help," I said. "When is he available?"

"Now."

"Where is he?"

Pete pointed up the stairway. "On the next landing."

"Bring him down."

Rosie, Nady, and I waited as Pete jogged up the stairs and returned a moment later with Vera. He was wearing jeans and a denim work short, both of which were covered in dust. He carried a lunchbox and a cell phone.

"I didn't have time to change," he said.

"No problem," I said. "You need water?"

"I'm fine."

"You sure you want to do this?"

"Yeah."

＊ ＊ ＊

Rosie stood at the lectern. "You were working on your car in your garage at approximately twelve-thirty on the morning of Saturday, October twenty-seventh of last year?"

Vera nodded. "Yes."

"Your garage was located directly behind El Conquistador restaurant?"

"Yes."

"You were up late."

"I work two jobs during the day and another on weekends."

She pointed at a rudimentary poster-sized drawing of the area behind El Conquistador that Nady had cobbled together. "El Conquistador was here?"

"Yes." Vera pointed at the apartment building across the alley. "I was here."

"Could you see anything outside?"

"No. The garage door was closed. It was cold outside."

"Did you hear anything?"

"Traffic on Valencia and music from a bar around the corner."

"Anything else?"

"Two people were arguing."

"Close by?"

"It sounded like it came from the area behind El Conquistador."

"How long did this go on?"

"Maybe a minute."

"Could you hear what they were saying?"

"Not clearly. One person said something like 'I can't believe you did this to me.' The other person said 'No' a couple of times."

"You definitely heard two voices?"

"Yes."

"Both male?"

"Yes."

"Mr. Vera, you're aware that our client, Ms. Tejada, has been accused of stabbing Carlos Cruz in the alley behind El Conquistador at approximately the same time that you heard the shouting, right?"

"Right."

"Is there any chance that you heard an argument between Ms. Tejada and Mr. Cruz?"

"No."

"May I ask why not?"

"Because I heard two male voices."

"Did you hear any female voices?"

"No."

"It's likely that one of the people that you heard shouting was Carlos Cruz, right?"

"Objection. Speculation."

"Sustained."

"And it's also likely that the other person you heard stabbed Mr. Cruz, right?"

"Objection. Speculation."

"Sustained."

"Did you report this to the police?"

"Yes."

"When?"

"They knocked on my door the following day."

"Did they ask you to provide a statement?"

"No."

"Did they say why?"

"I guess they didn't think it was important."

"Or maybe the information you provided was inconsistent with their belief that Mercy Tejada had stabbed Carlos Cruz."

"Objection," Harper said. "Ms. Fernandez is testifying."

"Withdrawn," Rosie said. "No further questions."

"Cross-exam, Mr. Harper?"

"Yes, Your Honor." He stood and spoke from the prosecution table. "Mr. Vera, you didn't see the people who were shouting, did you?"

"No."

"It's possible that it could have been people walking through the alley, right?"

"Right."

"And it's also likely that they had nothing to do with Mr. Cruz's death, right?"

"I don't know."

"All you know for sure is that you heard two people shouting, right?"

"Right."

"The only reason you're here is because Ms. Fernandez asked you to help her muddy the waters and confuse the jury, aren't you?"

"Objection. Relevance."

"Sustained."

"They're paying you to be here, right?"

"I had to take off work."

"How much?"

"Fifty dollars an hour."

"And you agreed to say whatever they wanted, right?"

"I came here to tell the truth, Mr. Harper. Truth still matters."

Harper appeared to be slightly taken aback. "No further questions."

"Redirect, Ms. Fernandez?"

"No, Your Honor."

"We're in recess until nine o'clock tomorrow."

* * *

Rosie and I were walking down the empty corridor when we saw Vera sitting on the bench, staring at his cell phone.

"You need a ride?" I asked.

"No."

Rosie sat down next to him. "We appreciated your help today, Mauricio."

"It was the right thing to do."

"Your life could get complicated if ICE comes looking for you."

"I'll deal with it."

She pulled out a business card, scribbled a number, and handed it to Vera. "This is my personal cell. If anybody ever gives you any crap about anything, I want you to call me right away—day or night. Understood?"

"Thank you, Ms. Fernandez."

She smiled. "Rosie."

He smiled back. "Rosie."

55
"I FOUND HER"

The light was buzzing in Rosie's office at nine-fifteen on Thursday night. "No trick-or-treating tonight," I observed.

Rosie looked up from her computer. "Next year."

"I just got a text from Tommy. He's handing out candy. He said it was a slow night."

"I knew that he would be useful someday."

"Hopefully, a hundred of his classmates aren't hanging out at the house."

"Seems unlikely. Tommy is like you—he isn't a big party animal."

"You need to watch the quiet ones."

"I've been watching you for almost twenty-five years."

We had just returned from St. Peter's. Perlita was relatively calm. The ICE guys were still in their vans. According to Gil Lopez, they had been instructed to sit tight for at least another day. In a gesture of goodwill, the neighbors had provided coffee and cookies. Hundreds of parishioners were surrounding the rectory. Neighborhood restaurants and markets (including Tony's) had donated more than enough to feed everybody. The mood had shifted from a tense standoff into a makeshift Halloween party.

Rosie checked e-mails and re-worked her closing argument. Nady was hunched over her laptop. Luna was stretched out in the corner.

Rosie looked at the big Keeshond. "No trick-or-treating for her tonight?"

Nady shook her head. "She doesn't like Halloween. No

campaign events tonight?"

"I don't have time, and I have a full schedule over the weekend. For now, I need to work on my closing. Did you finish our draft jury instructions?"

"Yes."

"You included a manslaughter instruction?"

"Yes."

"We'll see what the judge has to say."

* * *

An hour later, I was sitting at my desk when Pete's name appeared on my phone. I pressed the green button.

"I found her," he said. "Carmen Dominguez. The waitress."

"How?"

"A tip from her cousin, my auto parts supplier."

"Where are you?"

"Tony's market."

"Anybody else there?"

"Just Tony."

"We'll be there in twenty minutes."

56
"I NEED YOU TO DO SOMETHING FOR ME"

The room smelled of asparagus as Rosie and I walked up to the counter of Tony's market at ten-thirty on Thursday night.

"Where is Carmen?" I asked.

Tony handed me a can of Diet Dr Pepper. "In the back with Pete."

Rosie and I walked into the area near the loading dock which was illuminated by a single light bulb. The overhead door was closed. Pete was holding a can of Coke Classic. A young woman with waist-length hair and multiple ear piercings sipped a smoothie.

Rosie extended a hand. "Rosie Fernandez."

"Carmen Dominguez."

"Thank you for seeing us."

We exchanged stilted introductions. Dominguez was twenty-two, single, and undocumented. She looked a little like our daughter, Grace, who was about the same age. She said that her mother had made her way to the U.S. from El Salvador when Carmen was a baby. Her father travelled separately and got as far as Mexico before he was killed when he got caught in the middle of a shootout between rival gangs. When Carmen was fourteen, her mother returned to El Salvador to visit her ailing father, and never returned. Carmen lived with her cousins and cleaned houses. She hadn't filed for Dreamer status.

Rosie draped her jacket over the back of a folding chair. "Mercy needs your help."

No answer.

Rosie tried again. "I understand that you and Mercy were

friends."

"We were co-workers. We tried to look out for each other. She helped me sign up for classes at City College."

"What was it like at El Conquistador?"

"Hard work, crappy pay, no benefits."

"And working for Carlos Cruz?"

"Miserable."

"He hit on you?"

"Many times."

"Were you close to anybody else at the restaurant?"

A hesitation. "What did Mercy tell you?"

"Nothing."

"I went out with Carlos's brother for about six months."

"Did Carlos know?"

"Yes. He wasn't happy about it."

"Were you still going out with him on the night that Carlos was killed?"

"Yes."

"Are you still seeing him?"

"No."

"How did he get along with Carlos?"

"Carlos treated him like crap."

"Did you tell Alejandro that Carlos had hit on you?"

"Yes."

"When?"

"The night that Carlos died."

"Why didn't you tell him sooner?"

"It was Carlos's restaurant. Alejandro was afraid of him. So was I."

"Did Alejandro do anything about it?"

"He promised to talk to Carlos."

"Did he?"

"He said he did." She shrugged. "And then Carlos died. I broke up with Alejandro a few days later."

"It must have been hard."

"It was."

"Did you hear Mercy and Carlos arguing that night?"

"Yes."

"Did she threaten him?"

"It sounded like it to me."

"Did you see her take a knife into the break room?"

"No."

"Am I correct that you didn't see Mercy stab Carlos?"

"Correct."

Rosie lowered her voice. "We need you to testify."

"I can't."

"Yes, you can."

"No, I can't." Carmen's expression hardened. "ICE is watching me. If I show up in court, I'll be deported."

"It won't happen," Rosie said.

"I can't take the chance."

"We'll represent you."

"No."

Rosie took a deep breath. "Do it for Mercy and Perlita and all of the Dreamers and undocumented women who have been abused by their employers and hassled by ICE."

Carmen considered her options. "I need you to do something for me."

"What?"

"I need you to help me get out of town."

* * *

At midnight, Rosie, Tony, and I lugged crates of vegetables across Twenty-fourth toward the crowd at the rectory. We climbed the stairs and waited for Gil Lopez to unlock the door.

I turned to Rosie. "You sure you want Carmen to testify?"

"She helps our narrative that Carlos was a serial harasser."

"We've already established it."

"You never know what else I might get her to say."

"What are you thinking?"

"Just a hunch." She didn't elaborate.

I looked at the hand-made banner above the doors which read, "Justice for Mercy." "Are you really planning to help Carmen leave town?"

"No."

"Are you going to put her in touch with somebody who could?"

"No comment."

"Is your mother involved?"

"No comment."

"Father Lopez? Tony?"

The corner of her mouth turned up. "Don't ask too many questions."

57
"I'M GOING TO MAKE IT UP AS I GO"

Carmen took the stand at nine-thirty the following morning. In response to our request that she dress conservatively, she had chosen a modest gray top with a pair of black slacks. Her makeup was subtle, her hair pulled back.

"I worked at El Conquistador for almost two years," she said.

Rosie was at the lectern. "Did you enjoy your job?"

"It paid the bills."

"You knew Mercy Tejada?"

"We were co-workers. She helped me sign up for classes at City College."

"Was Carlos Cruz a good boss?"

"No, he was horrible." She took a drink of water and refilled her cup. "He was very demanding."

Rosie moved closer to her. "He made inappropriate sexual advances to you, didn't he?"

"Yes."

"How many times?"

"Dozens."

"What type of advances?"

"Uninvited hugging and kissing. He pinned me against the wall and fondled my breasts."

"I'm so sorry. It must have been awful."

"It was humiliating."

"You told him to stop?"

"Yes."

"Did he?"

"No. He threatened to fire me. He said that if I told anybody, he would report me to ICE."

Rosie waited a beat. "Did you report this to anybody?"

"The restaurant manager, Ms. Fong."

"How did she respond?"

"She said that the lawyers would look into it. She also told me that my only other recourse was to quit."

"You weren't in a position to do so, were you?"

"I needed the money."

"Did you tell anybody else?"

"Alejandro Cruz."

"Carlos Cruz's brother, the general manager?"

"Yes."

"When did you tell him?"

"The night that Carlos died."

"Why didn't you do it sooner?"

"It was complicated. He was Carlos's brother, my boss, and my boyfriend."

"You were concerned that if you accused Alejandro's brother of sexual harassment, it would have adversely impacted your employment and your relationship with Alejandro?"

"Yes."

"Is he still your boyfriend?"

"No. We broke up after Carlos died."

"How did Alejandro respond after you told him about his brother's harassment?"

"He was angry."

"Did he do anything about it?"

"He said that he would talk to Carlos and make him stop."

"No further questions."

"Cross-exam, Mr. Harper?"

"No, Your Honor."

"Any more witnesses, Ms. Fernandez?"

"Just one, Your Honor. The defense calls Alejandro Cruz."

* * *

Rosie and I were in the consultation room down the hall from Judge Vanden Heuvel's courtroom during the mid-morning break.

"Did Gil Lopez take Carmen back to St. Peter's?" I asked.

Rosie nodded. "They're on their way."

"ICE may stop them."

"Gil is going to have his driver pull in behind the rectory. The neighbors will form a circle around Carmen and Gil and make sure that they get inside."

"The ICE guys can stop them if they want to."

"It will be a bad look on TV if they manhandle a priest."

True. "You sure you want to put Alejandro on the stand?"

"Yes."

"What are you planning to ask him?"

"I'm not sure."

"That isn't much of a plan."

"Plans are overrated, Mike." She flashed the confident smile that appeared on campaign posters nailed to power poles all over San Francisco. "I'm going to make it up as I go."

58
"YOU LEFT HIM THERE TO DIE"

Rosie stood at the lectern at ten-thirty on Friday morning. "You're Carlos Cruz's older brother, right?"

Dressed in a navy blazer, a powder-blue oxford shirt, and a yellow tie with blue polka dots, Alejandro looked like a stockbroker. "Yes, I am."

It was only our fifth day of trial and our third day of testimony, but it felt like we'd been sitting in the steaming courtroom for weeks. The gallery was full. Jerry Edwards was in his usual seat on the aisle. Nicole Ward was sitting behind Harper. Rosie's mother was in her seat behind us, but Gil Lopez had stayed at St. Peter's.

Rosie strode to the front of the box. "You went to college, right? And got an MBA?"

"Yes."

"Your brother barely graduated from high school, didn't he?"

"He wanted to open a restaurant."

"You were selling real estate before he hired you as the general manager of El Conquistador, right?"

"Right."

"You got fired from your previous job, didn't you?"

"Objection," Harper said. "Relevance."

"Sustained."

Rosie leaned closer to him. "You didn't like working for your baby brother, did you?"

"I was happy to help."

"But it must have been humiliating for you, right?"

"No."

"He got a lot of media coverage, didn't he?"

"It was good for business."

"And he was paid a lot more than you were, wasn't he?"

"Yes."

"You were jealous, weren't you?"

"No."

"Not even a little?"

"Objection. Asked and answered."

"Sustained."

Rosie folded her arms. "Your brother was hard on his employees, wasn't he?"

"He was very demanding."

"And he was even harder on you, wasn't he?"

"At times."

"You resented being bossed around by your kid brother, didn't you?"

"We were business partners."

"He was your boss."

"We were collaborators."

"Right. And he always treated you with respect, right?"

"We had disagreements from time to time. That's how it works in business."

"You knew that he had been accused of making sexual advances, didn't you?"

"Yes."

"Several people complained directly to you, didn't they?"

"Yes. I reported the allegations to our lawyers. They conducted investigations and found no wrongdoing."

"It must have bothered you that your brother was a serial harasser, didn't it?"

"It was troubling."

"It was more than troubling, Mr. Cruz. It was illegal."

"Objection."

"Withdrawn. Did you talk to your brother about it?"

"Of course. I told him to be more careful."

Rosie's voice filled with sarcasm "More careful? That was the best that you could do?"

"Yes."

"The sexual harassment claims didn't stop after you talked to him, did they?"

"Uh, no."

"Let's be honest, Mr. Cruz. Your brother was a sexual predator, wasn't he?"

"Objection. The question is outside Mr. Cruz's area of expertise."

"Overruled."

Cruz was starting to sweat. "I don't know. Our lawyers investigated the claims and concluded that Carlos had not engaged in any illegal activity."

"What about immoral activity?"

"Objection. Making moral judgments is also outside Mr. Cruz's expertise."

"Sustained."

Rosie was becoming more animated. "You were working at the restaurant on the night that your brother died, weren't you?"

"Yes."

"You testified that you saw Ms. Tejada take a Messermeister knife into the break room, right?"

"Correct." He added, "She didn't bring it back."

"But you weren't in the kitchen the entire night, were you?"

"No."

"So you couldn't possibly have been watching her the entire

time, right?"

"Right."

"So she could have brought it back into the kitchen without your having seen it, correct?"

His lips turned down. "Correct."

"Or are you just lying about it, Mr. Cruz?"

"No."

Nady leaned over and whispered, "Where is she going?"

Not sure. "Be patient."

Rosie pointed at Cruz. "You know a woman named Carmen Dominguez, don't you?"

"Yes. She was a waitress at El Conquistador."

"She was also your girlfriend, right?"

Cruz poured himself a cup of water. "Right."

"Your brother knew that you and Ms. Dominguez were seeing each other, didn't he?"

"Yes."

"He was unhappy about it, wasn't he?"

"He didn't think it was a good idea for management to be dating staff."

"It seems that rule didn't apply to him."

Cruz didn't answer.

Rosie added, "Especially since he was harassing her, right?"

Still no answer.

"He wanted to sleep with her, didn't he?"

"I don't know."

Rosie was now in his face. "On the night that your brother died, Ms. Dominguez told you that Carlos had made another unwanted sexual advance, didn't she?"

Cruz tried to measure his words. "I would call it questionable touching."

"Questionable touching? Are you serious? He pushed her

against the wall and fondled her breasts and forcibly kissed her, didn't he?"

"I don't know."

"That's what Ms. Dominguez told you, didn't she?"

He swallowed. "Yes."

"Are you saying that she was lying?"

"No." He looked at Harper for assistance, but none was forthcoming. "I have no reason to believe that she was."

"You would therefore acknowledge that your brother's behavior was a lot more than 'questionable touching,' wouldn't you?"

Another swallow. "Yes."

"He attacked your girlfriend, didn't he?"

"I'm not sure."

"You believed her, didn't you?"

"Yes."

"If you did, it means that he attacked her. And you were angry about it, weren't you?"

"Yes."

"You should have been. Did you do anything about it?"

"I told Carmen that I would talk to Carlos."

"You did more than that, didn't you? You told Carmen that you would get your brother to apologize to her and 'make things right,' didn't you?"

"I don't recall my exact words."

"You argued with your brother, didn't you? You left the restaurant and waited outside for him, didn't you? And you continued the argument when he came outside, didn't you?"

"No."

"And you took the Messermeister from the drawer on your way out, didn't you?"

"No."

"You went outside and confronted your brother—the hot shot chef who treated you like crap and tried to rape your girlfriend, right?"

"No."

"And he denied everything, didn't he? Just like he always did, right?"

"Yes."

"So you *did* confront him, didn't you?"

Cruz reached for the empty water cup. "No."

Rosie's eyes were on fire. "Your brother looked you right in the eye and laughed at you about screwing your girlfriend, didn't he?"

"No."

"So you stabbed him, didn't you?"

"No."

"And you left him there to die, didn't you?"

"No. I told Carlos that we would talk in the morning. I got into my car and drove home."

"Sure you did."

"Objection. There was no question."

"Withdrawn." Rosie glanced at the prosecution table, where Harper and Lee were sitting in silence, then she turned back to Cruz. "I trust that you would have no objection if Inspector Lee wants to search your apartment and your car for evidence relating to your brother's death."

"Objection," Harper said. "Mr. Cruz is not on trial here."

"He should be," Rosie snapped.

Judge Vanden Heuvel held up a hand. "The objection is sustained, Ms. Fernandez. The question of whether Inspector Lee wishes to obtain a warrant to conduct a lawful search is not before this court."

Rosie shot a glance at Lee, then turned back to Cruz. "You

understand that even if you had your car power-washed with detergent and bleach, they can still find traces of blood, right?"

"Objection. Relevance. Mr. Cruz has no expertise in this area."

"Sustained."

"No further questions, Your Honor."

"Cross-exam, Mr. Harper?"

"Just one question, Your Honor. Mr. Cruz, did you stab your brother?"

"No, Mr. Harper."

"No further questions."

Judge Vanden Heuvel spoke to Rosie. "Any additional witnesses, Ms. Fernandez?"

"No, Your Honor. The defense rests."

"I want to meet with counsel in chambers to discuss jury instructions. Assuming that we can come to an agreement, we will begin closing arguments after lunch."

59
"LET THE JURY DECIDE"

Harper's normally unflappable demeanor showed a hint of frustration as he took his seat next to Rosie and me in Judge Vanden Heuvel's chambers. He spoke to Rosie in an uncharacteristically acerbic tone. "What the hell was that about?"

"I don't know what you're talking about, DeSean."

"Your direct exam of Alejandro Cruz was straight from *The Twilight Zone*."

"I was introducing legitimate evidence."

"You were making stuff up."

"I was providing a zealous representation for my client."

"We've been around the block, Rosie. That wasn't a legitimate SODDI defense."

"Yes, it was. The police never seriously considered Alejandro as a suspect. For that matter, they never seriously considered anybody other than Mercy."

"You were blowing smoke and throwing stuff against the wall to see if anything would stick."

"Let the jury decide," Rosie said.

Judge Vanden Heuvel was pretending to ignore us. She was reading our draft jury instructions, eyes focused, lips pursed. "I want to start closing arguments this afternoon. The only remaining issue is whether I will give the jury a manslaughter instruction."

The repercussions were significant. The minimum sentence for first-degree murder is twenty-five years; for second-degree, it's fifteen. The minimum for voluntary manslaughter is three years, with a maximum of eleven. For involuntary, the range is two to four, and the defendant is sometimes allowed to serve at the local county jail instead of state prison.

The judge took off her glasses. "Both sides have requested a manslaughter instruction."

Harper nodded.

Rosie glanced my way, then she turned back to the judge. "We've reconsidered, Your Honor. We would prefer that you limit your instruction to first- and second-degree murder."

The judge's eyes narrowed. "Why have you changed your mind?"

"This isn't a murder case. It never was. Mr. Harper hasn't proved murder beyond a reasonable doubt. It is therefore not in our client's best interests to give the jury a potential offramp to a lesser charge by giving them a manslaughter option."

"Your client could end up serving a minimum of fifteen years."

"I understand the potential ramifications."

She was more confident than I was.

The judge's eyes shifted to Harper. "How do you feel about this, Mr. Harper?"

"I still think it makes sense to give the manslaughter instructions."

He needed a conviction. So did his boss. Manslaughter was better than an acquittal.

The judge fingered her gold necklace for an interminable moment. "I'm going to give the manslaughter instruction. Let's let the jury decide."

* * *

A few minutes later, Rosie and I were walking back to court.

"Why'd you change your mind about manslaughter?" I asked.

"They haven't proved their case for first- or second-degree murder. Manslaughter gives the jury an easier option to a conviction."

"You sure?"

"Pretty sure. At the end of the day, it didn't matter. The judge had already made up her mind to give the manslaughter instruction."

"You good to go on your closing?"

"Yes."

"You think you can change any juror's mind?"

She flashed a confident smile. "I don't think I'm going to have to."

60
"YOU NEVER KNOW"

"Nice mass this morning," I said. "Big turnout."

Gil Lopez smiled. "We always fill the church on Sunday. This is the first time we've broadcast mass to a thousand people outside."

Father Lopez, Sylvia, Perlita, Carmen Dominguez, Rosie, and I were sitting at the table in the dining room of the rectory at eleven-thirty on Sunday morning. The ICE officers were still outside. So were the parishioners surrounding the building. The vigil was being streamed on the St. Peter's website, and the standoff was getting live coverage from cable news. The sun was out, the weather was warm, and the Niners game was being shown on the big-screen TVs outside. A couple of enterprising lads from the neighborhood were selling "Free Perlita" T-shirts.

Father Lopez turned to Rosie. "How long do you think the jury will be out?"

"Hard to say. They won't start deliberating until tomorrow morning. Sometimes it's a few hours. Other times, they'll talk for days. You never know."

On Friday afternoon, Rosie had delivered a heartfelt and—in my view—convincing closing argument to an attentive jury. Harper's presentation was more workmanlike. The jurors gave no indication which way they were leaning. Judge Vanden Heuvel read them the instructions and set them free until Monday morning. For now, all we could do was wait.

I took a sip of watery Folgers. "What are the guys from ICE telling you?"

"They're prepared to wait us out for as long as it takes," Gil said.

"How long are your people prepared to surround the building?"

"As long as it takes."

Rosie finished her tea and spoke to Perlita. "How are you and Isabel holding up?"

"We'll get through it. How are you feeling about the trial?"

"The jury was with us."

"The *Chronicle* said that they might convict Mercy of manslaughter."

"I'm confident." Rosie spoke to Carmen. "You okay?"

"You promised to get me out of here."

"We need you to be patient until the jury comes back."

"Then what?"

"We'll figure it out." Rosie shifted her gaze to her mother. "We'll give you a ride home."

"Tony will take me home later, Rosita. Where are you heading now?"

"A couple of campaign events. You may recall that there's an election on Tuesday."

* * *

The big Keeshond opened one eye, lifted her head, yawned, and finally summoned the energy to sit up. Luna extended a paw, which I shook. I removed a treat from my pocket, and she wagged her tail enthusiastically. I popped the treat into her mouth. She chewed and swallowed in one motion, licked her chops, and looked for more.

"Sorry," I said. "That's all that I have."

Her tail came to an abrupt halt.

Rosie, Nady, Pete, Luna, and I were sitting in Rosie's office at eight-thirty on Sunday night. Rosie had just returned from a campaign event in the Fillmore. Nady was trying to catch up on her other cases. Pete had stopped in on his way to tail an unfaithful husband who lived in one of the high rises near the new Warriors arena.

Just another Sunday night at the P.D.'s Office.

"How did your speech go?" I asked Rosie.

"Fine."

"Any blowback about Mercy's case?"

"No."

"How are you feeling about the jury?"

"Good. You?"

I have no idea. "Good."

"You're usually a basket case when the jury is out."

"I'm evolving."

"Right." She turned to Nady. "You think we'll get an acquittal?"

"Mike taught me not to make predictions about juries."

"That's good advice."

"He's a good lawyer."

"Are you going to trial on that assault case in the Mission?"

"*Alleged* assault. Trial will start in February before Judge Stumpf."

"How are you feeling about it?"

"Good."

Rosie glanced at the sleeping Luna. "How does she feel about it?"

"Good."

Rosie smiled. "She has excellent instincts."

Pete pulled on his bomber jacket. "Gotta get to work."

Rosie nodded with appreciation. "Thanks for your help, Pete."

"I'll send you my bill."

* * *

"Anything from the court?" I asked.

Rosie took a sip of Diet Coke. "The jury asked to see a transcript of Alejandro Cruz's testimony."

Her office was quiet at six o'clock on Monday night. The jury had been deliberating all day.

"Did they go home for the night?" I asked.

"Not yet." She frowned. "Maybe we should have taken the deal for second-degree. Mercy is only nineteen. She'd be out before she's thirty-five."

"She didn't stab Cruz."

"How can you be so sure?"

"I can't." I took a sip of room-temperature Diet Dr Pepper— Rosie authorized an extra can for the week. "You've always said that you shouldn't second-guess yourself at trial."

"Trial is over, Mike. We're just waiting for a verdict."

"The same principle applies."

"You know that I'm better at giving advice to others than following it myself."

True. "You really think we should have cut a deal?"

"No."

"Neither do I."

"It's nice that we agree, but we don't get a vote." She finished her soda, crushed the empty can, and tossed it into the recycling bin. "Even if we get an acquittal, ICE may decide to detain Mercy."

"We'll deal with it if we have to."

Terrence "The Terminator" filled the doorway. "I got a text from Judge Vanden Heuvel's clerk. The jury reached a verdict. The judge wants you in court nine o'clock tomorrow morning."

61

"THE GRAY GOOSE FLIES AT MIDNIGHT"

Judge Vanden Heuvel's voice was somber. "The defendant will please rise."

Mercy stood between Rosie and me. Nady stood to my left.

The judge spoke to the foreman. "Have you reached a verdict?"

"We have, Your Honor."

The foreman handed the verdict to the bailiff, who delivered it to the judge, who studied it for a moment, nodded, and handed the slip of paper to the clerk.

"Please read the verdict."

"On the charge of murder in the first degree, the jury finds the defendant not guilty. On the charge of murder in the second degree, the jury also finds the defendant not guilty."

Yes!

"On the charge of voluntary manslaughter, the jury finds the defendant not guilty. On the charge of involuntary manslaughter, the jury finds the defendant not guilty."

Yes!

Mercy burst into tears. She turned and hugged Rosie, then me.

Rosie's stoic expression didn't change, but I saw satisfaction in her eyes. Sylvia beamed. So did Gil Lopez. Nicole Ward headed out the door followed by Jerry Edwards.

Judge Vanden Heuvel asked the foreman if the verdict was unanimous.

"Yes, Your Honor."

"Thank you for your service." After the jurors filed out of

court, the judge spoke to Mercy. "You are free to go, Ms. Tejada. We wish you well."

"Thank you, Your Honor."

We all stood as Judge Vanden Heuvel left the courtroom.

Mercy sat down and tried to get her bearings. Finally, she spoke to Rosie. "I don't know how I can possibly thank you."

"You're welcome, Mercy."

For the first time in weeks, she smiled. "I want to see Mama and Isabel."

"First, we'll need to collect your belongings. Then Father Lopez will take you to St. Peter's. Mike, Nady, and I have to go back to the office, and then I have to go to a campaign event. We'll come over tonight."

"Thank you." She wiped a tear. "Do you think we could stop for ice cream?"

"I think Father Lopez can arrange it."

The bailiff escorted Mercy and Father Lopez to the back of the courtroom, where they waited for Rosie, Nady, and me to pack our briefcases. As we started making our way toward the door, Sylvia stopped us.

"Rosita?" she whispered.

"Yes, Mama?"

"You, Michael, and Nady did a good job."

"Thank you, Mama."

"Thank *you*, Rosita. There is going to be a gathering for Mercy and Perlita at St. Peter's at nine o'clock tonight. I know that you're busy with election day, but please try to come. I'm sure that they want to thank you."

"We'll be there after we watch the election returns. Hopefully, there will be a victory celebration."

"Hopefully." Sylvia flashed a sly grin. "The gray goose flies at midnight."

Rosie returned her smile. "We'll see you tonight, Mama."

* * *

"What was that about?" I asked.

Rosie picked up her briefcase. "It was an inside joke between my mother and father."

"Meaning?"

"Don't be late."

I suspected there might have been more to it.

62
"IT'S BETTER NOT TO ASK TOO MANY QUESTIONS"

At eight-thirty the same night, I approached Terrence "The Terminator," who was sitting at his desk outside Rosie's office. "We're watching the election results in the conference room. You should join us."

"I'll be there shortly."

"The news is good."

"I heard. Four more years."

I pointed at the closed door leading into Rosie's office. "She inside?"

"Yes."

"She wanted to see me."

"She said that you should let yourself in."

I opened the door and looked inside. The newly re-elected Public Defender of the City and County of San Francisco was sitting behind her desk.

"Come in, Mike," she said.

"We're having a little victory celebration for you in the conference room."

"I'll be out in a few minutes." She nodded at Harper, who was sitting in the chair opposite her desk. "DeSean and I were chatting. I thought you should be here."

I hadn't expected to see him. "Hello, DeSean."

"Mike."

Rosie pointed at the chair next to Harper. "Have a seat."

I did as I was told.

Harper adjusted his tie and spoke to Rosie. "Congratulations on the election."

"Thank you."

"Seems your decision to handle Ms. Tejada's case had no adverse impact. Sixty-four percent would seem to be a mandate. Some might call it a landslide."

"We're very pleased."

"You heard that Nicole won?"

"I did. Please give my best to our new mayor. Does this mean that you are now the acting District Attorney?"

"It does."

"Congratulations. I hope you will run for D.A. in the special election."

"That's the plan."

"Good." She eyed him. "Why did you want to talk to us?"

"There are some new developments regarding the death of Carlos Cruz. I thought you should hear about it from me before it hits the media."

"Thank you."

He lowered his voice. "Off the record."

"Understood."

"Inspector Lee pulled a warrant and impounded Alejandro Cruz's car. He had Lieutenant Jacobsen do a luminol test."

Luminol is a chemical that exhibits a blue glow when sprayed where blood is found.

"She found traces of blood on the driver's seat and the dashboard. It's the same type as Carlos Cruz's."

"It doesn't mean that it was Cruz's blood."

"There was enough to do a DNA test. We have a guy at the lab who can run DNA on short notice. It isn't official, but it looks like the blood in the car matches Carlos's."

"A good defense lawyer would point out that Carlos could have cut himself and bled in Alejandro's car long before the night that he died."

"And a good prosecutor would point out that Alejandro bought the car the day before his brother died. It makes your scenario unlikely."

"So it seems. Has a warrant been issued for Alejandro's arrest?"

"Keep your eye on the news."

"You're waiting for the results of a second DNA test?"

"Off the record, yes. How did you know that Alejandro killed his brother?"

"I didn't."

"You guessed?"

"I played a hunch. Alejandro was a little too adamant about having seen Mercy take the knife into the break room. He was the only person who did."

"You thought he was lying?"

"I thought it was possible. I sensed that there was some sibling rivalry—there always is. It was obvious that Carlos had harassed his employees. When I found out that Alejandro was seeing Carmen Dominguez, it wasn't a stretch to think that Carlos mistreated her, too."

"You figured that Alejandro was so unhappy about it that he stabbed his brother?"

"I didn't know, DeSean. I was just trying to get one juror to reasonable doubt."

"You got there." The Acting District Attorney of the City and County of San Francisco picked up his briefcase. "Looks like you got the right result."

* * *

An hour later, Rosie was waiting for me on the steps of the rectory of the modest Catholic Church in the Mission where she had been baptized fifty-four years earlier. Hundreds of parishioners surrounded the building. "You found a place to park?" she asked.

"The parking gods smiled."

"That's even more exciting than winning the election."

"Not quite." I took a deep breath of the cool night air. "Thanks for waiting."

"I thought we should go inside together."

I looked at the black SUV with government plates parked in the red zone. "Give me a minute."

"Sure."

I walked over to the SUV and tapped on the window, which lowered. "Evening, Doug."

The ICE agent forced a smile. "Evening, Mike."

"You want coffee?"

"That would be nice."

"You aren't planning to storm the rectory, are you?"

"Not tonight."

"Good. How long are you guys planning to stay here?"

"That's up to my superiors. In the meantime, I would appreciate it if you would inform Perlita Tejada that we'd like to talk to her."

"Can it wait until tomorrow?"

"I think so."

"I'll get you that cup of coffee."

* * *

Father Guillermo Lopez sat in the dining room of the rectory. "Coffee, Mike?"

"Thanks, Gil."

"Rosie?"

"Yes, please." She turned to her mother, who was knitting. "You okay, Mama?"

"Yes, dear."

Rosie looked at her brother. "You?"

Tony nodded. "Fine."

I spoke to Father Lopez. "I talked to Doug Nevins outside. He said that ICE wouldn't come inside tonight."

"Good. We'll invite him inside for coffee in the morning. It's the Christian thing to do."

"That could get complicated."

"No, it won't."

"Mercy, Perlita, and Isabel are still downstairs, right?"

"No."

"Carmen Dominguez?"

"No."

"Uh, where are they?"

"Gone."

Huh? "Where did they go?"

"I don't know."

"When did they leave?"

"It must have been earlier this evening while I was at prayers."

"They just walked out the door?"

"I presume."

"They didn't say goodbye?"

"Unfortunately, no."

"They managed to elude the ICE agents outside?"

"So it seems."

I looked at Rosie. "What's going on?"

"It's better not to ask too many questions."

I tried Tony. "You know anything?"

"Nope."

Sylvia was next. "You?"

She didn't look up from her knitting. "Afraid not."

I eyed Gil. "Hypothetically, how do you suppose four people might have slipped out of St. Peter's without being seen?"

"Attorney-client privileged?"

"And priest-parishioner privileged."

"This is an old church, Mike. It was built over some underground sewer lines that haven't been used since the 1800s. I've been told that one extends to Garfield Square. Another goes all the way to Potrero Avenue near San Francisco General. It would be very dangerous to walk through those lines today."

"Of course."

"Then again, if one did, I suppose that it's theoretically possible that one could have found an exit a few blocks from here without being seen by the ICE guys."

"Where they could have gotten into a car or truck?"

"Possibly."

I looked at Tony. "Or maybe a panel van without windows in the back belonging to one of the businesses on Twenty-fourth?"

"I don't know anything about it."

"And they could have been driven to another part of California or another state? Or perhaps even all the way to Canada? Am I getting warm?"

"Anything's possible, Mike."

I shifted my gaze to Sylvia. "You have no idea how any of this happened?"

The corner of her mouth turned up. "It's better not to ask too many questions, Michael."

63
"WE'RE ALL DREAMERS"

I took a sip of Cabernet. "You won the election and got an acquittal. Mercy and her mother and sister and Carmen are on their way out of town. That would seem to warrant a modest celebration."

Rosie's eyes gleamed. "It does."

"Our usual way?"

She kissed me. "Absolutely."

At one o'clock the following morning, we were sitting on the sofa in her living room. A log glowed in the fireplace. Tommy was asleep. The TV was tuned to election results, the sound off.

I touched her cheek. "You knew that Mercy, Perlita, Isabel, and Carmen were leaving last night, didn't you?"

"I don't know what you're talking about, Mike."

"You going to tell me the truth, Rosita?"

"The truth can be elusive, Michael."

"I'll make it worth your while."

"Are we in agreement that everything we talk about stays in this room?"

"Absolutely."

She sipped her wine. "Yes, I knew that they were leaving."

"And you made sure that we were at the P.D.'s Office celebrating your election victory when they departed, didn't you?"

"Deniability is generally a good thing."

"Your mother knew this was coming down?"

"The gray goose flies at midnight."

"Gil?"

"Yes."

"Tony?"

She nodded.

"They took the sewer tunnel to Tony's market?"

"I think so."

"He drove them?"

"Probably not."

"But they used one of his vans?"

"Probably. My guess is that they were dropped off somewhere in the East Bay. Somebody else took them from there."

"Do you know where they were heading?"

"It's better not to know."

"Your mother and Tony and Gil could get into serious legal trouble."

"People in the Mission have been looking out for each other for a hundred and fifty years. It isn't going to change."

I poured myself another glass of wine. "Why did you really decide to try this case yourself?"

"Mama asked me. It was personal for her."

"Because it was Perlita's daughter?"

"In part. The story is a little more complicated."

"I have time."

"You need to understand a few things about our family's history."

I waited.

"Mama always said that she and my father were sponsored by her cousins when they came up here from Mexico. As far as I know, they came here legally, but I'll never know for sure. I do know for sure that they became U.S. citizens."

"What about Tony?"

"His birth certificate says he was born at Saint Francis

Hospital."

"Then he's a U.S. citizen."

"Except that it's dated a year before my parents came here."

"He was born in Mexico?"

"Could be. Either way, he has a birth certificate from Saint Francis Hospital."

"I take it that you've never asked him about it?"

"And I never will."

"He would have been a Dreamer."

"He's a U.S. citizen, Mike. His birth certificate says that he was born here."

Right. "And you?"

"My birth certificate says that I was born at Saint Francis Hospital, too."

"*After* your parents came here?"

"Yes."

"So you're a U.S. citizen?"

"Absolutely. But if the timing had been different, I could have been a Dreamer, too."

"I'm not completely surprised."

Her tone turned philosophical. "We're all Dreamers, Mike."

"Yes, we are. Is that why you decided to take Mercy's case?"

"In part."

"What's the other part?"

"Mama asked me to do it, and it was the right thing to do."

"I'm not completely surprised by that, either."

We looked at the fire for a long moment.

"What about you?" she asked. "Did all of your ancestors come here legally?"

"According to Big John, my great-grandmother was allowed to come to the U.S. for an arranged marriage to my great-grandfather. They met fifteen minutes before their wedding."

"Did money change hands?"

"Probably. It worked out pretty well. They were married for fifty-seven years."

"Go figure."

"If they hadn't gotten together, I wouldn't be here."

"I'm glad they did."

"So am I. Big John said there were others who may have come here illegally."

"They did what they had to do to feed their kids, Mike."

"Just like your mom and dad."

"And Perlita and her husband." Her eyes reflected the light from the dancing fire. "Things could get complicated if anybody finds out that Mama came here illegally."

"She's a U.S. citizen, Rosie. So are you. You have a birth certificate from Saint Francis Hospital to prove it."

"I'm not going to worry about it tonight."

"Neither am I." I raised my glass. "To Sylvia."

"To Mama."

"And to Mercy, Perlita, Isabel, and Carmen."

"And Mauricio Vera," she said. "He took a big risk by testifying."

"Yes, he did. To Mercy, Perlita, Isabel, Carmen, and Mauricio."

She tapped her glass against mine.

"And here's to the re-election of the Public Defender of the City and County of San Francisco."

"And to the co-head of the Felony Division. May we continue to keep innocent people out of jail—for one more term."

"You aren't going to run for a third term?"

"Two will be enough."

"You might change your mind in four years."

"I might."

"You aren't planning to retire, are you?"

"I'm not planning to run for re-election, but I'm never going to retire."

"Neither am I."

"Good. You'd be bored out of your mind and drive me crazy." She leaned over and kissed me. "Here's to us, Mike."

"Here's to us, Rosie."

"I love you, Mike."

"I love you, too, Rosie."

THE END

A NOTE TO THE READER

I hope you liked **THE DREAMER**. I enjoy spending time with Mike & Rosie, and I hope that you do too. If you like my stories, please consider posting an honest review on Amazon or Goodreads. Your words matter and are a great guide to help my stories find future readers.

If you have a chance and would like to chat, please feel free to e-mail me at **sheldon@sheldonsiegel.com**. We lawyers don't get a lot of fan mail, so it's always nice to hear from my readers. Please bear with me if I don't respond immediately. I answer all of my e-mail myself, so sometimes it takes a little extra time.

Many people have asked to know more about Mike and Rosie's early history. As a thank you to my readers, I wrote **FIRST TRIAL**. It's a short story describing how they met years ago when they were starting out at the P.D.'s Office. I've included the first chapter below and the full story is available on my website: **www.sheldonsiegel.com**.

Also on the website, you can read more about how I came to write **THE DREAMER**. In addition, you will find excerpts and behind-the-scenes stories from the other Mike & Rosie novels. A few other goodies!

Let's stay connected. Thanks for reading my story!

Regards,
Sheldon

ACKNOWLEDGMENTS

Over the course of writing eleven Mike Daley/Rosie Fernandez stories, I have been fortunate to have an extraordinarily generous "board of advisors" who have graciously provided their time and expertise. I can't thank everybody, but I'm going to try!

Thanks to my beautiful wife, Linda, who reads my manuscripts, designs the covers, is my online marketing guru, and takes care of all things technological. I couldn't imagine trying to navigate the chaos of the publishing world without you.

Thanks to our son, Alan, for your endless support, editorial suggestions, and thoughtful observations. I will look forward to seeing your first novel on the shelves in bookstores in the near future.

Thanks to our son, Stephen, and our daughter-in-law, Lauren, for being kind, generous, and immensely talented people.

Thanks to my teachers, Katherine Forrest and Michael Nava, who encouraged me to finish my first book. Thanks to the Every Other Thursday Night Writers Group: Bonnie DeClark, Meg Stiefvater, Anne Maczulak, Liz Hartka, Janet Wallace, and Priscilla Royal. Thanks to Bill and Elaine Petrocelli, Kathryn Petrocelli, and Karen West at Book Passage.

A huge thanks to Jane Gorsi for your excellent editing skills.

A huge thanks to Linda Hall for your excellent editing skills, too.

Another huge thanks to Vilaska Nguyen of the San Francisco Public Defender's Office for your thoughtful comments and terrific support. If I ever get into serious trouble, you're my guy.

Thanks to Joan Lubamersky for providing the invaluable "Lubamersky Comments" for the eleventh time.

Thanks to Tim Campbell for your stellar narration of the audio version of this book (and many others in the series). You bring these stories to life!

Thank you to Lala Gavgavian for the stunning cover photo.

Thanks to my friends and colleagues at Sheppard, Mullin, Richter & Hampton (and your spouses and significant others). I can't mention everybody, but I'd like to note those of you with whom I've worked the longest: Randy and Mary Short, Chris and Debbie Neils, Joan Story and Robert Kidd, Donna Andrews, Phil and Wendy Atkins-Pattenson, Julie and Jim Ebert, Geri Freeman and David Nickerson, Bill and Barbara Manierre, Betsy McDaniel, Ron and Rita Ryland, Bob Stumpf, Mike Wilmar, Mathilde Kapuano, Susan Sabath, Guy Halgren, Ed Graziani, Julie Penney, Christa Carter, Doug Bacon, Lorna Tanner, Larry Braun, Nady Nikonova, Joy Siu, and DeAnna Ouderkirk. A special thanks once again for the inspiration to our late colleague, mentor, and friend, the incomparable Bob Thompson. Thanks also to the late Cheryl Holmes, my longtime secretary, mentor, co-conspirator, location scout, and friend. We miss you.

Thanks to Jerry and Dena Wald, Gary and Marla Goldstein, Ron and Betsy Rooth, Jay Flaherty, Debbie and Seth Tanenbaum, Jill Hutchinson and Chuck Odenthal, Tom Bearrows and Holly Hirst, Julie Hart, Burt Rosenberg, Ted George, Phil Dito, Sister Karen Marie Franks, Brother Stan Sobczyk, Chuck and Nora Koslosky, Jack Goldthorpe, Peter and Cathy Busch, Steve Murphy, Bob Dugoni, and John Lescroart. Thanks to Lloyd and Joni Russell and Rich and Leslie Kramer. Thanks to Gary and Debbie Fields. Thanks to the wonderful Mercedes Crosskill. A special thanks to my late friend, Scott

Pratt, who was a terrific writer and a generous soul.

Thanks to Tim and Kandi Durst, Bob and Cheryl Easter, and Larry DeBrock at the University of Illinois. Thanks to Kathleen Vanden Heuvel, Bob and Leslie Berring, Jesse Choper, and Mel Eisenberg at Berkeley Law.

Thanks to the incomparable Zvi Danenberg, who motivates me to walk the Larkspur steps.

Thanks as always to my family: Ben, Michelle, Margie, and Andy Siegel, Joe, Jan, and Julia Garber, Roger and Sharon Fineberg, Scott, Michelle, Kim, and Sophie Harris, Stephanie, Stanley, and Will Coventry, Cathy, Richard, and Matthew Falco, and Julie Harris and Matthew, Aiden, and Ari Stewart.

And to our mothers, Charlotte Siegel (1928-2016) and Jan Harris (1934-2018), whom we miss every day.

FIRST TRIAL

A Mike Daley/Rosie Fernandez Story

1

"DO EXACTLY WHAT I DO"

The woman with the striking cobalt eyes walked up to me and stopped abruptly. "Are you the new file clerk?"

"Uh, no." My lungs filled with the stale air in the musty file room of the San Francisco Public Defender's Office on the third floor of the Stalinesque Hall of Justice on Bryant Street. "I'm the new lawyer."

The corner of her mouth turned up. "The priest?"

"Ex-priest."

"I thought you'd be older."

"I was a priest for only three years."

"You understand that we aren't in the business of saving souls here, right?"

"Right."

Her full lips transformed into a radiant smile as she extended a hand. "Rosie Fernandez."

"Mike Daley."

"You haven't been working here for six months, have you?"

"This is my second day."

"Welcome aboard. You passed the bar, right?"

"Right."

"That's expected."

I met Rosita Carmela Fernandez on the Wednesday after Thanksgiving in 1983. The Summer of Love was a fading memory, and we were five years removed from the Jonestown massacre and the assassinations of Mayor George Moscone and Supervisor Harvey Milk. Dianne Feinstein became the mayor and was governing with a steady hand in Room 200 at City Hall. The biggest movie of the year was *Return of the Jedi*, and the highest-rated TV show was *M*A*S*H*. People still communicated by phone and U.S. mail because e-mail wouldn't become widespread for another decade. We listened to music on LPs and cassettes, but CD players were starting to gain traction. It was still unclear whether VHS or Beta would be the predominant video platform. The Internet was a localized technology used for academic purposes on a few college campuses. Amazon and Google wouldn't be formed for another decade. Mark Zuckerberg hadn't been born.

Rosie's hoop-style earrings sparkled as she leaned against the metal bookcases crammed with dusty case files for long-forgotten defendants. "You local?"

"St. Ignatius, Cal, and Boalt. You?"

"Mercy, State, and Hastings." She tugged at her denim work shirt, which seemed out-of-place in a button-down era where men still wore suits and ties and women wore dresses to the office. "When I was at Mercy, the sisters taught us to beware of boys from S.I."

"When I was at S.I., the brothers taught us to beware of girls from Mercy."

"Did you follow their advice?"

"Most of the time."

The Bay Area was transitioning from the chaos of the sixties and the malaise of the seventies into the early stages of the tech boom. Apple had recently gone public and was still being run by Steve Jobs and Steve Wozniak. George Lucas was making Star Wars movies in a new state-of-the-art facility in Marin County. Construction cranes dotted downtown as new office towers were changing the skyline. Union Square was beginning a makeover after Nieman-Marcus bought out the City of Paris and built a flashy new store at the corner of Geary and Stockton, across from I. Magnin. The upstart 49ers had won their first Super Bowl behind a charismatic quarterback named Joe Montana and an innovative coach named Bill Walsh.

Her straight black hair shimmered as she let out a throaty laugh. "What parish?"

"Originally St. Peter's. We moved to St. Anne's when I was a kid. You?"

"St. Peter's. My parents still live on Garfield Square."

"Mine grew up on the same block."

St. Peter's Catholic Church had been the anchor of the Mission District since 1867. In the fifties and sixties, the working-class Irish and Italian families had relocated to the outer reaches of the City and to the suburbs. When they moved out, the Latino community moved in. St. Peter's was still filled every Sunday morning, but four of the five masses were celebrated in Spanish.

"I was baptized at St. Peter's," I said. "My parents were married there."

"Small world."

"How long have you worked here?" I asked.

"Two years. I was just promoted to the Felony Division."

"Congratulations."

"Thank you. I need to transition about six dozen active misdemeanor cases to somebody else. I trust that you have time?"

"I do."

"Where do you sit?"

"In the corner of the library near the bathrooms."

"I'll find you."

* * *

Twenty minutes later, I was sitting in my metal cubicle when I was startled by the voice from the file room. "Ever tried a case?" Rosie asked.

"It's only my second day."

"I'm going to take that as a no. Ever been inside a courtroom?"

"Once or twice."

"To work?"

"To watch."

"You took Criminal Law at Boalt, right?"

"Right."

"And you've watched Perry Mason on TV?"

"Yes."

"Then you know the basics. The courtrooms are upstairs." She handed me a file. "Your first client is Terrence Love."

"The boxer?"

"The retired boxer.'

Terrence "The Terminator" Love was a six-foot-six-inch, three-hundred-pound small-time prizefighter who had grown up in the projects near Candlestick Park. His lifetime record was two wins and nine losses. The highlight of his career was when he was hired to be a sparring partner for George Foreman, who was training to fight Muhammad Ali at the time. Foreman knocked out The Terminator with the first punch that he threw—effectively ending The Terminator's careers as a boxer and a sparring partner.

"What's he doing these days?" I asked.

"He takes stuff that doesn't belong to him."

"Last time I checked, stealing was against the law."

"Your Criminal Law professor would be proud."

"What does he do when he isn't stealing?"

"He drinks copious amounts of King Cobra."

It was cheap malt liquor.

She added, "He's one of our most reliable customers."

Got it. "How often does he get arrested?"

"At least once or twice a month."

"How often does he get convicted?"

"Usually once or twice a month." She flashed a knowing smile. "You and Terrence are going to get to know each other very well."

I got the impression that it was a rite of passage for baby P.D.'s to cut their teeth representing The Terminator. "What did he do this time?"

She held up a finger. "Rule number one: a client hasn't 'done' anything unless he admits it as part of a plea bargain, or he's convicted by a jury. Until then, all charges are 'alleged.'"

"What is the D.A. *alleging* that Terrence did?"

"He *allegedly* broke into a car that didn't belong to him."

"Did he *allegedly* take anything?"

"He didn't have time. A police officer was standing next to him when he *allegedly* broke into the car. The cop arrested him on the spot."

"Sounds like Terrence isn't the sharpest instrument in the operating room."

"We don't ask our clients to pass an intelligence test before we represent them. For a guy who used to make a living trying to beat the daylights out of his opponents, Terrence is reasonably intelligent and a nice person who has never hurt anybody. The D.A. charged him with auto burglary."

"Can we plead it out?"

"*We* aren't going to do anything. *You* are going to handle this case. And contrary to what you've seen on TV, our job is to try cases, not to cut quick deals. Understood?"

"Yes."

"I had a brief discussion about a plea bargain with Bill McNulty, who is the Deputy D.A. handling this case. No deal unless Terrence pleads guilty to a felony."

"Seems a bit harsh."

"It is. That's why McNulty's nickname is 'McNasty.' You'll be seeing a lot of him, too. He's a hardass who is trying to impress his boss. He's also very smart and tired of seeing Terrence every couple of weeks. In fairness, I can't blame him."

"So you want me to take this case to trial?"

"That's what we do. Trial starts Monday at nine a.m. before Judge Stumpf." She handed me a manila case file. "Rule number two: know the record. You need to memorize everything inside. Then you should go upstairs to the jail and introduce yourself to your new client."

I could feel my heart pounding. "Could I buy you a cup of coffee and pick your brain about how you think it's best for me to prepare?"

"I haven't decided whether you're coffee-worthy yet."

"Excuse me?"

"I'm dealing with six dozen active cases. By the end of the week, so will you. If you want to be successful, you need to figure stuff out on your own."

I liked her directness. "Any initial hints that you might be willing to pass along?"

"Yes. Watch me. Do exactly what I do."

"Sounds like good advice."

She grinned. "It is."

There's more to this story and it's yours for FREE!

Get the rest of **FIRST TRIAL** at:

www.sheldonsiegel.com/first-trial

ABOUT THE AUTHOR

Sheldon Siegel is the New York Times best-selling author of eleven critically acclaimed legal thrillers featuring San Francisco criminal defense attorneys Mike Daley and Rosie Fernandez, two of the most beloved characters in contemporary crime fiction. He is also the author of the thriller novel The Terrorist Next Door featuring Chicago homicide detectives David Gold and A.C. Battle. His books have been translated into a dozen languages and sold millions of copies. A native of Chicago, Sheldon earned his undergraduate degree from the University of Illinois in Champaign in 1980, and his law degree from Berkeley Law in 1983. He specializes in corporate law with the San Francisco office of the international law firm of Sheppard, Mullin, Richter & Hampton.

Sheldon began writing his first book, SPECIAL CIRCUMSTANCES, on a laptop computer during his daily commute on the ferry from Marin County to San Francisco. A frequent speaker and sought-after teacher, Sheldon is a San Francisco Library Literary Laureate, a former member of the Board of Directors and former President of the Northern California chapter of the Mystery Writers of America, and an active member of the International Thriller Writers and Sisters in Crime. His work has been displayed at the Bancroft Library at the University of California at Berkeley, and he has been recognized as a Distinguished Alumnus of the University of Illinois and a Northern California Super Lawyer.

Sheldon lives in the San Francisco area with his wife, Linda, and their twin sons, Alan and Stephen. He is a lifelong fan of the Chicago Bears, White Sox, Bulls and Blackhawks. He is currently working on his next novel.

Sheldon welcomes your comments and feedback. Please email him at sheldon@sheldonsiegel.com. For more information on Sheldon, book signings, the "making of" his books, and more, please visit his website at www.sheldonsiegel.com.

ACCLAIM FOR
SHELDON SIEGEL'S NOVELS

Featuring Mike Daley and Rosie Fernandez

SPECIAL CIRCUMSTANCES

"An A+ first novel." *Philadelphia Inquirer*.

"A poignant, feisty tale. Characters so finely drawn you can almost smell their fear and desperation." *USA Today*.

"By the time the whole circus ends up in the courtroom, the hurtling plot threatens to rip paper cuts into the readers' hands." *San Francisco Chronicle*.

INCRIMINATING EVIDENCE

"Charm and strength. Mike Daley is an original and very appealing character in the overcrowded legal arena—a gentle soul who can fight hard when he has to, and a moral man who is repelled by the greed of many of his colleagues." *Publishers Weekly*.

"The story culminates with an outstanding courtroom sequence. Daley narrates with a kind of genial irony, the pace never slows, and every description of the city is as brightly burnished as the San Francisco sky when the fog lifts." *Newark Star-Ledger*.

"For those who love San Francisco, this is a dream of a novel that capitalizes on the city's festive and festering neighborhoods of old-line money and struggling immigrants. Siegel is an astute observer of the city and takes wry and witty jabs at lawyers and politicians." *USA Today*.

CRIMINAL INTENT

"Ingenious. A surprise ending that will keep readers yearning for more." *Booklist.*

"Siegel writes with style and humor. The people who populate his books are interesting. He's a guy who needs to keep that laptop popping." *Houston Chronicle.*

"Siegel does a nice job of blending humor and human interest. Daley and Fernandez are competent lawyers, not superhuman crime fighters featured in more commonplace legal thrillers. With great characters and realistic dialogue, this book provides enough intrigue and courtroom drama to please any fan of the genre." *Library Journal.*

FINAL VERDICT

"Daley's careful deliberations and ethical considerations are a refreshing contrast to the slapdash morality and breakneck speed of most legal thrillers. The detailed courtroom scenes are instructive and authentic, the resolution fair, dramatic and satisfying. Michael, Rosie, Grace and friends are characters worth rooting for. The verdict is clear: another win for Siegel." *Publishers Weekly.*

"An outstanding entry in an always reliable series. An ending that's full of surprises—both professional and personal—provides the perfect finale to a supremely entertaining legal thriller." *Booklist.*

"San Francisco law partners Mike Daley and Rosie Fernandez spar like Tracy and Hepburn. Final Verdict maintains a brisk pace, and there's genuine satisfaction when the bad guy gets his comeuppance." *San Francisco Chronicle.*

THE CONFESSION

"As Daley moves from the drug and prostitute-ridden underbelly of San Francisco, where auto parts and offers of legal aid are exchanged for cooperation, to the tension-filled courtroom and the hushed offices of the church, it gradually becomes apparent that Father Ramon isn't the only character with a lot at stake in this intelligent, timely thriller." *Publishers Weekly.*

"This enthralling novel keeps reader attention with one surprise after another. The relationship between Mike and Rosie adds an exotic dimension to this exciting courtroom drama in which the defense and the prosecutor interrogation of witnesses make for an authentic, terrific tale." *The Best Reviews.*

"Sheldon Siegel is to legal thrillers as Robin Cook is to medical thrillers." *Midwest Book Review.*

JUDGMENT DAY

"Drug dealers, wily lawyers, crooked businessmen, and conflicted cops populate the pages of this latest in a best-selling series from Sheldon Siegel. A compelling cast and plenty of suspense put this one right up there with the best of Lescroart and Turow." *Booklist Starred Review.*

"An exciting and suspenseful read—a thriller that succeeds both as a provocative courtroom drama and as a personal tale of courage and justice. With spine-tingling thrills and a mind-blowing finish, this novel is a must, must read." *New Mystery Reader.*

"It's a good year when Sheldon Siegel produces a novel. Siegel has written an adrenaline rush of a book. The usual fine mix from a top-notch author." *Shelf Awareness.*

PERFECT ALIBI

"Siegel, an attorney-author who deserves to be much more well-known than he is, has produced another tightly plotted, fluidly written legal thriller. Daley and Fernandez are as engaging as when we first met them in Special Circumstances, and the story is typically intricate and suspenseful. Siegel is a very talented writer, stylistically closer to Turow than Grisham, and this novel should be eagerly snapped up by fans of those giants (and also by readers of San Francisco-set legal thrillers of John Lescroart)." *Booklist.*

"Sheldon Siegel is a practicing attorney and the married father of twin sons. He knows the law and he knows the inner workings of a family. This knowledge has given him a great insight in the writing of Perfect Alibi, which for Siegel fans is his almost perfect book." *Huffington Post.*

FELONY MURDER RULE

"Outstanding! Siegel's talent shines in characters who are sharp, witty, and satirical, and in the intimate details of a San Francisco insider. Nobody writes dialogue better. The lightning quick pace is reminiscent of Elmore Leonard—Siegel only writes the good parts." *Robert Dugoni, New York Times and Amazon best-selling author of MY SISTER'S GRAVE.*

SERVE AND PROTECT

An Amazon rating of 4.5/5. Readers say: "A strong, thought-provoking novel. It is a page-turner and well worth the time and effort." "His stories are believable and entertaining. The main characters are written with human foibles. With everyday problems they reflect real life." "Sheldon keeps the reader involved, wondering and anxious to read the next line... And the real magic is the ability of the author to keep the reader involved up to and including the very last page."

HOT SHOT

With over 150 amazon reviews and an average of 4.7/5 stars. "The reader gets an inside view of Silicon Valley and is allowed us to see its very dark side. What a hornet's nest of cutthroat people only concerned for two things - themselves and money!"

"Sheldon Siegel is a great storyteller... One of my favourite parts of this series is reading what Mike thinks — I love his sense of humour!"

Featuring Detective Gold and Detective A.C. Battle
THE TERRORIST NEXT DOOR

"Chicago Detectives David Gold and A.C. Battle are strong entries in the police-thriller sweepstakes, with Sheldon Siegel's THE TERRORIST NEXT DOOR, a smart, surprising and bloody take on the world of Islamic terror. As a crazed bomber threatens to shut down American's third-largest city, the Chicago cops, the FBI, Homeland Security and even the military sift through every available clue to the bomber's identity, reaching for a climax that is both shocking and credible." *New York Times* best-selling author Sheldon Siegel tells a story that is fast and furious and authentic." *John Sandford. New York Times Best Selling author of the Lucas Davenport Prey series.*

"Sheldon Siegel blows the doors off with his excellent new thriller, THE TERRORIST NEXT DOOR. Bombs, car chases, the shutdown of Chicago, plus Siegel's winning touch with character makes this one not to be missed!" *John Lescroart. New York Times Best Selling Author of the Dismas Hardy novels.*

"Sheldon Siegel knows how to make us root for the good guys in this heart-stopping terrorist thriller, and David Gold and A.C. Battle are a pair of very good guys." *Thomas Perry. New York Times Best Selling Author of POISON FLOWER.*

ALSO BY SHELDON SIEGEL

Mike Daley/Rosie Fernandez Novels
Special Circumstances
Incriminating Evidence
Criminal Intent
Final Verdict
The Confession
Judgment Day
Perfect Alibi
Felony Murder Rule
Serve and Protect
Hot Shot
The Dreamer

David Gold/A.C. Battle Novels
The Terrorist Next Door

Connect with Sheldon

Email: sheldon@sheldonsiegel.com
Website: www.sheldonsiegel.com
Amazon: amazon.com/author/sheldonsiegel
Facebook: www.facebook.com/SheldonSiegelAuthor
Goodreads: goodreads.com/author/show/69191.Sheldon_Siegel
Bookbub: bookbub.com/authors/sheldon-siegel
Twitter: @SheldonSiegel

Milton Keynes UK
Ingram Content Group UK Ltd.
UKHW020638260923
429382UK00021B/417/J

9 780999 674789